WARRING SUNS

INTERNATIONAL BESTSELLING AUTHOR

YD LA MAR

First paperback edition March 2021
Second paperback edition December 2021

Book Cover: YD La Mar
Editor: Dark Raven Edits

ISBN: 9798729251520

ACKNOWLEDGMENTS

To my wonderful husband, who never bats an eye when I come up with crazy ideas, but instead just adds to it, making my stories come alive. My children, who tell me every day that they are proud of me.

Thank you to everyone who was a fan of my Goodreads' reviews; the ones who pushed me to start writing. It was the kick in the butt I needed. Thank you to all the new author group members and authors who helped me get my bearings. My dark group, who have been with me through the cover process! It was a long one.

To my beta readers. You guys are the real MVP. Thank you for sticking it with me through the initial phases of my writing journey. All of your feedback has inspired me to better myself and my writing ability. Dana, Vicky, Maria, Alex, Megan, Sasha and Sue, thank you for bouncing ideas with me. **December Rose**! Without you, I would not have felt as confident to shape the main female character in this book! Your advice was crucial and indispensable. Beth, Gloria and Ana! Thank you for taking the time to beta my extended version.

To all my readers, thank you for giving me the chance. I hope I can continue to make you guys proud.

BLURB

Living my life as an independent woman in the city, I never expected to become the object of a stalker's obsessive fixation.

Then, I found a strange talisman tucked inside my work bag. What did it all mean?

One moment, I'm at home, Netflixing and chilling solo, and the next, I wake up in an unfamiliar place—without my glasses, of all things.

Everything is a blur, but the heat and the unfamiliar surroundings make me feel like I've somehow ended up in Africa... except, there are two suns overhead. Definitely not Africa.

I have no control over these random teleportations, and soon, I find myself stuck in the middle of a brutal war between three men from warring tribes... and my stalker.

Can I find the strength to convince these men to put aside their bloodshed and consider peace in a land steeped in violence, or will this be the final battle their people ever see?

COURTESY WARNING

This book may contain triggers for some. Triggers may include but are not limited to violence, DESCRIPTIVE NON CON BY ONE OF THE MEN IN THE HAREM, dub-con, bondage, torture, decapitation, themes of war.

PROVERBS/TERMINOLOGY

Worse things happen at sea - Said in a resigned tone when we find ourselves in an awkward or difficult situation, or when we have to put up with something less than we expected.

Ye ishq nahi asaan Bas Tina samjh lijiye Aag ka dariya hai Aur dob ke jana hai - *(translation)*

This love ain't easy…just understand this. It's a river of fire and you have to swim through it.

Har kali raat ke baad ek ujli subah hoti hai - *(translation)* After every dark night arrives the brightest morning.

Antedeer - a cross between earth's antelope, zebra, and deer, with a deep even tan-colored skin tone.

Golden leer - a cross between earth's lion and hyena. Its golden fur and hide are a golden color.

Sparcra - a cross between earth's vulture and crow, has black feathers.

Gugull - seabirds related to earth's seagulls, spotted with tan flecks on their feathers.

Cycles - equivalent to earth's years.

Seasons - equivalent to earth's seasons

Come of season - when a male warrior reaches the age of "adulthood" in order to join in with the other warriors in the hunt/wars

Light spear - lightning

OTHER EARTH CHARACTERS

CHINTKKU TRIBE

DUMA - at 49 cycles, he is the oldest warrior of the tribe. Known for their barbaric ways of torture and warmongering.

JOMO & CHIKU - the youngest warriors in the tribe.

KWAME: THE SIGHT SEEKER - a village seer, keeper of tales, keeper of prophecies passed down through the generations.

Gamja! To Guergalo - Salute! To war!

MATALO'TOA TRIBE

CHIEMKO - at 35 cycles, the youngest warrior to lead the tribe on hunts and fights. Known as warriors of the waters for their ability to navigate boats and take down prey. Good with short distance range and hand-to-hand combat.

ISSA - right-hand warrior to Chiemko, at 38 cycles. Short-range weaponry and hand-to-hand combat.

NAMWANA TRIBE

GAMBA - at 45 cycles, the main warrior to lead the tribe in strategy and tactics. He is best with his long-range weaponry and strategy. Namwana tribe is known for their mixed weaponry and strategic war tactics.

JAHI - long-distance shooter of the Namwana tribe.

KELLAN - sprinter and spearman of the Namwana tribe.

KAIKURA - Spearman of the Namwana tribe.

Gbamke! Oiye! - Salute! Yes!

Ma
Chintkku
Nam

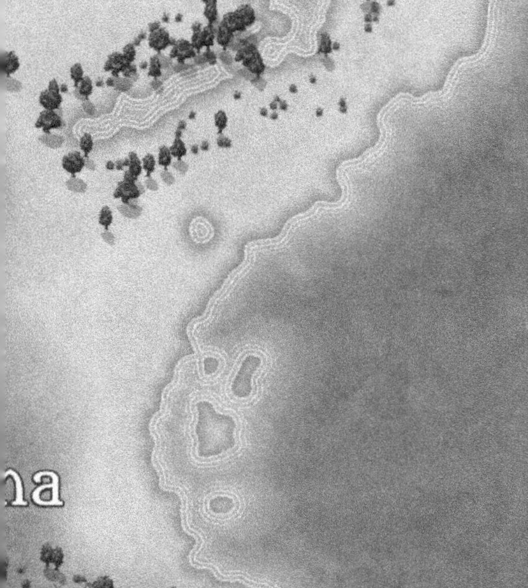

'toa
Other Earth
na

AUTHOR'S NOTE

I was hunting high and low for a specific type of reverse harem and never could find it.

SO I WROTE IT.

It is not everyone's cup of tea, I know.

I've had a reviewer mention the grammar is funny. but honestly, it was meant to be this way because it was meant to simulate *'authentic/fictional authentic speech'*.

The thing with most readers who concentrate on grammar is that...you almost choose to believe that everyone in the world speaks the same, when they don't. There's nothing wrong with wanting perfect grammar in your books. But there's also nothing wrong with wanting to represent things more authentically in books.

Thus why I choose to try and represent minorities in all the tales I weave. It's not common. But I feel like it's my calling.

This tale is about a second earth that runs parallel to the earth as we know it - a parallel universe.

I chose to write it in first person because I wanted the readers to feel just as lost in the moment as our heroine. To see how things unravel *with* her. In reality, we don't always understand things and we don't always find the answers, but we must find ways to move forward and live on anyway.

To the men of color.
To the ones who aren't common in the average dark reader's fantasies.
You were always in mine.

PROLOGUE

GARY

You thought I forgot, Juri. I really didn't. I just wanted to see you again, to feel you. That beautiful shade of your skin, and your damn eyes. The intensity of the feeling in my chest hasn't gone away since I first saw you in our Cybernetics building. You were new and Anderson grabbed you right up quickly to add to his harem of assistants. The bastard is a greedy fucker, and he removed you from my area too soon for my liking. We could have been something, you and I. You didn't notice me, but I noticed you. The way your skirt hugs your ass and legs. The way your hips swayed when you walked in those heels for me. Makes me want to rip my fucking heart out.

You were shy; I know that's why you didn't talk to me. But I knew you were it for me, every time you walked by my cubicle that first month. Anderson, the fat fuck, is lucky to be related to the higher ups. I would have killed him for you, you know? Bathed you in my love, in his blood. All for you.

You like to play hard to get though. And I think I'm enjoying our new game together. You run, I catch. You think you get away when I just like watching you run faster. It thrills me. You pretend to like nice guys, and I tried that for you, I did. But you didn't like it. You wanted it rougher. Who knew you'd be a little kinky thing? I'll do whatever you want baby because it's just me and you. You're mine.

Staring into your window as you sleep makes me feel things. Lifting up your window that I unlocked earlier, my senses are assaulted by the unique fragrance that's you. The carpeting in this apartment complex helps to hide my footsteps, brings me closer to the bed with just a whisper.

JURI

Nightmares are plaguing my mind, everything is red and the only thing I could see is a sea of dead faces staring back at me accusingly. The smell of dust and copper surrounds me, burning my nostrils.

My heart is breaking for the guilt I feel for what I've caused.

The memory of my mother's wise words comes to mind: "Ye ishq nahi asaan Bas Tina samjh lijiye Aag ka dariya hai Aur dob ke jana hai."

This love ain't easy…just understand this. It's a river of fire and you have to swim through it.

Little did I know, just how right she would be.

ONE

JURI

I'm falling asleep at my desk. I just know it. I think I felt my head nod and almost hit my computer monitor a few times. Judging by the way my monitor is still shaking a little, I probably saved myself from a bruise. I'm not cut out for office work, sitting in a cubicle for long hours, my life is draining away. This will probably give me spider veins. No one wants spider veins. I mean, I could always wear leggings. But still, an ounce of prevention is worth a pound of cure, as they say. And with my last ounce of coffee in my cup, I think it's time I head on home and call it a day.

It's a good thing I don't live that far from work. I could use the walk too. The tingly sensation I'm getting on my calves down to my feet tells me my limbs were on the verge of going numb. Time to walk. It will wake me up a bit more and get some circulation back in my legs. I'll probably be walking a little funky for a minute, but that's alright. As long as I get out of here. That's why I always pack my flats in my work bag. Yes, I'm a bag lady. I carry a lot of junk; you know, just in case. Probably gives me buff shoulders though, I'm not trying to brag. I need them, in case I have to punch someone in the face if they try something on me while I'm walking home. You'll never know what you run into on a normal walk home from work.

I should pick up Yoga to get some of these kinks out of me though. All those years in a university, to end up as a personal assistant to some cocky CEO at this Cybernetics Industry. Lord, my eyes are about to cross with all the data and mumbo jumbo I have to sort through. The numbers on the screen are starting to meld together despite still wearing my glasses. Rubbing my eyes, I shake my head and then log off. I swear the CEO, Mark Anderson — the lazy bastard, is just sitting back in his room taking a damn nap when he's not forwarding all his work to me and the other girls.

Standing up, I stretch my back a little and wiggle my toes before putting my heels back on. Turning around, the other girls still have their heads towards their screens, concentrating on whatever they're doing. Clearing my throat and breaking the keyboard clacking, the girls give me their attention. I wave my goodbyes to my fellow office mates because, of course, Anderson needs 3 personal assistants for who knows what reason. An all-female office harem.

My toes are sliding into the front of my heels with every step, only serving to make me more anxious to get out of here. I get into the elevator and press the button for the bottom floor. Rubbing the back of my neck to try and relieve the tension of the day, I think about when my next vacation will be. *Never. My next vacation will be next Neveruary.* Sounds about right. I put my head back on the elevator wall with a thud, letting out a big sigh and closing my eyes. I hear the elevator door open up and someone steps in. He smells masculine but my mind is still chastising me about getting myself into this position with Anderson. Not paying attention, I keep my eyes closed.

"Long day?"

My eyes flutter open and close again, the readjustment to the light bringing on a small headache. I bring my head back down to see who's talking to me. Once I adjust my glasses, I open my eyes to find a clean-cut, handsome guy in a suit. At least that's what he would be described as by most of the female species. Clean cut, pressed suit, blond hair combed and gelled back a bit, a little smirk on his face, playful baby blue eyes. But to *this* female, he looks like every other guy in this building.

"You can say that." I'm not really one for conversation when you know what they're trying to do. Now, I'm not trying to toot my own horn or anything, but everyone in this building is just straight thirsty. Men and women alike; everyone here is practically single and just ready to mingle in the copy room and closets. It's like sitting in an office too long amps up their mating instinct or something, and I just don't have time for that. Plus, I'm at the office enough. I don't want any more reason to stay in this damn building. I just want to go home and watch some mindless TV shows while eating my weight in popcorn.

He's clearing his throat like he doesn't know what to say to my response. *Good.* I don't need him to say anything. I just need to get out of this elevator.

Ding!

Oh, and look at that, here's my stop.

I try to at least be polite and smile at him as I exit. "Have a nice day!" Fake enthusiasm is usually appreciated around these parts. And I can play the part like the best of them, even when I don't feel it on the inside.

Quickly stepping out of the elevator, my feet lead me towards the front of the building. I stop in the middle of the lobby to switch out into my walk-friendly shoes. Ahhh, now things are starting to look up; My feet are thanking me. Throwing my pumps into my bag, I walk more briskly out the front glass doors, craving the fresh air, anxious to leave this building behind for another day.

It's just about 4:30 in the afternoon by the time I exit the place. Should I drop by the store to buy some liquor? Some brandy? Not sure how well that will mix with my planned popcorn binging, though. I guess I'll just head straight home then.

The sound of the city carries with the cool breeze coming across my skin, the hustle and bustle of the usual work day. Walking down the street in the city, you see how alive it becomes the closer it gets to happy hour. But, I'm not really a sociable person and you can't hang out in these places barefoot and in just a t-shirt. So home will just have to suffice for me; no complaints about it either.

Getting into a nice comfortable cadence to my walk, crossing the crosswalk with a small smile on my face, I think of how delicious that popcorn is going to be in my loungewear. Just then, someone bumps into my shoulder, throwing my body back a step. *Ouch!*

Rubbing the ache in my shoulder, I try to apologize to the person. "Oh, dear! I'm so sorry," I try to tell whoever it is.

Once I rearrange my glasses back to their rightful place, I open my eyes to find… No one. *Huh?* I turn around 360 degrees and it doesn't look like anyone is stopping or rubbing their shoulder from the impact. The foot traffic is lightening around me and when I look up, I only have a few more moments to cross the street completely. Oh well, sorry anyways whoever you are.

The sight of my apartment door makes me giddy. Popcorn here I come! I make it into my apartment, kick off my shoes and make sure to lock the doors — then double-check I locked them. Look, it may not be considered a bad neighborhood where I live, but I am a single young female in a complex that has men as well. One can never be too careful, right? Plus, I don't want anyone stumbling into my house drunk, thinking it was their apartment because the doors looked similar. If they haven't realized ALL the doors look exactly the same by now … I just don't know. They shouldn't probably be living here.

My apartment in this complex is one of the simpler ones, being just a single bedroom with a bathroom attached. The living area is an open concept with a modest kitchen. My small four chair kitchen table fits right in the middle, with enough space to walk around. The perfect size for just *me*.

Chucking my clothes on the floor in my bedroom, I go to start the bathwater. The sound of the water flowing is a welcoming rumble. I can feel the warmth of the liquid in the air, making me breathe it in deeply. This should relax my muscles and cramps enough to actually enjoy my TV binging later. Stepping out of the bathroom, I shut the door a little to keep the steam in. When I go into my work bag to look for a cleaning cloth for my glasses, I find something that wasn't in there before, not from what I remember packing this morning.

My fingers caress the shape and the grooves on the surface. I take what looks like a coin or a circular disk of some sort into my hands and just cradle it. It looks ancient or looks to have been made to look old, like some sort of antique. I can't make out the engraving on it. Looks like it's made out of some sort of wood or bone, perhaps? I don't know how I feel about that. When my fingers caress the top once more, it feels as smooth as ivory. The Carving is so intricate in its details. *Strange. Hopefully, it's not made out of ivory.*

I gently place it on my dresser to check out later because seriously it's bath time, and the steam is already drawing me in and calling my name.

Clean and dried, I put on one of my most comfortable t-shirts and some boy short panties. I let my wavy black hair air dry naturally because I heard towel rubbing will give me more split ends than I care for. Picking up my discarded clothes with my towel, I deposit them into my dirty laundry hamper when my eyes land back on that coin-like thing I found in my work bag.

I reach to pick it up again, trying to see it from different angles. It looks important. I wonder how it ended up in my bag? My bag is usually next to me or on me at all times. I stand about 5'4", so unless someone is 6 feet or taller purposely dropped it, I have no clue. I mean, even the person who bumped into me didn't feel that tall. They felt about the same shoulder height as me. I can't help but caress the top of it though, it's magnificent — other-worldly. The design is just so intricate and must have taken a lot of time and talent from the artist to complete it. I place it back on my dresser carefully because I don't want to ruin it since I guess it's mine now. Finders keepers and all.

When was the last time I called my family to check in? I probably should do that and see how they're doing. Grabbing my phone, I scroll until I see my mother's name.

"Hello?"

"Hey!"

The conversation was a short one. As usual, my intentions were to ask them how they're doing but instead the conversation turns towards me and why I'm still single. My parents, who are still in India, always worry if I'll end up alone. They've been kind enough to let me live my life out here in the states, pursuing my dream. They really have nothing to worry about because I'm not worried about it. Once the conversation is done, I end the call and think over what show I should catch for tonight's binge.

Leaving my bedroom to the living room, I sit in front of my TV and start browsing shows on my only TV. The softness of the couch is really making me relaxed. I'm unable to listen to the conversation on the screen as I find my eyes fluttering closed after only a short period of time, missing parts. I realize I didn't even end up making my popcorn before I inadvertently fell asleep on the couch for a few minutes. I must be really exhausted. That's alright. I'm just going to lay my head down on my couch right here…

TWO

DUMA

It's hotter today. The suns peak sooner and fall later this season. That will give us plenty of time to find meat for our people. I'm leading this hunting group today into the plains.

"We venture farther into the west plains this day. We need to find more meat to bring back to the village."

My warriors nod their heads in understanding and agreement. We usually find good hunting near our village but it is good for all warriors to gain experience in different parts of our lands. I count the men with me today and it looks to be 5 seasoned warriors and 2 who just came into season. That is a good number for what we need to do.

I whistle to indicate we should check all of our belongings and make sure we all packed sufficient water hides before leaving the village. It will be a longer trip than usual, it is good to have enough water for us to make it back carrying our kills. With my spear in my grip, I give the men a few moments to get their weapons into their hands before leading the way out of our village.

The two warm suns bake the land, making it warm under our toes. That's good. This will help with our trek and keep our blood flowing well along our path.

"What do you think we will catch today, Chiku? A big antedeer? They are fat this season, preparing themselves for the upcoming cool weather." Jomo and Chiku are our new warriors who join us today, newly seasoned. They grew up together and tend to always banter back and forth, a habit from their younger days. It is good to have such a close-knit group. It helps us to read each other's cues and faces when we must remain quiet during the hunt.

"I do not know Jomo. Whatever it is, I hope it is something big enough to feed our village for a while. That way the men in our group can stay home for a while to enjoy the spoils instead of coming out soon again after the hunt. Then we can also tell the women of our prowess in the hunt." Chiku is wise for his age of sixteen cycles and has not yet found an attachment to one of the village women — every warrior's goal.

Being too picky with the hunt may not provide us with what we truly require, and we are required to take care of the people back in our village. Taking care of our people will help us continue to grow as a tribe, keeping the belly of the mothers and children full.

Unlike the young warriors like Jomo and Chiku, my season has already come and gone for longing to be bedded by one of the village women. It has been ten years since my female was caught in the middle of one of our tribal wars of old — ten years and I have not had any feelings for any of the other women, though they try. They have all recently stopped trying these past few seasons I have come to notice, and I am grateful for it. I only live for the hunt now — it gives me more than enough purpose.

The younger men can have their pick of the females, there is plenty to go around. Our men tend to attach themselves to one female, devoting themselves in cherishing her all her days under his protection. If my female was still alive, I would be doing the same. But it seems the gods chose a different path for me. The end of these hunts brings me home to an empty hut but a full belly.

"You two need not worry. We will find something this hunt; I can feel it. The sun is smiling down on us this eve." With that, I pick up the pace for my men to follow into the hunting grounds to the west. I am the most seasoned warrior among us at forty-nine cycles, and they trust where I lead them. I will not let my men or my village down.

GAMBA - ON THE OTHER SIDE OF THE PLAINS, EAST

The warm breeze feels cool on my skin. We have been blessed this day. The hunting party and I are just coming back to our village. We are ten warriors strong today. A good size to take down enough to feed the hungry mouths of the children that await us back home. We have captured a very good amount of meat this day. Two antedeer and a foal that got caught in the crossbows during the hunt. We were lucky for it, though. This will tide us over until the next dark days, when the night sun no longer shines.

My body still buzzes with the chase we had — the energy inside of me still dancing from our take down. My mind replays the scene of another successful hunt.

"Jahi! Up on that tree right there. I will stake out on the cliff overlooking the path the beasts will run across. Kellan, behind the herd! If beasts are falling behind, make sure to make good on your position. Take down whatever is within your reach with your spear. You have the

The memory fades and my smile can still be felt on my face.

We reach the village to find the women and children preparing for our arrival with good spirits and seasonings for the meat. We are a very efficient tribe; stronger together. The men who return with me are already relaying tales of their prowess in the hunt, hoping to catch the eye of one of the unattached women.

I have come home to no one, but some of the women are following me as I make my way towards my hut, hoping to catch my eye. It is the same after every hunt.

"Gbamke! Oiye! We have returned with gifts!" scream the younger warriors, proud of our success. The village roars and the drums start to beat for our arrival and good blessings. It is good to be a warrior this day — a good day to be alive.

CHIEMKO - ON THE ISLAND ACROSS THE WATERS, NORTH

"How is it looking out there, Chiemko? Do we ride the waves this day or do we wait for tomorrow? We await your word." Issa is my right-hand warrior. He is one who is always on these hunting trips with me; he has never said no since he came of season these many cycles past. I am glad for it; I would not wish for another to remain by my side and watch my back.

Some of our warriors have retired from the hunt and instead wish to stay behind in the village to protect the women and children we leave behind. The older warriors keep watch of each corner of the shores in case of attack from directions we may not be expecting. I have been made the lead on our hunts now, the youngest to be made lead in many moons at thirty five cycles. But the old warriors say my agility and ability to quickly adapt hunting and fight tactics is something they have not seen in many years. I had no choice. I had to be faster, quicker, stronger and smarter than those around me because both my parents died in the last tribal war of old. My village raised me as their own, but I had to make sure I not only survive but survive well in respect to my parents and my people. They died to protect the village. I will not be one to let them or my village down if war ever comes to our island again.

The breeze picks up and the sound of the flat leaves rustling on the trees tells me our sails will move our boats quickly over the currents. The sound of the waves calls to me like a secret lover.

"Issa, my friend. I think we will be leaving this day when the suns are cresting the trees at the edge of the island. Gather the other warriors and start setting up the boats. If we find luck, we may return home with a good weight of meat to feed the village for many days! I am feeling a blessing on us this day." And I tell him the truth for I can feel it deep in my bones.

Today will birth something great. Something we have been waiting for. Something that will challenge us and make us better warriors upon our return.

THREE

I awake with a start. What happened? The grogginess of my mind makes me groan. I wonder what woke me up? I had the strangest dream. All the faces were distorted and unclear; the same way things look without my glasses on — a blur. Maybe this will convince me to start that special savings account to get some corrective eye surgery done. I always tell myself I should, but every time I get to work I seem to forget everything but what Anderson throws at my desk.

This dream, though. It was hot, wherever it was. I can almost still feel the heat on my skin. And I think the sky was dark? Could it be? There was still so much light, even though it felt like it was nightfall. The moon was almost as bright as the sun but to its right I spotted another very small ball of light as well about ten percent of its size. Two moons? *Weird. Just plain weird.* The people that did appear in my dream were blurry, but I could tell their skin was bronzed by the hot sun rays. Varying shades of warm, tan, rich umbers and browns. But I just couldn't make out their faces.

Readjusting the glasses on my face, I look around and I find that I ended up dozing off on the couch. I really shouldn't sleep with these glasses on, it's such a bad habit of mine. The clock on the wall says it's nearly three in the morning and I seem to have left the living room lights on during my nap. This is definitely going to increase my utilities. Turning off the lights, I head to my actual bed. I might as well just get a little more sleep before I have to wake up for work.

I swear I feel like I just closed my eyes for five minutes, when I'm woken up to my alarm clock. How can I feel more tired right now than when I woke up last night at 3:00am? *Ugh.* Despite how I feel, it doesn't stop time from creeping forward, so I drag myself out of bed and start my morning ritual before work. Maybe it's like this for everyone who hits their thirties. I still feel young inside though, I guess that makes it a little bit better. *Think young thoughts, Juri. Alright, get your butt up and get yourself to work.* Do we start to talk to ourselves more as well when we hit this age? Physically shrugging my shoulders to myself, I continue to get ready.

After throwing my pumps into my work bag, I run out the front door, but not before locking it behind me. I'm cutting it close, but I think I'll make it on time. Throwing my keys into my bag, I start walking down the hallway towards the stairs when I bump my head into something hard. *Ouch.*

"Oh dear, I'm so sorry!" I adjust my glasses and look up to find the same gentleman I think I ran into in the elevator at work. I had no clue he lived in the same apartment complex. "Hey, don't I know you? Were you the one in the elevator at the Cybernetics Industry building yesterday?" He looks sheepish and I'm squinting my eyes a little bit at him but still trying to maintain a nice-person smile.

"Yea, that was me. And that was you. I'm Gary, by the way. It's a pleasure to finally meet you."

Finally meet me? Is this guy following me around? I just saw him yesterday. Is he really a resident here? I'm trying not to let my internal paranoia show on the outside, but I'm feeling a little red flag waving at my face right now. There's something not right about this situation. This is a big city. What are the odds…?

"I'm Juri. But I have to get going before I'm late for work. It was nice meeting you." I quickly turn around and briskly walk down two flights of stairs in my flats and make it out onto the streets. I'm not that tall, but I have a pretty fast-walking pace and good people dodging skills. It gives me some mean calves. It's just the way it is when you have to walk everywhere. I didn't want to waste my money on a car and car insurance if I didn't have to. Not only do I get to keep my body in some sort of shape, I can also put some of that money back into savings. I don't plan on living in the city forever. *My mother would be smiling right now if she knew.* I don't blend too well in the nightly city scene, being as antisocial as I am. But a girl's gotta do what a girl's gotta do to get where she's destined to be.

Making it to my work building at record speed, I stop to slip on my pumps when I get to the front lobby. Who decided that heels were office attire anyway? Taking a deep breath in and out, I try my best to look like I didn't just fast-walk/jog my way here. My hair is probably out of its low bun with wayward flyaways about my face, but whatever.

Once I reach my floor, I step out of the elevator and greet my fellow office mates who look like they probably slept here all night long. Anderson is giving us way too much work. Isn't there something in our employee clause about abuse of the workers? *This guy.* Living the life of the man on top while we peasants are down here slaving away. I heard through the grapevine that he is somehow blood related to the person who's at the very top of this food chain, so he gets a lot of passes. He also makes a lot of passes when he's not passed out on his chair in his office. The guy has a gut that makes his shirt cry on his best days. *That's what happens when you're just pigging out and sleeping at the desk, Anderson.*

I reach my desk, throw my bag on the floor by my feet and take a small 360-degree spin on my office chair. I made it with five minutes to spare. I will gladly take those five minutes to just take a breather before I dive into the world of computerized mumbo jumbo and fancy jargon. I close my eyes for a moment, taking in the air conditioning, when I hear a male voice calling my name.

"Miss Chakrabarti, I need the email I sent you last night done today."

Anderson's greasy presence is a little close for comfort right now.

I pop my eyes open to see him staring down my shirt. I have average C cups and I wear a pretty modest bra to deemphasize them at work. My buttons are done pretty high up as well, so I have no idea why he looks like he's about to need a napkin to wipe the drool that's about to form in the corner of his mouth. This guy reminds of that wolf character you sometimes see in the old Looney Toons cartoon. Always whistling and howling at anything on two legs. Except this guy's gut is almost touching my hand and I'm trying really hard not to move my hand in case he moves too and takes it as something else.

"Yes sir, I was just about to boot up my computer. I'll have it on your desk by this afternoon." I say as I straighten my body up in my chair ever so slowly so I don't touch any part of him. Lord, his eyes are blazing up; he looks like he enjoys what he thinks to be a show of my breasts sticking out for his pleasure. *Uh, no.* If I push my feet ever so slowly, I could possibly roll my chair a bit farther back. I'm just about to execute my plan when Anderson's gaze lands on my legs poking out of my pencil skirt.

He's clearing his throat like there's a family of frogs stuck in it before he says, "That's good, Miss Chakrabarti. That's what I like to hear. You keep up the good work and I'll see you at noon."

Uh huh.

Why does he make it sound like we just booked a date together? I'm just dropping off paperwork. I let out an exhale once he decided to leave and go check out his other assistants. I don't know how much longer I can work here. Some days are easier than others, but days like today really almost break the camel's back. First that elevator guy—who I swear is stalking me, and I have pretty good predator instincts — and now Anderson. *Greasy gut Anderson.*

Feeling like a real blue ribbon winner right now.

The day passed by fast and I was able to sneak in his office to drop off the paperwork when I saw him take a restroom break. I do not want any more of his creepy stares my way.

I make it back to my desk before he even exits the restroom. *Crisis averted.* Sitting back at my desk, I reach into my bag for my lunch. The weight of the glass container in my hands makes my hunger increase. I grow a very small garden by my window at home. I love having fresh vegetables in my salads. Throw a big fat juicy grilled chicken breast on that thing and it gives me enough energy to survive the day at the office. Homemade salad dressing made from my freshly grown herbs make my cubicle smell fabulous. With all these thoughts floating around my head, my stomach rumbles.

"Hey, do you have any plans this weekend Juri? We were thinking about having an assistant's night out. Get us out of this place. I swear I see it in my dreams. Jessica was suggesting this new club that just opened up a few blocks down. It used to be something or other but this grand opening has been the hottest topic this past week."

Amy and Jessica, my office mates, are the other girls who also have to endure Anderson's stares. It would be good to get out, I guess. Hottest topic? I haven't heard anything about it. But I'm usually fast walking right back home after work, so I guess it makes sense that I didn't.

"Yeah, sure. What time are you girls thinking about?" Do I have a dress in the back of my closet that's appropriate? Shoving a forkful of chicken salad into my mouth, I chew and try to mentally envision the contents of my closet. I haven't looked in the back of the closet in a while. Whatever I have probably has moth holes in it.

As I'm sitting here pondering if I should just go buy something new, Amy says, "how about 8:00 tonight? We can drink a few drinks, dance and stay until whenever you like. Might find some hot single guys that's from somewhere other than this building. I swear the men here have made their rotations at least three times by now." Amy scrunches her face and I shiver just thinking about what she said.

That's just nasty. This is exactly why I swear off anyone from this building.

FOUR

JURI

I did end up buying a new dress. A soft satin, blush colored dress that comes to my mid-thigh. Enough give and slink to it that I can still move comfortably. The straps are smaller than what I'm used to or am comfortable with but so is going clubbing, might as well go big or go home, right? Then I had to convince myself that I shouldn't stay home in a baggy t-shirt and panties. I'm thirty, I should go live it up a little. This dress doesn't allow me to wear a bra, so I just bought a couple of pasties and prayed it'll hold. I'm not the skinniest girl around, but I think I fill out this dress nicely despite my buffer shoulders and calves. *Dang, look at me, huh? All dolled up for once, letting the girl's loose, literally.* It feels kind of liberating.

Jessica and Amy are meeting me here at the apartment so we can all arrive together. I'm just applying some lip gloss when I hear my doorbell ring.

Ring! Ring!

I answer it by the next ring. These girls are so impatient. *Sheesh.* I open my door to find the girls dressed to impress.

"Woah. Are we at the right house? You look nothing like Juri." Jessica's looking back and forth between me and my apartment number.

Amy's eyes are wide and looking me up and down multiple times. I don't usually doll myself up much. All they've ever seen me in is my usual boring work attire. "I never knew you had curves like that, even though you constantly wear a pencil skirt. I think those loose tops are hiding a lot of secrets there, Juri."

The girls are giggling as they walk through the door. This easy banter uplifts my spirits a little. I know I hide behind my boring librarian look. This night will be a good thing.

Amy and Jessica are all primping and fixing whatever it is they think they need fixing in front of the mirror I just vacated in my living room. They already look dressed to the nines, what more can they possibly do? Even though I'm dressed up for tonight, I decided to not put on too much makeup. Just a little lip gloss and some mascara to emphasize my lashes and brown eyes. I don't want to look like a melting mess if we start sweating on the dancefloor. The image of the wicked witch of the west from The Wizard of Oz comes to mind. *All they'll find is my heels.*

With all the time I had to spare during my get ready process earlier, I decided to make a hole in that circular disk I found in my bag the other day. There was an awl tool hidden in the desk that came with the apartment. I often wonder who used to live here before me. Attaching a black strap, I made the disk into a choker to complete my outfit. It might not match, but I don't mind all that much. I just wanted it on me tonight for some reason. I kind of missed it near me — two lost pieces in this big city.

"Alright ladies, are you ready to party?" Jessica's pumped. Her energy is kind of spilling over to us and we're all full of smiles as we exit my apartment and head to this grand opening everyone seems to be talking about.

This club is hopping and I'm feeling the energy. There's a calm and yet exciting ambience to the place all at once. I decided on a light drink, sipping it slowly to start off. I don't want to be drunk within thirty minutes of arriving. The girls are already on their second drink, casting looks all about the room like they're hunters hunting for male prey. I laugh inwardly at the image of office women in the wild, trapping men like cave-women. The single life can be a hard one. It seems the older women get, the more fierce they become in the hunt. At least in *this* city this is true from what I've seen. Amy and Jessica are also proving me right when they both zero their sights on a broad body that has stopped right by us at the bar.

I'm squinting again because I swear this is the elevator boy, though I might be wrong since I've never seen him dressed so casually before; the last two times I saw him, he was polished up and in a pressed suit. He pushes his loose blond locks away from his eyes and lifts his face to my direction. Yup, baby blue like an undisturbed ocean. *Worse things happen at sea,* but these eyes are right in the middle of the whirlpool that is about to pull you to your impending doom. This is definitely the same guy. Is he stalking me or is he just here for the grand opening as well and he really does live in my apartment complex? My left hand is playing and fingering my homemade choker. I don't feel comfortable with this guy either way, and I really don't like the way he's oogling my body despite the attempts my friends are making to get his attention.

The sound of their voices drown out with the sound of the music around us. Maybe letting the girls loose was a bit too forward of me. No matter how much my office mates toss their hair back, stick their chest out and flirtatiously run their fingers on his arm, he's still staring at me all while having what looks like a full conversation with them. It's quite unnerving, really. In order to break eye contact, I clear my throat, look away and lean over the bar to try and get the bartender's attention.

Bartender man quickly homes his sights on my cleavage and is walking over my way. Are my pasties working? I play with my choker again, hoping to indiscreetly hide my cleavage with my arm over it; I'm really not used to this kind of attention.

"Hey, what can I get you beautiful?"

Hey indeed.

"Can I have a Sangria?"

"Sure thing."

After getting my drink with a wink from the bartender, I take a sip and turn back around to my friends only to find the elevator guy making out with Jessica. But the kicker is that his eyes are open and still staring at me, even though Jessica looks like her panties are about to combust from his kiss. *What the hell? I can't be the only one seeing this, right?* Amy is looking back and forth between us with her forehead wrinkled because she notices this too. *Good. I'm not going crazy.* My hackles are raised. I do *not* like elevator boy at all.

I give Amy a look I hope she can read: be wary. She can't read it; We haven't hung out enough for her to know me that well; it seems.

Quickly finishing my drink, I excuse myself to the restroom, making sure I hold my clutch tightly in my hand. All I brought was my ID, a credit card, my keys, a travel perfume spray and a small pepper spray. Look, like I said, I'm a single woman in the city and I don't like letting my guard down. I needed a breather from the looks elevator boy throwing my way. It feels like he stabbed me with a mental spear and is about to bring meat home for some barbecue. It's a strange feeling, a bit intense.

There are a few girls lingering in the restroom fixing their clothes in front of the mirror. Paying them no mind, I make my way into one of the stalls. When I finish using the restroom and wash my hands, I take a look at myself in the mirror. I've been told I have pretty big brown eyes. These are the eyes I inherited from my mother. My tanned Indian skin has the usual olive undertone that is contrasting nicely against the blush pink I'm wearing. Thick black waves and curls fall down my back; I love my hair. Trying to tame the tresses of my hair tonight was only going to lead to disappointment, especially with the potential of sweating while dancing. I might as well flaunt it. I'm in my prime and single, but I really don't feel bad about it. I worked hard to get where I am today. All me. Blood, sweat, and tears. My family constantly reminds me that my stubbornness to succeed is a blessing and a curse because you don't always win every challenge. Is it a curse, though? I haven't run into anything that would make me think so. I haven't failed at what I set my heart to yet. But again, I still feel young in my eyes and my heart. Young and full of life, full of things to offer.

Alright Juri, you've pumped yourself up enough. I'm feeling good. Time to head back out there and face what the night has to offer.

Once I exit the restroom doors, the sound of the music seeps into my skin and syncs with the beat of my heart. Bodies are writhing and everyone around me is having a good time. Keeping my eyes forward, I carefully make my way towards the bar without running into anyone with a drink in their hand.

The girls are right where I left them, and it looks like they finished the drink they were nursing prior to my departure to the restroom. Elevator boy is nowhere to be seen. Maybe he needed a bathroom break too. *Good.*

"Hey! You're finally back. I thought Gary was sneaking off to meet you at the restrooms or something."

I'm confused by her statement. "Why would you think that?"

"Because he excused himself right after you left. We learned he's thirty-five and single. His immediate departure after you looked that way to me. Thought he snuck off to have a little quickie with the way he was eye-fucking you earlier."

I can feel myself making a face at her statement.

"So, you didn't see him then?"

"No, I don't think I did. I just came straight here; I wasn't really looking around much on my way back." This is something I'm going to have to remedy because this guy gives me the creeps. He could have been right next to or behind me on my walk back for all I know. I let my guard down, thinking that nothing crazy would happen with so many people here out for a good time. I need to do better.

"Well, I'm done hanging around the bar. You girls up for a turn on the dance floor?"

"Hell yes! I did not wear this outfit to just sit around. Come on, Juri!"

Not waiting for me to answer, Jessica grabs my hand and starts strutting towards the middle of the room with our other office mate right beside us. The girls are advertising their rocking bodies with each step they take and with each hip sway they give towards the men that look our way.

This is definitely the best time to be single in the city: during a grand opening of a club.

We end up dancing the night away and I have to admit that it was pretty fun to just let loose for once. All the top hits are remixed into sultry and upbeat compilations, making it easy to move to the beat. I can feel my body heating up as the girls and I dance together, rubbing our bodies against one another. My hair is a little curlier and frizzy from the sheen of sweat that's accumulated on the skin of my neck, but I don't mind. Our bodies continue to move to the beat and we're laughing the night away.

It's surreal, and it feels amazing, liberating. Men are congregating around us, trying to get a taste of what we have to offer. If any of the men get too close, we start ignoring them and just dance with each other, grinding away in sultry moves that will leave all the wanting men drooling on the dancefloor. The art of the tease.

Hitting up the bar for some water, I lean back and smile at the girls.

"How long do you plan on staying?" Looking at my officemates, they have a nice light sheen of sweat across their faces as well. Whatever makeup they have on tonight is really holding up well.

"I'm getting pretty tired and my feet are killing me."

"Always choose dance heels over stilettos, girl. It's something you learn over time."

"Ugh! Why didn't you tell me that when I went to your house?"

"You looked so excited, and we had to go to Juri's."

"Whatever."

Smiling at the girl's banter, I finish my last gulp of water. I can feel the coolness go all the way down my throat. "I'm pretty beat. I'm good to call it a night if you girls are."

Pushing the glass towards the bartender, he gives me a hooded eye look before looking me up and down again the way he's been doing all night. After taking my glass, he writes his number on a napkin and slides it over to me with a cocky grin.

"Call me."

I don't plan on it, but it's nice to be appreciated nonetheless. Biting my lip, I give him a friendly smile and take the napkin out of courtesy. He's a good practice for my rusty flirting skills. He probably gives his number out to plenty of women each night, but I'm not one to just be a notch on someone's bedpost. So innocent flirting is all he'll be getting from this girl. I want a man who's over the top crazy about me and makes me just as crazy about him.

The girls drop me off outside my apartment complex after sobering up a bit at the club. We're all full of laughs as we talk about the men who were trying to steal dances with us on the floor. I'm still feeling the buzz of energy from the night as well.

"Thank you guys again for inviting me. I had a lot of fun. I haven't had fun like that in a long while." I make sure to show them my appreciation in case they plan on any more future assistant's nights out.

"Of course, Juri! The three amigos have to get away from Anderson as much as we can. I'm tired of just seeing his face and gut all day. I need some fresh meat to look at." The girls and I are still laughing as they drive away. I wave at the retreating car with a lingering smile on my face before taking off my heels and try to go up two flights of stairs to my apartment floor.

It's nasty and I shouldn't be walking barefoot, but man, my feet hurt. It was all worth it, though. I'm almost at the last few steps when I hear a voice saying my name. Snapping my head up, I look around in the darkness with my heels still hanging on my fingers. Sounds like it's coming from where my apartment door is located. When I make it to the top of the steps, my feet falter a bit when my eyes land on the elevator boy right in front of my door like he's been waiting for me this entire time. How long has he been standing there? I pretend to look like I'm getting out my keys — which I will be — but instead I am making sure my hand has a secure hold on the pepper spray I have in there while I'm walking towards my door. My heart rate is steadily increasing the closer I get with each step.

"Hey Juri. I was wondering if you wanted to hang out tonight. I mean we kind of did at the club for a bit, but I know you're more of a homebody so — "

How does he know this?

"I mean; we could just watch some movies or something to wind down from the night. How does that sound?" He looks so hopeful, but it sounds like I'll have to make sure he knows he's never welcome back here.

When I'm almost upon him, I move to position myself in front of my door, separating him from it. He hasn't made any moves yet, but I swear I can feel him sniffing my hair.

"Um.." I'm stalling, because I have to quickly be able to unlock my door, then grab my spray. I do just that as Gary takes me by surprise by spinning me to face him and putting both of his hands on either side of my head against my door, caging me in.

Thud thud. Thud thud. My heart is about to beat itself right out of my chest.

"Juri, I would like to get to know you better. You have to give me a chance. What are neighbors for, if not to hang out when we're home around the same time? It's not like we have to worry about waking up somewhere we don't recognize."

Woah, Nelly.

Clutching my spray in my dominant hand, I prepare for whatever it is he thinks he has in store for me. The crispness of the night air is sending chills all over my skin. From the look on his face, he's still drunk from the club and drunk people have no filters. They start getting brave when they're not usually when they're sober.

Suddenly, his hand is on my neck, squeezing tight. His warm grip is firm and steady despite him being inebriated. This might have been sexy if I wasn't so scared shitless right now. My eyes widen as his face comes closer and closer. He's forcing a kiss on my lips, his lips soft but dominating against my own.

"You've always been mine, Juri. I had to bide my time until you were ready, but I can't wait anymore. You look so beautiful tonight."

He's whispering all this crazy talk against my lips and I'm beyond confused. This guy is crazy. I barely even know him. What does he mean by biding his time? How long has he been stalking me?

"Juri, you taste so good on my lips. I wonder what you taste like between your legs."

Okay, I was going easy on him by not making any drastic moves yet, but this is crossing the line. Sounds like he's about to rip my dress off right here, he's got it all figured out, planned and everything.

With quick reflexes, I bring the spray bottle to his face and press the button down with firm pressure while giving him a knee to the groin. His groan tells me I've hit my target. He lets go of my neck and I'm able to take in a few breaths before I run into my apartment and slam the door on his crumpled form laying on the ground. That will leave him confused as to what pain he should be concentrating on. I lock my doors and double check the locks again. Scrambling for a chair from my breakfast table, I jam that under the door too, just in case. I'm breathing hard and I'm getting goosebumps despite getting out of the cold night air. I feel dirty and shaky at what almost happened. My hand smells strongly of my perfume. I must have used the wrong spray, but it worked to distract him either way.

With one last shiver, I shake off the feeling and strip out of my clothes so that I can hop in the shower to wash the night away. To wash the feel of his hands and lips on my skin away.

The hot water and steam helps to relax me enough to bring my heart back to a steady rhythm. Washing the sweat from the night away, I turn off the water and grab the fluffy towel that's hanging right outside the shower door. Drying myself while staring into the mirror, I take a deep breath in and out. Once that's done, I feel a lot better, but I'm still keeping my ears open and aware of any weird noises outside my door. Back in my preferred house wear, I decided to put my homemade choker back on. Something about it gives me a feeling of peace. And after what happened tonight, I need to feel some peace.

Laying down on my bed, I rewind the day back in my head, trying to figure out what brought all this craziness on, if I led him on in any way. I swear, I just met the guy, though. The drinks I had tonight make my eyes flutter faster than they should, sending me into sweet oblivion.

FIVE

JURI

I feel warm. Warmer than I usually am with my blankets on me. Warmer than it usually is during this time of the year. There's a concentration of warmth on only one side of my body. Rolling onto my back, I hear some crunching noises and something is poking my skin. *What the?* This cannot be possible. I know for a fact that my bed is like sleeping on pillows, I made sure of it. I force open my eyes but have to shield them right away because of how bright the sun is in my face. Gosh, I'm so confused right now. How much did I drink last night? Rubbing my eyes to get rid of some of my grogginess, I'm reaching around for my glasses, but it's nowhere to be found. A spike of fear runs through me. Oh no. Reaching around again expecting to feel my nightstand or something familiar, all I feel are pebbles, dry sharp grass and dirt beneath my hands no matter which directions I lead them to.

What in the world? Did I pass out outside somewhere? That still doesn't make any sense. I live in a city.

I sit myself up and look around. Okay, I really should have gotten corrective eye surgery because this is a frightening worst-case scenario: being somewhere and everything is a *blur*. Unless I pick up items and bring them about a foot or so from my face, I can't see anything clearly. Sun or not, the world looks like melting watercolors of different warm tones. The colors are blending in together and I'm a little afraid because not only can I not see clearly, I don't recognize where I am — nothing about what's around me is ringing any memory or mental images. What do I do?

I hear something scuffling to the left of me, but when I turn my head, I see nothing moving. Even though things are blurry, I can still kind of see the movement of some of the grass in the breeze. The wind is picking up the smell of dry warm dust. Another sound to my right has my head spinning that direction. My heart rate is picking up. Am I surrounded by something? The hairs on the back of my neck are rising and my gut is telling me there's a predator nearby. It's the same feeling I get when Gary's around. I also just realized in this moment, that I'm still in what I wore to bed. Great, not much protection there. But at least that means I didn't pass out drunk somewhere because how else would I have gotten into my sleepwear? I don't have my pepper spray either, can this get any worse? *Please don't answer that whoever is watching over me right now.*

I feel a chill go down my spine like an invisible warning and all of a sudden there is a change of air current a few feet from the front of my face, moving my hair with it.

Holy...

Something just moved by in front of my face, going right; something big that moved by *fast*. I hear something strike at what sounds to be flesh and a roar that must have come from the creature that was struck to my right. A yelp escapes me, but I'm too afraid to move from my position. My heart is utterly erratic right now. Of all the times to not have my glasses! I can't do anything but stay as still as I can in case there's something else that goes flying by around me. I don't want to get hit either. That has to be what that thing was, some sort of weapon for it to make that creature roar like that.

Crap, what if that creature is still alive and blames me?

"..Uh.. hello?" My voice is almost stuck in my throat at this point from the fear I feel. This hot sun is not helping me one bit either, my mouth is so dry. Suddenly, I hear grass and pebbles being disturbed by something coming from my left. The direction the thing flew from. *Do I turn to look? Dammit, how did I get myself into this position?*

I jerk a little from the feeling of someone touching me. Who's there? Suddenly I'm being dragged up to my feet by really strong — and really warm — arms. Warm, like this person must have been in the sun all day. He's standing really close to me and I can see him clearer because of it. It has to be a he for this person to be this big. The skin in front of my face is such a dark and even shade of a deep, deep umber. A deep dark chocolate with abs full of what looks like raised scarring on his skin in patterns going up to the start of his chest. This is something I've never seen before. *Wow.* I slowly bring my gaze up — and up — and I'm taken aback by the intensity of his gaze. It's very stoic but also very sharp, so I can't decipher what he's feeling or what he's thinking. His head is still turned towards the direction of the beast. Is it dead? Better yet, is this guy a friend or foe? The moment my eyes catch his, he takes a very subtle step back, like he's afraid to show weakness in front of me and catches his own reaction quickly.

"Your eyes," says the deepest rumble of a voice I have ever heard, like rolling thunder, and it just kicked my heart up to second gear in a different way. Holy hell, I could melt to that voice. It's authoritative and sure, confident. So is his gaze. He looks over my face; the same way I'm trying my best to look over his. He's more than a head taller than I am and my near-sightedness can only help me see so far. There's sounds coming from the necklace he's wearing when he moves. It reminds me of hollow wood hitting each other like a wooden wind chime, but even through the blur the shape reminds me of unnaturally large fangs. Fangs don't sound like hollow wood when they hit each other, do they?

Where the heck would this guy get fangs this large anyway? My mind suddenly goes back to the beast from before.

His voice breaks me away from thoughts of getting mauled and eaten alive with teeth that big. "Where is your village, little one? Have you lost your way? These are very dangerous areas to be wandering. The golden Leers wander these planes. These are their hunting grounds."

Golden what now?

His hand raises a little to the right of us and I still have no idea what he is talking about after cycling through my memory of all the animals I've heard of. I mean, I understand what he is saying, but I have no answers to what he is saying. I'm still trying to wrap my mind around what the hell is happening to me right now as my fingers automatically fiddle with my choker for some form of comfort. Suddenly, he leans down towards my neck, making me lean back a bit because this guy has no respect for personal space.

But this close, I see his face clearly — very clearly. And my good-ness is he *striking*. Dark, haunting eyes above a strong broad nose that has a piercing through his nostrils. His lips are full and the same color as the rest of him. He reminds me of a black jaguar, lethal grace and a body full of rippling muscles in motion. The only thing contrasting his features are the whites of his eyes. It's a striking juxtaposition against each other.

A thought in my mind clicks. Wait, was he the one that threw something to strike that creature? Looking at his bare chest and necklace again, my mind slowly begins to piece things together.

Did he just throw a spear in front of my face?

DUMA

What tribe does one hail from to have eyes like this? Eyes like the light spears that come from the heavens when the heavens are crying. In all my hunts and travels, I have never seen one such as her. Her skin looks like she is from our lands, darkened but only kissed by the sun. Too light to be from the Chintkku, the tone seems different to the skin of other nearby villages as well. I have never seen a coloring as soft as the female before me. It is *alluring*.

Does my mind fool me? It seems at times, she looks to be forcing her eyes to sharpen by squinting and narrowing her sight so the blacks of her eyes change in size. Perhaps her eyes are not as good as a hunter's eyes then. This is not good. That means she cannot see predators that may happen upon her, not until it is too late.

It is a good thing, I happened upon the golden leer when I did.

My eyes look over her once more, something I find myself enjoying more than I should. She is wearing a strange covering, something I do not recognize. It covers a lot of her with holes for her arms and I am surprised she does not burn up under it. The suns here can be merciless in certain seasons, and the rainy seasons would add weight to her outside wear, making it hard to move quickly, putting her at a disadvantage to the predators.

Many village women hope to catch themselves a warrior, but this little one seems she desperately needs one to keep her alive.

It is lucky that I happened upon her during my walk. I was trying to clear my head and breathe away from the village celebrations of our return with meat from the hunt. It can, at times, be too much for me — seeing all of my warriors happy with spirits and drink, chasing the unattached women. It has been many seasons since I've been where they are.

But it seems I was not in control of where my feet were taking me, even though I thought I was; my feet were being guided by higher beings towards *this female*. This small woman left to the elements of the plains. And for the first time in a very long time, my heart has a yearning to protect her and take care of her, especially because she does not have good eyes.

I gently place my hands on her arms and she feels like she's been warmed by the sun. Her skin prickles and her hairs are standing with my touch. "What are you called?"

She smells very good and her skin is as soft as the hide of some of the beasts that roam the plains. When she brings her sights back to my face, her eyes widen, and I am caught in the color of them again.

"Juri."

Though I heard her call out earlier when she was on the ground, being this close, I can feel the air of her voice caress my skin. She has a soft voice, not a voice of one who should be left out here defenseless. She is not a warrior.

"Come. We had good hunting today. There should be plenty for you to join us. If you are lost, you can stay with me until we find your village."

I shall provide for her while she is here, keep her safe.

SIX

I'm captivated by the deep rumble of his voice and by his presence of how sure he is of everything. He seems seasoned, a lot older than I am. The combination of his voice and presence makes my instincts feel like I can trust him. I always trust my instincts, so I guess I will be joining him back to his village. What else can I do? I don't know where the hell I am and what the hell is going on anyway. It wouldn't do well for me to be stumbling around out here. What if another beast finds me?

"Where are we?" I can't help but ask because this place looks like and feels like someplace in Africa, but it also doesn't. My mind is telling me there's just something a bit off.

"I do not understand your question. We are not far from the hunting plains to the west. I am a warrior of the Chintkku tribe. My village is just a few foot spans from where we are standing. This is where you are."

I am wracking my brain to see if I recognize any of the names he's telling me, but I honestly don't find any hint of familiarity anywhere in my mind. Where the hell am I? My hand fiddles with my choker again the longer I think.

"You wear a mark on you that I do not recognize as well. What tribe are you from? The talisman around your neck seems familiar but I cannot place a name to it." He's staring where my hands are near my neck and I realize the talisman he is referring to is the choker I'm wearing.

"Talisman? This thing around my neck? It came to me out of nowhere. I don't know why I always feel drawn to touch it. It brings me comfort." What else can I tell him? I don't know anything about this either.

He hums but doesn't respond just yet. What? What is it? What am I missing here?

"The village sight seeker may be able to help us find out more about it then." He continues to lead me towards this village he speaks of, but my eyes don't see anything resembling one just yet. "He does not join our festivities much, so it will be easy to find him in his hut. I will take you to see him." His pace is quick and I have to almost jog to keep up with him. He notices and starts to slow down. I can see the white of his teeth, I think. Is he laughing at me? "Have no worry, little Juri, you are safe with me. I am a warrior of many generations. My fighting blood goes back to the original tribal wars. You can trust me."

He is so earnest in what he says that even though I don't understand half of it, I *feel* what he's saying. He is of a warrior bloodline that is bound to honor. That's good, right? I'm almost huffing and puffing by the time I kind of see what looks like the top of huts, maybe?

Catching my breath a little, I look at him and offer him a friendly smile. I'm about to enter into new territory, better start making friends quickly. "Okay, I trust you. But what's your name, I don't think you've mentioned it."

His smile broadens. I know this because his white teeth are such a high contrast to his skin tone. He leans down closer to my face — almost like he knows I can't see well — and tells me, "I am called Duma."

KWAME - THE SIGHT SEEKER

I feel it. It has begun. There is a ripple. A shiver. A chill. Something is different. Something has touched our lands that has not touched before. Something not from here. My eyes, they only see the color of light spears from the sky.

Tales passed down from my youth flit through my mind. The ancestors have spoken of this. The tales around the fire have slowly become tales for children, our history slowly fading with each new blood brought into this world. But my memory serves me well, and the stories are not stories at all but a foretelling. It is said the lands will be united by the strongest of light spears that hail from the skies. The last tribal war; the war to end all wars and unite our people as one. To finally bring peace to the lands.

The shiver runs through me again. It is the touch, the touch of the sight seeker passed down through my bloodline. The ancestors spoke true. It is here, and it is time.

Beasts as yellow as the suns. Something round from the times of old, from the time of the beginning. A time broken by blood will be created whole once more. All of our blood will be united as one.

Duma's destiny will play a big part in this war. Thank the blessed suns it is he who was chosen. He is one of the last seasoned warriors who shares blood with warriors from the original tribal wars.

The blood of the beginning.

His time has come. And he cannot fail.

DUMA

I lead Juri to Kwame's hut, ignoring the other villagers calling out to us to join in feast. Some of them stare at the visitor with curious eyes but say nothing. They know better than to question me. There is smoke billowing out the top opening of the small hut in front of us, signaling he is indeed resting inside with fires to warm his home. Once we stand in front of his door, I scratch the outside wall of his hut beside the opening to tell him we wish to see him before we enter his space.

"Kwame! I have —"

Kwame's voice booms over mine before I can finish. The excitement in his voice gives me surprise. "Duma! It has begun and your destiny starts now. It has been foretold and passed on to me since the beginning of our people. Since the time of our first bloodborn. It is you Duma who must take the path towards the light spear that will hail from the skies to unite our lands!"

What is the old one speaking of? I am unsure of what Kwame is going on about but he has never steered us wrong as the sight seeker of our people. He is shaking his walking stick towards the skies with his frail arm while he exits his hut to tell me this. His body language and speech wishes for me to listen, so I will.

"What must I do, Kwame?"

"Duma, it is you who must lead us in this!" Some of the villagers are looking our way curiously. "I can only tell you that your paths must cross others and that this will be the war to end all wars between the tribes."

I take his words as written in stone. He is one who has been blessed by the suns in this skill. "Kwame, what of little Juri? I have come upon her in the plains and do not know which way to take her back home."

Is there a reason for this? For why I have stumbled upon this female.

"Juri? Who is Juri?"

She must have been standing behind me for Kwame to have questioned me like I am speaking falsely. Turning, I find her like one who plays behind trees in their youth. I gently grab her shoulders and bring her in front of me to face our sight seeker.

"This is Juri, Kwame." The moment she brings her head up to look at him is the moment Kwame takes in a hard breath. I felt the same the first time I saw them.

"Duma, her eyes! They are the color of light spears." He leans in and stares at her sharply making little Juri lean back a little. "Where did you say you found her?"

"What are you talking about? I have brown eyes."

Little Juri must have been under the suns longer than I first thought.

"I do not know how she came to be in the plains, but it is where I felled a golden leer that would have eaten her alive if I was not close by. She does not have the hunter's eye, and so I brought her back to the tribe to look over her."

Kwame is still staring into her eyes and now is mumbling something that I cannot hear clearly. "Kwame, what do you speak of? Speak louder, old man."

"Beasts as yellow as the suns." Yellow as the suns? The suns are more gold than yellow, I know this, for I have hunted many seasons for our village. Does he speak in tricks of the tongue? Gold… a golden leer?

Kwame is slowly coming even closer to little Juri, and she steps back, bumping into my body with hers. I place my hands on her shoulders for comfort and I can feel her body relaxing. This makes my chest swell with pride, her trust in me. Old man Kwame can be strange at times. When the old sight seeker comes close enough to her, I give him a look to let him know he has taken enough steps to frighten prey that currently wishes to flee. It is only my hands that keep her still.

Kwame reaches towards her neck, and my reflex brings my grip around his wrist, stopping him. My heart is starting to run inside my chest, for I do not like the thought of another touching what I am protecting. Not when she shrinks even closer to me at his movement in fear.

Kwame is still mumbling something, not minding my firm grip on his wrist. When I strain to sharpen my ears, I hear it.

"Something round from the time of the beginning."

He is speaking of the talisman around little Juri's neck. I am glad to have stopped his hand then. I do not like thinking of him touching her *there*, a place so vulnerable.

"What are you mumbling about, old man?" Some days I wonder if he has many more cycles left. He's been an old man to me since my youth, and I have already seen forty-nine cycles.

"Duma, it is *you*. *You* must lead her. It is her! It is said the lands will be united by the strongest of light spears that hail from the skies. I have never seen eyes as these."

"What's wrong with my eyes?"

If I am understanding his ramblings, I am destined with little Juri to unite the lands? How can this be? The lands are not broken. Juri does not even have the hunter's eye. She does not belong in any war. Kwame's interest in touching her makes my inner beast growl. It is time to end this moment.

"Thank you old sight seeker, we bid you good feast on this day." I remove his hand from her space and replace mine back on Juri's shoulders, leading her away from Kwame's hut. I feel like a beast that gets its first meal and protects its kill.

We both breathe out when we leave the vicinity of the old sight seeker's hut, the crisp air of the plains bringing with it the smells of cooked meat. My beast calms inside of me with Kwame's distance.

"Duma, I don't know how to get back home."

"It is okay, little one. You can remain with me until we find a way." I will be her warrior until we find out what old man Kwame is talking about.

CHIEMKO

We fared well in the hunt today. The waters brought many creatures close to our shores, giving us not only meat but hides. My people will make good use of all the materials these creatures bring us. Despite the success of our catch and my chest filling with pride, there is something in the air that is different from the other days of hunting — *I feel it*. Something is calling me back out to the waters, even though the hunting trip is over. My body looking back over the waters again and again out of my control, searching for something. My warriors all want to go back home and have a feast from our spoils, so they do not feel the same pull I feel.

"Come Chiemko! It is time to celebrate. You led a good hunt this day!"

"It is all of us, Issa, that made it a good hunt. All the warriors did well."

"Don't humble yourself too much, Chief. Your leadership is what brings success."

Humble. No, I only speak truth. It is not just a leader that brings victory but the people behind him and their loyalty.

We make it to shore and jump out of our boats to pull them up away from the waves. It takes extra men with the spoils we bring back home. The women and children from the village come rushing towards us when they see some of their men come back home. The children all cry out for the tales of our ventures, their eyes sparkling with interest. They are future little warriors of our tribe. Though they are young, they learn quickly that working together makes the meat get on the tables faster and into their bellies. The old warriors we left behind are patting those returning from the hunt on their backs for another job well done.

My tribe are a happy people. Our lives are simple and content on the island.

I do not have family and so the welcoming tribe members are usually just friendly to me upon my return, but no more than that. The sound of the waters makes me turn back to look again, like a whisper of promises and secrets. Something is calling to me, pulling my heart to return and I am unsure of what decision I should make. The joyous cries of the people snap my head back towards the men and women around me. There will be high festivities this night with what we brought back and late nights around the fire with tales of the water creatures and battles.

The whispers of the shores float to my ears again. I will give myself a night to think on this. If the feeling does not leave me, I will go where the winds and water call me.

GAMBA

My legs carry me away from my village, the sounds of their happy cries dying upon the wind. I needed a break from all the festivities. The unattached women of the tribe can be overwhelming when they are hunting males. It used to be fun ten cycles ago, but now at forty-five cycles, I find that I tire of the games they play. They are fun but they cling, wanting something I do not think I can give them. I am too old for their chase of me, and my heart seeks something more than games. The only problem is, I do not know what it is seeking. Tonight's festivities brought something new out of me, something I haven't felt before.

A yearning. What is it that I have to yearn for when the hunt fulfils me? The women are plentiful and the feeling inside of me only pulls me away from them instead of towards them. What are the gods trying to tell me?

My feet continue their trek across the warm ground. When the ground becomes harder, I know I am close to my destination. The cries of the creatures overhead sound far away, just like the sounds of my people. Readjusting the bow across my shoulders, I continue my climb. No sense in coming out to find peace and getting caught by surprise to find a predator waiting. When I make it to the spot, I let out a relaxed breath and look around to make sure I am not being followed by any friend or foe. When the immediate surroundings remain clear, I lower myself to sit on the main rock in one of my secret areas away from the village, surrounded by trees and looking over the pass. I come here when I want to think alone, to find peace, to clear my mind for upcoming hunts — to think of strategies for quicker hunts. Staring down onto the plains, I feel a cool breeze pick up, sending up the scents of the beasts nearby. *You will live this day, for we have plenty of meat to last many moons.*

But despite the joy I feel from the happiness my warriors and I brought to our village, there is something different about today. The feeling of yearning for something unknown still echoes inside of me alongside the peace I feel in this very moment. This strange inner calling — it is what led me to seek this place during the festivities away from everyone. It is a tug inside. Do the gods speak to me? What are the blessed suns trying to tell me? Is there a need to be ready for something?

I look to my side to make sure my bows and arrows are within my arm's reach. Being a lone hunter can be a dangerous thing on these lands, and I am not a fool. This pull might bring me towards something dangerous, but I will be ready for it.

SEVEN

JURI

Duma takes me through the festivities of the village and all eyes are on me, especially from the women, I just feel it. It seems Duma has a fan club that he's either oblivious to or is just straight ignoring because he only stares straight ahead as he leads the way. The hairs on the back of my neck are rising from some of the looks I'm getting, even if I can't see it that clearly. I don't care where I'm at right now. Women are women, and women can be vicious when they want to be. I feel a potential catfight stirring, so I scoot closer to Duma's back. He must feel my uneasiness because he places a hand on my lower back to bring me ahead of him in a protective gesture. I'm grateful for it.

Looking around the village, I notice that Duma must be one of the older men here in regards to "warriors" as he says. His body is more worn and hardened, his bulk much wider than the other men in the tribe from what I can see through the blur, something I've come to notice when men age beyond a certain point. He definitely seems much older than I am, perhaps in his mid to late forties if I took a guess. But younger than the sight seeker, who reminds me of Rafiki from The Lion King. His large presence behind mine stirs something inside me. It's kind of sexy.

After walking what feels like a few yards, Duma goes into what I assume is his personal hut. It's far away from the village, almost on the outskirts of it. Strange in a way, for a man who is so well known. To be that popular but to be on the out fringes of the village? Like a lone wolf who seeks solitude.

Once we pass the hanging cloth and enter through the doorway, I take a look at the surroundings inside and notice it is very sparse. A fringy light tan mat lies on the floor to one side, some pottery looking items to another and what my eyes assume to be weapons in another corner. It screams bachelor pad, tribal style. Has he not connected with any of the village women? At his age, I don't see him as a sort of player, not with the way he ignored all the attention that was thrown his way. He seems too aloof and reserved. Maybe that's what the village women are attracted to? His mysterious nature. What woman doesn't like a man who is tall, dark and mysterious?

"We must share the mat for now, little Juri. It is not much, but it is all I have."

I'm not sure how I feel about that. Though I feel safe with him, I haven't really shared a sleeping space with a person of the opposite sex before. Well, it's not like I can be picky. No time better than the present. It's better than being eaten by whatever that creature was that Duma slayed for me. That's kind of sweet the more I think about it.

Duma leans down towards his cluster of his pots and brings out what looks to be beef jerky of some sort out of one of them, and brings it closer to me as an offering.

"If you hunger little Juri, I have plenty of meat from my stores to share with you this eve."

What a gentleman. There is just something about him that makes me not as nervous as I probably should be. This is just a dream anyway, might as well make myself feel good and eat something. Extending my arm to take it, I feel his eyes on me even if I cannot see him as clearly as I would like. Something about the way he makes my skin feel.

"Thank you, Duma. I am kind of hungry." Taking a bite out of the jerky, I'm amazed by the flavor and spices this little stick packs. Wow, is it because this is dreamland that everything tastes so much more intense? I inadvertently moan a little, not realizing how hungry I was. It makes sense since I haven't eaten since the night before. Chewing contentedly, I close my eyes and just savor the flavors in my mouth.

DUMA

I have never seen one eat in such pleasure. My loincloth is starting to shift and I am trying to keep my hunter's calm. Little Juri is making sounds that mess with my senses and thoughts. My inner beasts purr in response. I cannot help but stare at her mouth as she enjoys the food I provide for her. That in itself makes my chest swell with pride. To be able to provide for a female again, especially one who appreciates it so.

Juri has beautiful features. Her skin is kissed by the sun so evenly, like she wanders the plains without coverings, but still remains so much lighter than the Chintkku women, a softer color. I have never seen hair as full of life like hers; it moves with every step she takes and shifts with the breeze. Her body is more rounded than the women of the village as well and it makes my hands yearn to touch her again. Her eyes, by the blessed sun, her eyes. I only wish I can find a way to help her hone her hunter's eyes. She is too vulnerable as she is.

Why does she keep saying that her eyes are brown when they are so clearly not? I am unsure of the color name, but it is not how I would describe a light spear.

She moans again and I shift my thighs to try and push down my cock. Clearing my throat, I hope she understands that the noises she is making are a bit too forward for an unattached female. Is she doing this to call to my beast? It makes me wonder what other kind of noises she would make when one takes her between her legs. Gah, my loincloth can only do so much to hide my hardness and so I turn around to try and calm my thoughts.

As I close my eyes and try to think of hunting out in the unforgiving blaring suns during the hotter seasons, making all the warriors feel like meat roasting over the open flame. My cock starts to go down until I feel small hands in a light touch on my back, making my skin prickle. Juri has the softest fingers. I do not know what she is doing, but I am afraid to move in case she stops. The thought of her marking me with her scent has my beast purring in pride.

Her hands travel over my warrior marks. As one becomes of season, we receive a blooding ritual that marks us as warriors. The cuts are deep enough to leave raised scars that become patterns indicating how many seasons we are in our hunt and prowess. Being the oldest of the warriors in this tribe, my back and front are full of patterned cuts and raised scars that are only particular to me and my bloodline — one that goes back to the days of the old wars.

"What happened to you, Duma?"

Her voice is as soft as the breeze on a good hunting day. The sound of it rings a touch of sadness to my ears. What is there to be sad about? Surely, her tribe has seasoned warriors such as I?

"They are my warrior markings. They tell the tale of my seasons and the bloodline I carry. I am the last of the original warriors kin from the time of the first tribal wars. I am the eldest warrior of the Chintkku tribe." My breath catches when her hands continue to feel me in a soft caress. It has been so long since I've felt the touch of an unattached female. My heart beats like the sound of war drums and my breathing slows, like I am anticipating the hunt.

"Duma, there are so many. So you're saying, only you have these particular markings in this pattern here?" Her hands go from the expanse of my back and now travel across my sides to the front of me. I am unsure of what my next move should be. In a hunt, I will either go in for the kill or run and save my hide for another day. But little Juri is no predator.

She leans in closer to me. I know this because her body heat is now bouncing close to mine. She does not have a hunter's eye and must come closer to make sure of what she can see. I find this frustrating and endearing at the same time, making my heart feel full. The breath that leaves her mouth runs across my skin with how close she is to me. I remain still as to not startle her.

It must be hard to not be able to see predators close by, living by death's embrace. How did she stay alive this long?

When little Juri moves to the front of me, my cock stirs once more with how close she is leaning in, touching my warrior marks. When her hand slides up my body towards my chest, my heart skips a drum beat and my skin feels like a chill has shot through me from the inside.

"Duma, I'm glad you have these. It means that even when I can't see you, I will always know you by touch. Kind of like braille in a sense. It rests my mind to know that I won't be tricked because of my eyes."

Little Juri makes my chest tight with these words. How did she fare for so long without a warrior's protection? I do not know what this braille is, but I can imagine it means that her fingers will allow her to see truth in front of her.

The beast inside me tells me we must protect little Juri.

EIGHT

I'm lost in the intricate details of Duma's body. He must have had to suffer so much with all these cuts. They probably happened at different times, I'm sure. I shouldn't feel sad about it. He seems proud. My fingers trace the curve of one of the more prominent scars that leads to the middle, just below and between his pecs, when Duma's hands halt my movement. It startles me a bit and I lift my eyes up to his. Did I make him mad?

His voice sounds a little gruffer than usual when he says, "Little Juri, you may rest on the mat. I will head out and make another one for your comfort. You will not take up too much space on it, but I am not a small warrior. Wait for my return." As quickly as he spoke, he turns and leaves me standing there wondering what just happened.

What is there for me to do, but exactly what he says? Moving towards the mat, I lean down close to see what it's made of. It seems like some sort of dried grass that's not as prickly as you would think. The way it's woven, the grass' blades are flattened with the smooth parts touching where you lay down on. *Okay, I can do this.* Laying down in my t-shirt and panties, I try to make myself comfortable. I must have been more tired than I thought because I don't remember closing my eyes.

I hate that feeling of limbo, when you're in and out of dreams but unsure if you are really awake. Trying to rouse myself, I finally wake up with a start. Since I knew I didn't have my glasses the last time I woke up, I didn't bother to even search for them. With a yawn, I make myself sit up and rub my eyes, but something is different; I feel it. Whatever I'm lying on feels like I'm sleeping on pillows and feathers. That can't be right. That grass mat was flatter than a prison mattress. When I attempt to look around, things look eerily familiar. It looks like I'm back in my bedroom. What is going on? Was that just a really vivid dream? But Duma's warm skin felt so real.

Reaching towards my nightstand, I find my glasses where they usually sit and put them on. Looking for my phone that's still attached to the charging cable nearby, I bring it awake to see what day and time it is. I feel so out of whack. The phone tells me it's Saturday, the day after our assistant's night out. Huh, I guess it was a dream after all? Maybe all the craziness with Gary got to me, so I dreamed someone like Duma up? The perfect man, one that wants to protect you and make you feel cherished. My hand reaches towards my neck and I let out a small exhale once I feel my choker still there. It is so strange that I'm always called to touch it when I want to feel comfort. Now, touching it reminds me of Duma's face when he leaned down to look at me. I feel heat creeping up my neck at that thought and decide I need to shower and get this grogginess out of my brain.

Gently taking it off and placing my choker on my dresser, my t-shirt is the next to go. When I go to take off my panties, there's something scratchy caught between my waistband and buttcheek. Feeling around for whatever it is, I bring it to the front of my face and see that it's a blade of dead grass that's the same color of Duma's sleeping mat. *What the?*

Once I'm showered and refreshed, I browse on my laptop and start looking up information on corrective eye surgery. That dream really left me feeling vulnerable. I couldn't see a damn thing unless it was right up in my face, how *disturbing*. The things we take for granted in a first world society like always having access to glasses, no matter where you live.

Ten to twenty web pages later, I'm a little overwhelmed with what I'm reading on the screen because it does not boil down to the actual price. All I am getting is that I need to come in for a consultation because it depends on how bad my vision is. But something good I did catch while reading was that when an appointment is made, the procedure is quite simple and quick. They do suggest having someone help you out, at least for a day, to make sure you're alright. That stumped me a bit because I live alone and the rest of my family is back in India. I'm not sure I trust the other cubicle mates just yet; we've only gone out together that one time. I guess corrective eye surgery will have to be put off again until I can figure out what to do about the recovery period.

Well, with the rest of the day off, I need to think about how to spend it. Do I watch some Netflix? Go out somewhere? No, I don't feel like leaving my apartment today. Gary might be watching my every move. I need to figure out what I'm going to do about him. Maybe I should start leaving at different times of the day and changing up my routine so he can't anticipate when I leave. That will have to do for now until I can figure out a more permanent solution.

The afternoon sun is spilling into my apartment and bringing in warmth from the season. It's the beginning of summer and the cool air is starting to dissipate earlier in the day. Getting up from my kitchen table and my laptop, I explore what I have in my refrigerator. Finding a cool bottle of water and shutting the refrigerator door, I head to my bedroom for a little cat nap because why not? After taking a few swigs of water and placing my bottle onto the dresser, my eyes land back on my choker. I had forgotten to put it back on when I got out of the shower this morning.

Placing my glasses down on my dresser, I wrap the black string around my neck by feeling and start towards my comfortable white bed. The combination of the sun streaming in and my sweatpants might make me too hot during my nap, so I strip myself back down to panties before I crawl into the clouds of blankets and pillows. The moment my head hits the fluff, my eyes drift off to sleep.

My legs feel wet and it wakes me up. Did I just pee on the bed? When I put my hands down to push my body up, my hands sink into something grainy. The air also smells different. Bringing one of my hands up to my face, I think it's sand I see. The sound of crashing waves brings me back to the water and wetness issue. Am I on a beach? Am I dreaming again? A beach doesn't seem too bad.

My legs, panties and half of my t-shirt are wet by the time I situate myself into a standing position. Bending over at the waist to brush the sand off my legs, I feel something watching me. It's that gut instinct again. I really hope it's not like the last dream with that golden whatever creature trying to eat me. Dammit, another dream without my glasses. My head has been bent down to brush the sand off and nothing has fallen off my face. I always seem to find myself in the strangest predicaments. What is my mind or subconscious trying to tell me? That I'm being stupid by putting off that corrective eye surgery?

That has to be it.

"You've wandered a bit far from the village, were the festivities too much for you too?"

The cadence of the voice is masculine and very confident. Again, how do I keep finding myself in these situations? Suddenly a gust of air comes towards me and, who I am assuming is the stranger, grabs me from my midsection and throws me over his shoulder at the same time as he jumps backwards. The movement jostles my body and slams my gut into his shoulder. Damn, it's a good thing my stomach is empty. Gosh, what is happening right now?

"That was close, the creature almost got your foot. It slithers quietly and is attracted to the heat of its prey. The bite can be poisonous."

What the hell did he just say?

The stranger makes a move to put me back down, but now that he's essentially described what sounds like a snake, I wrap my legs around his midsection so my feet *don't* hit the ground. Is he crazy? He just said it almost got my foot!

His strong arms band around me once he figures out I'm not letting him put me down and we both look at each other for a moment, face to face. Well, this is awkward. With my arms around his neck and shoulders, it's the perfect distance for my nearsightedness to give me a clear view of his features. *Dear lord.* He's got golden bronze skin, thick eyebrows and dark eyes that are captivating. When he catches me looking over his features, he smiles and a dimple shows up on his right cheek. His hair is straight, short and sticking up every which way. He looks young, perhaps a little younger than me — or maybe he's around my age, I'm not too sure. His hands feel calloused, hands that are currently holding onto my very naked and wet ass cheeks. These panties aren't doing much at all to hide anything. *How embarrassing.*

Internally grimacing, I try to figure out a way to get down without getting bitten by snakes I can't see.

"I do not recognize you from the village. I am Chiemko."

His voice softens with how close we are. His eyes are roaming my face and stopping at my eyes. His stare is searing into my soul and I can feel heat creep up my cheeks. The ones on top.

Clearing my throat, I move to try and get out of this intimate hold we've found ourselves in. Before my feet touch the ground though, I make sure to look around as best as I can in case I catch any movement below me. Only when my feet touch the sand, do I let go of his neck. Oh, from down here I see that he is quite taller than I am. His hands are still holding my arms as if he is just as reluctant to let go of our initial connection as well.

"What shall I call you?" He gives me another smile, and the dimple is distracting.

"Juri. I'm not from around here. I mean, I'm not from your village." Did Duma have a beach too? I don't remember smelling the sea or any sort of large bodies of water the last time.

His smile falters and he's tilting his head to the side in thought. A little frown forms between his eyebrows before he says, "How can this be? The village is on an island. How did you come upon it? I do not see a boat here. Were you lost in the waters?"

He suddenly brings his face down so close to mine, the tip of our noses are almost touching, making me sharply inhale.

"Have the sun and water spirits led you to me?" What? "Did the Gods place you here? Is this what was calling to me? My heart was being pulled back to the waters once the hunt ended, and now that feeling is gone." His eyes flick to my lips and I stop breathing for a second. "Gone since I've met you, my Juri."

His eyes are boring into mine again and it's quite unnerving. My heart is picking up a little bit but my fight or flight isn't kicking in. Why is that?

He straightens up but continues to look at me with interest. "My gut has never led me wrong, my Juri. It is why I was chosen to lead the seasoned warriors on the hunt." A leader? He quickly leans back down towards my face and his voice becomes lower. "I think we were meant to meet this day, and I have to say, you are the best catch I have ever had the pleasure of bringing home."

Very confident, indeed.

NINE

CHIEMKO

I have never seen one such as her. There are so many things about her that are the same but different from the women in my village. Her skin is kissed by the sun, but has a touch of something more, a different tone. From far away, she could pass for one of us — islanders. But this close, with eyes that remind me of the skies and storms, she stands out like the unique beauty she is.

In my thirty-five cycles, I still have not been able to get used to the village festivities. Even if I am the cause of them at times. They are too much for me. Families gathering and warriors courting available females. I was never fully able to connect to my village after my parents' death, only through the hunts I lead do I feel the connection to my people as I should. But once my duties are done, my soul feels lost again, trying to find its next reason to search and find whatever it is the village needs from me. All the women of the village only see me as Chiemko, the young warrior who lost his whole family — the seasoned warrior who now leads the people.

This is the first time my heart feels settled, a calm I've never had since coming into season. But now, in front of this female before me, there is no need to go, no need to hunt in the unknown waters. The pull is gone, the water's whispers no longer promising the unknown. There's no longer a need to lose myself in something just to keep my mind from drowning in loneliness. I find that my Juri fills the aching hole that was left in my chest.

She probably does not know this, not from the way she is looking left and right, trying to gather her surroundings.

There is something strange about her. For her to not be able to sense and quickly see the creature as dark as night slithering on the light sand by her feet. If I had not been walking the shores, she would be in a very bad position and not walking at my side after a bite to her leg. She does not stray too far from my body either, not that I mind, but unattached females do not usually stay this close to another person when they are walking. It is such an intimate gesture that I find myself wondering, for the first time, what it would be like to have someone for myself. Someone other than the waters and my boat.

"Wow, it sounds like a big party is happening right behind those trees."

"Yes, it was a good hunt, and we were able to bring much meat to the village. You are welcome to join." I look over at her and feel my body heat rising from the sway of her hips when her feet dig into the sand.

"Oh. You are a warrior then? I'm not sure if I want to join the festivities. I'm not sure if I have the right things to say when people talk to me. I'm not exactly from your island, you know?" She looks at me with sad eyes and I feel a tug in my chest that tells me I need to protect her, even if it's only from the prying conversations of the village.

"My hut is not far from the shore; we can rest there until the village celebrations are done." *Thud thud.* My heart feels a fear I haven't felt since my childhood. The fear of her answer to what I am asking of her feels the same as the first time I hunted in the waters.

"That sounds really good, Chiemko. I think I would be too embarrassed with my wet outfit to show up at the party. Your hut sounds like the perfect place to rest."

Why does my heart feel like this with her answer? It's tight, it hurts, and it feels relieved all at once. It makes me smile, even though it doesn't feel that good. *Her* smile is like the rising suns over the waters when the day brings good luck for a hunt, its colors overflowing onto the waves. It makes my heart glow.

Leading her to my hut on the outskirts of the main village, I point it out with my hand. "This one here, it is mine. I do not share it with anyone, so I have one of the smaller huts on the shore." Hopefully, my Juri finds it adequate. I can always make a bigger one, if she asks. I did see some dried wood by the shore on my walk earlier.

When we reach the front, I put my hand on her back to urge her up the steps that take her into the front door.

"Why does your home have to be up on stilts with a ladder?"

What a strange question. How else can one have a hut left when the water and tides rise over the shores? With a little encouragement and a push, Juri walks up the stairs slowly and carefully. My gut tells me she does not trust her eyes as a hunter does, so I make sure to be right behind her to comfort her climb. How has Juri fared this long without help? And for her to be found alone wandering the shores of an unknown island to her? Thinking of another male helping her makes my beast inside angry.

When we make it inside, she stands still for a moment, looking around. My hut is small, made from strong wood that drifts from the waters and baked by the suns. The opening in the back wall of my hut looks over the waves that call to me during my solitude.

"The sound of the water is soothing. You must find a lot of rest when you're in here."

If only it were true. My heart has never truly rested until this day, and there has never been such a beauty as what is standing before me.

"The waters calm me and call to me. I can never stay still in one place too long. I always find myself walking the shores, getting closer and closer to my boat with no place in mind to go." How sad is this truth, now that I have said it out loud?

"Oh. That sounds very … lonely."

She is right. It does, and I have not thought about it that way until now. She makes me want what I never thought to have. I will make her my female.

Taking that last step up to get inside the hut beside her, I face her and take her hand in mine. Giving it a soft kiss, I hear her take in air through her beautiful lips. Does she feel the same yearning I do? The string to my heart that now pulls tight.

She turns to me with a confused look and I find the feeling in my chest turning into something different. "Chiemko, I do not belong here. Will you help me get home?"

But I've only just found you. My beast inside is raging against my mind with the thought of her leaving me before even having the chance to claim her. I need to calm my thoughts.

"You wish to ride the waters with me? In my boat? Do you hail from the mainland across the waters, then?" Maybe that is why she looks a little different from the people on my island? Reaching into my memories of the people I've come across during my rare visits, she does not look like anyone on the mainland either.

"I don't know how to explain it, but I do know that I don't belong on this island. Would it be okay if we try?"

When her eyes stare into mine the way it does now, I would take her anywhere she asks. I'm lost in their depths — a monster being called home into the deep waters. The thought of her wanting to leave my side has my chest aching and arms flexing to ready for battle to keep my prize. But I nod my head anyway and her smile has my chest feeling something else.

How can I survive all these new emotions crashing inside of me? It is a strange thing to want to dive into the unknown, head first — knowing it could possibly mean your death. Letting her hand fall from my grasp, I turn to lead her towards my door. I lead her path, going down the ladder first. When my feet touch the ground, I look up to wait for her. She is coming down slower than when she went up. Is it from fear? When I see her foot take a misstep, my body moves before I can tell it to.

A small cry leaves her lips right as she lands in my arms. We find our faces close together again in another type of embrace. My heart is being pulled on the string I cannot see and my blood is still pumping furiously from the fear of watching her fall. Without a second thought, I press my lips to hers. I have never done this before, but I have seen the other villagers do it when they are courting.

Now I see why.

Her lips are soft and I become more curious in discovering more about them. When I go to do it again, she breathes in and her arms are holding me tighter as if she is afraid to fall again. *I would never let her fall.* Her lips are just as soft against mine this time as they were the first time and I crave to taste her with my tongue.

Suddenly, she pushes off me and puts her feet on the ground, turning quickly to look out to the rolling waves. Does she fear my predator inside? Her reactions are only making me want to hunt her more. *Maybe this is what she wants.*

"So, where is your boat I keep hearing about, hmm?" She pretends to put her hand over her eyes when I know she cannot see that well from the way she's been moving around my hut and the ladder.

I will give into her game; I will give chase.

"I will return to my hut and get my hunting tools in case we need them. Once I return, you will follow me and I will bring us to my boat." I do not want to leave her standing here alone, but we cannot travel the waters without having something to protect us with.

The festivities towards the center of the island are still going, and drums can be heard over the laughter and cheers of my people. But I would not miss being near my Juri for anything, or the calm her presence gives my heart. When I return with my weapons, we make it to my boat that has been brought up to the shore after our most recent hunt. It is a bigger boat I use to lead the other warriors.

"Wow, okay. I was thinking of something else, but this will do."

I am unsure of what she means.

Helping her into the boat, one foot at a time, I move myself to the back so that I may move it into the waters that await our travels. With one big push, I find my footing and rhythm. My muscles move from memory. Each step becomes easier and easier the closer we get to wet sand.

When the front half of the boat is in the water, I run and jump into it before it gets swept in the waves. My Juri startles at my leap and laughs. It is the most beautiful sound that buries itself under my skin. *I need more of it.*

The waters push us along in a steady rocking movement. My hunting spears and weapons are close enough to me that I am able to grab it quickly if needed. When I look over to Juri, she is gazing out into the night sky. The moons here offer enough light to hunt, but with Juri not having good eyes, I am unsure of what she sees.

"My Juri, do your eyes not see well?"

She quickly turns to me, staring for a moment of silence. "…how did you know?"

What do you fear, Juri?

"It is okay, Juri. It is a hunter's instinct to watch for strengths and weaknesses. But I will protect you." *And I will kill anything that tries to take her from me.*

Her voice comes out low in a soft whisper. "You sound so much like him."

I do not like the sound of this 'him' she is talking about. My beast inside claws at my mind again and roars.

TEN

JURI

Are all the men in my dreams manifestations of my subconscious yearning for a man to take care of me? It's so strange that Chiemko's thoughts and actions remind me so much of Duma and his lethal grace. They're both warriors of their tribes, that's for sure. I wonder if they know each other?

I have no idea where we are going, but I know that whatever I need to find is not going to be on an isolated island. I thought, perhaps, the best course of action is to go *somewhere* and not just remain where I woke up.

My thoughts go back to Duma, and that old man in his village. He seemed to know more than we do about what I'm here for. Maybe if I could just find Duma's village again? Assuming I'm dreaming up the same world. That's possible, right?

"Chiemko, do you know Duma?"

"His name does not sound familiar. Is he from my village?"

Is Chiemko grimacing? It's blurry, but I swear he is. "No, I don't think so. He looks a little different from you. Much darker skinned. He's a warrior of his tribe as well. He has… scars on his body that distinguish him from the other warriors. He called them his warrior markings."

The change in Chiemko is immediate, and he sneers with a little growl. *Woah, what is this about? It's just a question, man. Calm down.*

"The warriors you speak of are from the Chintkku tribe, on the mainlands. They are ruthless in their ways and continue to practice barbaric carvings on their skin to mark their people. Blood as rituals and warriors whose spears are said to always aim true. But they have never met *me*. I am the youngest of the Matalo'toa tribe, but I lead one of the greatest warriors we've ever seen." He tells me this all through gritted teeth and I'm kind of sorry I brought it up.

Wow, okay, sore subject. I mean, he sounds really proud and confident about his position with his people, but there seems to be some sort of beef between the two tribes. Maybe it's not a good idea that I'm making him bring me to Duma. But what if that old guy knows something that will help me get back home faster? *It's a dream, I know.* Maybe I just need to go to sleep somewhere and wake back up? How do you wake yourself up from dreamland, though? Maybe that old sight guy has some magic mojo he can throw on me to send me home faster? Some sleeping sand? I need to at least try. But first, I need to calm this guy down.

"Your tribe sounds strong. I just need to find Duma, please." Does please work here like back home?

Chiemko's sneer is slow to go away and his frown remains. I'm not sure what else to say to get him back to his jovial demeanor from before. He really can be scary as hell when he wants to be. Maybe that's his warrior aura coming off him right now. I personally wouldn't want to go up against him. Looking down at my panties, I internally grimace myself. *At least I didn't wake up in one of those dreams where you're naked in class.*

"Are you an attached female then? Do you belong to this... Duma?" He almost spits Duma's name when he says it.

Okay, my mind is going in all different directions with this question. Attached? Like married? Belong? Like property? Tribes are known to do things a little differently, but I never even entertained the idea. I just want to go home back to my soft bed.

"I don't know how to answer that, Chiemko. I don't belong to anyone but myself. I'm just trying to get home." There, that's not offensive or anything, right?

He moves his now stoic gaze from my face and lips and looks out onto the water as he stands at the opposite end of the boat, the pole of the sail separating us. I can see his body deflate a little from an exhale. It's a bit blurry, but I could have sworn it moved that way. I'm not sure if I let him down or relieved him with my statement. Maybe I should get the attention off me and onto something else, like him.

"Chiemko, are *you*... attached? Do you have a female that belongs to you?" If he was, I need to punch him in the face from those kisses he stole from me under his hut. How inappropriate.

I can see his body move a little bit, in a blurry expansion from his back. Chiemko is naked from the waist up, like most of the other village men I've seen from Duma's camp. He wears a sort of colorful fabric covering over his waist, tied by what seems to be dry blades of grass. From finding myself in his arms the few times I did, I noticed arm bands around his biceps. I don't know what those are for. He was barefoot, like I was, when I found myself on the island shore.

I must have been lost in my mental musings because his voice snaps me out of my thoughts.

"I am an unattached warrior. None of the females within my tribe have made my heart want to give chase. I chose my time alone instead, to just lead my men to hunt for food and help our village carry on with our lives. I lost my parents when I was young. I do not have anyone."

My heart goes out to him. That sounds like a very lonely existence indeed. Maybe that's why he happened upon me when I arrived. Was he walking along the shore in his solitude?

"You have been the only one to bring my heart to settle, my Juri. Perhaps the Gods' had me wait out here alone until your arrival." He turns his face to look at me and his eyes are intense and emotional. "And you are worth the wait."

Thud thud. Thud thud.

My heart is beating hard. Is it getting hot in here? I've had my fair share of pickup lines thrown at me. People like Gary, who come on like a bulldozer. But Chiemko feels different.

His words get to me and pierce my heart with something sharp.

The waves carry us and cradle us at the same time. Our prior conversation ended with his statement echoing in the wind. How does one escape an awkward conversation in such a small boat? Speaking of boats, when he spoke of it, my mind was imagining something much, much larger than what we're in. But what do I know? I'm not a sailor or anything.

The one we're in reminds me of the boats the Polynesians rode in their travels. I learned something about it during my time in college. What did they call their water traveling skills? Wayfinding? Chiemko is definitely doing something of that sort since he hasn't pulled out any sort of navigation device since we entered the waters. He only stands confidently, looking out upon the waves and into the skies now and again.

It's admirable to watch someone so confident in their abilities to not get lost. Unlike myself, who finds herself lost just by closing her eyes.

The sound of birds overhead tells me we're getting close. I think, in the blur of my sights, I see something resembling the top of trees. Good, I'm not sure how long I can take sitting in a large cradle essentially — the lulling movement getting to me in not so good ways. When our boat gets closer to the opposite shore, Chiemko jumps out with a splash and starts to pull our boat further up the sand. He is a really strong guy to be pulling the boat with me still in it.

Looking over at him, watching the way his muscles flex with every tug, I'm thinking he may be the same age as myself, but not much older. Maybe? I should ask. Would that be rude? His body and muscle memory remind me of a person who has done this since their childhood. Smooth grace without any doubt about which way his arms and legs are supposed to move.

Once the boat is far enough onto the shore that the lapping waves won't inadvertently pull it back out, Chiemko comes to my side and picks me up out of the boat like I don't weigh one hundred and fifty pounds. *Wow, they make the men here strong and hard worn.* He doesn't even breathe any harder after placing me back onto the sand. My toes sink in and he hasn't let go of me just yet. *Oh boy.* With a little push against his chest, he releases his grip on me with a grin. There's that dimple again.

I clear my throat and start walking away from him. He's intense and makes my stomach flutter with nerves. He catches up quickly with my stride without even having to break into a jog. His thigh muscles and calves must have become used to maneuvering on the sand, unlike mine.

We walk for a good while towards the expanse of trees in front of us. They look different from the ones on the island. The trees there look more tropical, while the ones here are just regular trees. Can crossing waters really make that big of a difference in foliage?

Once the sand ends, our feet start stepping on more solid ground and rocks. I almost forgot the fact that I am still barefoot when little pebbles get stuck between my toes sending small spikes of pain through me. Hissing under my breath with each step, I turn to look at my companion. It doesn't seem to bother Chiemko much at all. He must be used to going around barefoot. I'm a city girl. The most torture I put my feet through is wearing heels. Even then, the bottoms of my feet are protected from rocks.

I can feel myself start to slow down, trying to avoid fallen branches and anything else found on our path. The smell of the water is slowly going away, the warmth of the breeze bringing the smell of dust and something else I can't put my finger on. Bending down to try and pick a little branch from between my big toe and second toe, my balance shifts and I almost fall over on my face until Chiemko's strong arms come around me, saving me from humiliating myself. Once more, my face is heating up with the position we're in. This time it's me bent over at the waist and him pressed right up against my ass like we are about to start something right here in the wilderness.

That sounds kind of hot, but I really need to get home.

"Thanks," I mumble, but Chiemko isn't moving a muscle. "You can, uh, let me go now. I'm okay." *You are way too tempting.*

Suddenly, I feel him bend over further right on top of me and I'm enveloped in his warmth. He smells of salt water and something masculine and musky. My resolve becomes even weaker when he rubs his nose in the back of my hair, sniffing me, giving me goosebumps all over my skin. Something hard is pressing up against my ass crack and a shiver goes through my body. Lord, help me with all these virile men I keep running into in these dreams of mine. It must be another part of my subconscious telling me this dry spell is killing me from the inside and I need to do something about it.

Using whatever ab muscles I have, I straighten myself up and turn in his arms, politely shoving him a good arm distance away from me. His eyes are fixated on my choker, but he doesn't say a word. I turn again and start walking along the path we started, pretending that awkward moment didn't just happen between us.

We walk, slowly, for about an hour or so until the trees begin to become sparse. The dirt on the ground is turning into more of a hard solidified rock of the same color and there are more open plain areas. The creatures before me baffle my mind. It has to be my eyes playing tricks on me. The four-legged creatures ahead of us look like a cross between some sort of antelope/stripeless zebra/deer. I've never seen anything like it. At least that's what my mind is telling me through the blur of my vision. For all I know, they might be something totally different and my eyes have fooled me again. I think I see their heads hanging downwards eating grass though, so that's something. Strictly herbivores, hopefully. The last thing we need are strange creatures on a bloodlust once they notice us within their vicinity.

"I have hunted these before, on one of our trips to the mainland." The nearness of his voice to my ear startles me for only a second. "One had strayed close to the shores. It was a good feast and brought much festivities that night." Chiemko is keeping his voice low near my ear, his face right beside mine, as we both continue to gaze out onto the plains where the animals are grazing. I trust his judgement, so I try to keep as quiet as I can as well.

Chiemko begins to lead us in a slightly different direction, keeping to the areas that contain more trees, most likely for camouflage. We don't want to spook anything with big teeth. Flashes of Duma's necklace go through my mind. I wonder what he's doing right now? Do dream people do things when they're not in your dreams? Walking for about thirty more minutes, I feel the air shift near me and my hair moves with the direction of the breeze. The deja vu makes my heart rate pick up.

Duma?

Chiemko is quick on his feet, his movements much too fast for my mind to comprehend as he shoves me a bit before leaping backwards a step himself. The sound of a loud *thud* near us snaps my eyes down to the ground where we were both *just* standing a moment ago. That was close — way too close for comfort. Crap, it's still too close. Something thin sticks out of the hard rock. It's definitely not one of Duma's spears. Judging by what looks like feathers of some sort coming off the end, I would assume that the blurry thing in front of me right now is a damn arrow.

An arrow that was shot *right for us.*

I'm still thinking about this fact when Chiemko grabs me by the midsection and lifts me in a leap and starts running, making my head spin from the abrupt change in position. I'm still trying to catch my breath from the leap and in a few moments, I hear something else sail into the air in a *woosh* sound. The cogs in my mind turn at the familiar sound. *Something larger than the arrow, then.* Chiemko is maneuvering around rocks and trees so quickly, I'm sure everything is a blur for him too. The *thud* and crack of the ground nearby tells me the target was us again and I don't know whether to panic or not because I don't know what exactly we're running from. I can't see who's throwing it and Chiemko is running at a constant speed, zigzagging through the trees and covering distance fast. Over his other shoulder, on the opposite side of me, he carries his weapons but hasn't reached to use them yet. That's a good thing, right? He's not that worried enough to start fighting back.

The blur of moving trees ends when Chiemko stops his run and we find ourselves in a small clearing on a hill or ledge of some sort. The ground is a tan color that reminds me of the deserts in the middle east but this rocky cliff is darker in shade. I think we just hit a dead end, unless we're planning on jumping over the ledge. Bad eyes or not, that looks like a far way down and I don't feel like dying in my dreams. Does that make you die in real life too?

My hands grip onto my companion tighter, afraid of his decision. He must feel my worry because he rubs a little right before he puts me down carefully and keeps me towards the ledge side as he turns to face whatever is coming our way — facing whoever was trying to kill us. It has to be a who, right? *Please don't tell me there are creatures here that can wield a spear and bow and arrow.*

My ears pick up the sound of grass shifting and pebbles being moved. The sound of very light footsteps approach. You would almost miss it if your adrenaline wasn't making your senses amplified and sensitive. This is it. Who is this person? What the hell makes a person just start shooting at a bunch of strangers anyway?

"A warrior of the waters." His voice is gruff and cocky. Is he talking about Chiemko? "A Matalo'toa this close to my village." His cocky voice suddenly changes into one full of menace. "I am going to kill you before you lead your men towards my people."

I don't recognize this voice, not that I have much to go on, but the venom in it tells me he hates Chiemko and the islanders for whatever reason. What is up with this place? Is no one on friendly terms?

Peeking around Chiemko's back, I place my hand on his arm and try to look around us. I don't see anyone or anything moving. Where did the voice come from? Right when the question crosses my mind, someone emerges from the last scattering of trees before us. He's of a similar tan complexion to Chiemko, but different at the same time. It seems those on the island have a different undertone to their bodies, probably from living by the waters. This man, or shall I say warrior, has long dark dread-locks piled on top of his head. Naked from the waist up seems to be the name of the game for all the warriors here — a required nakedness. His loincloth, I'll call it, is bigger than what Duma had on but smaller than Chiemko's. It's blurry, but the color of it tells me it's possibly leathers from a hunt with how stiffly it moves. It reminds me of the color of the skin on those weird deer things we were spotting on our way in. He also has some sort of light armband on each arm, just like Chiemko, and it contrasts against his skin color. There is paint on his face, forehead and chin. The necklace he is wearing is more of a choker than the one that hung off of Duma's neck like a string of fangs.

So different, yet in so many ways the same.

Something glints in the sun a bit and catches my eye. In one of his hands is the spear he threw at us. Something else is around his other shoulder, leaving that arm free. I'm assuming it's a bow since we were being shot at with arrows earlier. *The bastard.* My squinting only helps so much from where I'm standing but I know what I'm looking at — the asshole who's been after us this whole time.

Chiemko's stance tenses up, and he's crouching a little bit more, his legs hip width apart, readying for battle. This is bad, if these guys get too crazy up on this cliff area we're standing on, I'm going to fall to my death and no one will be the wiser.

Making a split-second decision, I touch Chiemko on the back and poke my head out from behind him with a little wave.

"…Uh, hi there! We're just trying to find someone I know, so that I can get back home. Sorry if we… uh… stomped on your terri-tory or whatnot. We didn't mean anything by it, just walking through." That sounds neutral, right? Chiemko's back stiffens as the other man stares right at me. His arm comes back slightly to protect me from whatever might happen that I can't see. *Sorry buddy, I'm not ready to die today, even if this is dreamland.*

"Mata warrior, what are you doing with this female? She does not look to be of your people. Did you steal her from another tribe?"

Wait, what? People steal females around here? What in the world? How did this situation just escalate when it was supposed to start diffusing? *Quick Juri, think of something!*

"No, no, nothing like that! I'm looking for the — the chin — chintk tribe? Something like that?"

Growls erupt from both of the men making me jump and I am just at a damn loss now. *What did I say?* The heat from the sun is starting to beat down on us out in the open like this. There's also a breeze coming from below us, reminding me of the potential fall that might still happen. Stuck between a rock and hard place, or in this case — an enemy warrior and a cliff of doom.

"The Namwana tribe does not talk to bloodthirsty barbarians like the Chintkku." Dang, he hates Duma's people too? "Any Matalo'toa warriors found close enough to my village are taken care of as well. We protect our own, it is how we became as strong as we are."

Okay, that is way too many tribal names for me to remember.

Closing my eyes and taking a deep breath, I pinch the bridge of my nose and think. So Duma is from Chintkku, Chiemko is from the Matalo'toa and this guy right here is of the Namwana tribe. One thing I'm *not* confused about is the fact that they apparently all hate each other and want to kill each other on the spot, but they don't seem to enjoy hurting women. *Lost women like me.* A lightbulb goes on above my head.

This is a dream, after all — it's just a dream. Mentally putting on my big girl panties, I step from behind Chiemko, much to his distress by the sound coming out of him. Placing myself in front of his body with my arms crossed over my chest, I let this guy right here have it. I'm getting tired of all this craziness and I just want to go home, or just find a way to wake myself up from this mess. Is that too much to ask?

"Look, guy from Manwawa or whatever, I don't know who you are, and I don't really care. I *need* to get home. I need to find that old guy from Duma's tribe. What did you call it? The Chintkku tribe. So please just point us in the right direction and we'll be on our way." *There. Plain and simple. All laid out, you can't get confused by anything.*

Both of the boys are looking like I've lost my damn mind and maybe I have. I'm getting tired of these boys trying to fight over the metaphorical sandbox with grudges that go back to who knows when.

"I am Gamba, of the Namwana tribe."

I think I see his lips moving. I don't know if he's laughing at me for standing in front of a guy who's much bigger than I am, or at the audacity I seem to have in front of a bunch of warriors.

"I would soon spill the blood of this Mata right here before I bring him anywhere near my people. I would be more than happy to help you on this journey, little one." His lips curl directly at Chiemko and I feel a little offended on his behalf. "But this warrior needs to die, or go back to where he hails from."

His lips move again; I'm going to assume it's a smirk because his tone of voice sure as hell sounds like he's smirking at me. *Asshole.*

Eesh, these boys and their need to kill each other. I step away from Chiemko and towards this new person in front of me with a fire I haven't felt before since having these crazy ass dreams began. But a girl can only be nice and submissive for so long, you know?

"My Juri!" Chiemko is hissing these words out of his teeth, his hands grazing my arm and his fingers gripping me, trying to prevent me from getting any closer. I twist my arm out of his grip and step right up to this guy who thinks he's going to stop me from finding Duma again. Standing close enough that I can finally see his face clearly, I poke him in his hard and warm chest with my finger as firmly as I can muster.

"You are not going to stand in my way, tough guy. I *am* going home. You guys can stay here and fight all you want. That. Is. Not. My. Damn. Problem. My problem is that I need to go home!" *I am woman, hear me roar.*

This guy is way too attractive for his own damn good too, with his five o' clock shadow and his beautifully tanned skin. Why does every man here have to be damn shirtless? How is anyone supposed to keep their cool and make their intentions known when all this muscle is distracting them — okay, me. Distracting me. I am still pissed though. His sexy dreadlocks be damned, with his stupid smoldering dark eyes, thick eyebrows, thick juicy lips and stupid smirk on his face be damned. *I knew he was smirking at me.*

A breeze comes through the clearing and it reminds me that I am still in my damn t-shirt and panties. Makes me think of those stupid dreams again where you wake up in a classroom naked. At least my mind gave me the decency of some clothes, even if they're my nightwear. It could be worse, right?

When Gamba moves his free arm towards me, the shift in wind comes quick and Chiemko pushes me behind him hard, creating a barricade between my body and Gamba's. *Holy shit, that is some lightning quick reflexes.* I hear Chiemko growl under his breath in Gamba's face.

I tell ya, these guys need to rein this crap in.

"One more move and I will slice your throat right here, Namwana."

Oh snap.

I didn't even see the knife Chiemko has on Gamba's neck. But Gamba doesn't even flinch, he's still standing there with a calm posture. These guys are serious, aren't they, with this whole warrior spiel. With more quick movements, Chiemko throws an elbow into Gamba's face only to have him lean back and block it with his forearm. Both of Gamba's weapons are long-range ones, so I don't know what the outcome of this fight is going to be.

Taking a few steps back in case an elbow comes my way, I make sure to not take too many and fall off the cliff accidentally. Wouldn't that just suck? What happens when you die in a dream, anyway?

Grunts and growls surround me as fists are being thrown back and forth. I assume that's what's happening since both of their bodies are a blur from where I am standing. The men are aggressive in their movements, one tan body on top of the other and then vice versa. Two beasts fighting for dominance on top of a damn cliff. The dust kicks up around us adding to my blurry vision and I try to hold back my cough from it going up my nose. I can hear the sound of flesh on flesh, making me cringe, as they land blows on each other.

None of them speak, choosing instead to say all they need to say through the fists and blows they land on each other. It looks like Chiemko makes a quick bend of the knees for a leg sweep and throws an elbow down onto Gamba's chest, knocking him back. Quickly turning, he runs towards me and throws me over his shoulder again, starting just as equally a quick pace back the way we came.

Hold up, I know damn well the way to Duma is not this way! The island isn't going to get me back home! I need the old man!

My chest is slapping against his shoulder as he runs, knocking the breath out of me and making me unable to utter a word in protest. Dammit! The pain starts to become a little unbearable with each leap he takes over whatever he's jumping over. My head is starting to spin and I think I'm about to get motion sick. I don't know how he does it, but Chiemko makes it back to the boat in twenty minutes flat.

"Ahh!"

He unceremoniously tosses me into the boat and runs to the back to push it towards the waves.

"Chiemko!"

"Juri, keep your head down in case he releases arrows. I'll keep you safe, trust me." His voice is so steady like this is an everyday occurrence. Should I be worried about that fact?

By the time my breathing slows down from the run, he's already jumped into the boat himself and is paddling us out from the mainland quickly. Geez, how did this turn around so fast? One minute I feel like we're almost where I need to be, the next I'm back at square one with this stupid dream — back in the water. I'm frustrated and relieved at the same time.

I mean, was Gamba really going to kill us or just take us back to his people? What am I saying? Is that even a good thing? Staring at Chiemko's serious expression as he paddles us away from the shore, my mind tells me that it wouldn't fare well for Chiemko at all. I might survive, but then I might also be the reason for someone's imminent death sentence. I can't have that on my conscience, dream or not.

The weather has started to turn and the skies look greyer by the minute. What the hell is going on? How does the weather turn this fast when it was just sunny a minute ago? This dream is going to drive me nuts. Was that thunder in the distance?

Something comes out of the water right next to me with a splash, and the boat tips just enough to knock me completely out of the boat.

Splash.

I'm breathing in a mouthful of water. I'm floundering in the water and tumultuous waves and my body feels heavy, sinking lower and lower. I know how to swim, but that came out of nowhere and my mind hasn't caught up yet. I'm trying to kick my legs and the water lights up with what looks like lightning from the skies. I scream but all that happens is another mouthful of water. My logical mind is telling me it's a stupid move but my body is reacting automatically to what's happening right now. *I need help! Someone, anyone!* A muffled splash reaches my ears as my arms begin to tire from fighting against the weight of the water. This is it, isn't it? This is how I will die in my dream and wake up? Maybe I should just let myself die. Suddenly, I feel arms go around me, hauling me towards the surface for some much needed air.

When we both break the surface, I take a big breath into my lungs and feel Chiemko throw me back inside the boat. *This guy, always tossing me like a damn rag doll.* But I'm grateful for it in this instance. Coughing up water into the boat, I struggle to get a good breath in. *Dammit, am I going to get pneumonia from this? Can you get pneumonia from a dream?* The waters continue to get angry and choppy, the waves tossing the boat to and fro. Not only am I still struggling to get a good breath in, I'm probably going to get sea sick. Chiemko struggles with the brewing storm but is able to bring himself into the boat. Dropping himself onto his back, he takes in a few deep breaths like I did. We both lie in the same position for some time, the pounding of the oncoming rain landing on us like spikes and bullets. When Chiemko finally catches his breath, he jumps up and continues to paddle us back towards the island.

Damn. What a champ. Sitting up, I look around for another paddle but don't see one. I'm not helping at all. *Dammit, Juri. What good are you? The man probably just saved your life.*

I'm too exhausted from the day's events. I don't even remember eating since I woke up here this time around. The rain continues to pound down on us with an aggression that's uncalled for. Laying back down, my eyes are drifting close from exhaustion. I don't know how long I drift in and out but I start to feel light sprinkles of rain on my face instead of the initial bullets.

Just a few minutes of rest is all I need — I'm so tired. A loud crack of thunder sounds again, but my mind finally starts to drift towards the darkness with the rocking of the boat.

ELEVEN

I wake up with a gasp. *Please lord, tell me I'm where I want to be.* Looking around for a few moments, I know I'm back in my room. My sheets are a rumpled mess and half of it's on the floor. *That was something else.* Bringing my hand back to my choker, I sigh in relief and tell myself I need a shower.

That weird feeling of deja vu goes through me again. But I need to wash this panicky feeling away. *I almost died. I almost drowned. It felt so damn real.*

Reaching toward my nightstand, I find my glasses and put them on. Looking for my phone that's still attached to the charging cable nearby, I bring it awake to see what day and time it is. I feel so out of whack. The phone lights up and tells me it's Saturday, the date after my assistant's night out. *Wait, how can that be?* Looking around, the sun is still out, and the phone tells me it's 10:00 in the morning. *Didn't I lay down around noon? I'm going out of my damn mind.*

Taking off my choker and glasses, I undress and head into the shower. Shucking off my clothes by the hamper, I let them fall

"

where they may and tell myself to worry about laundry later. Once my feet reach the tile in my restroom, I feel grittiness on the bottom of my feet. *What in the world?* Leaning one hand against my sliding glass shower door, I pick up my foot closer to my face. *Is that fucking sand? Okay, okay, Juri. Let's just shower.*

Shaking my head to clear it, I continue into the shower. I need to sort out my thoughts. *It's Saturday, the weekend. Let's get a clean start and look into that corrective eye surgery I keep putting off.* All these situations where I'm running around in a blur are messing with my equilibrium and giving me a damn headache.

The hot water from the shower feels good against my muscles. I must have slept the wrong way and gotten a few kinks in my shoulder and back because I'm feeling sore in some places. Shampooing my hair with one of my more expensive bottles, my senses soothe down even more with the smell of lavender mingling with the steam. *This is what I needed.*

Once done, I carefully step out onto my shower mat and grab my white fluffy towel that's hanging nearby. The softness calms me and I close my eyes and I just feel it gliding across my skin, drying me up.

Letting the steam of the room release as I open the restroom door, I walk towards my dresser and look for something comfortable. Dressed in a loose but form fitting t-shirt and yoga pants, I make sure to put my choker and glasses back on. They've subconsciously become two staples in my routine. The good thing about living alone for so long, I've become meticulous with where things are so that everything is easy to find even without my glasses. It never occurred to me how much my life had to adjust because of my vision issues.

Walking into my living area, I look around for my laptop. It's sitting on the kitchen table and that weird feeling of deja vu hits me again. Shaking it off, I sit down at the kitchen chair and power up the computer. I see that the page for corrective eye surgery is already up and opened. *What the? Did I do this? When? Friday? No way, not after the night I had with the girls drinking, dancing and the craziness with Gary.*

Reading over the information online about corrective eye surgery, I find that I can't seem to get an exact price. I need to set up an appointment because the cost varies depending on the severity of the problem. *Okay, fine, whatever.* Free consultation, it says. Getting out of my kitchen chair, I walk towards my kitchen where I have an old school printed calendar hanging.

When was the last time I took a little vacation? *Never.* Then maybe it's time, at least for this consultation. Grabbing a nearby marker, I circle the upcoming Friday as my day off. That will give work at least more than four days' notice. The girls can handle things while I take one day off.

Walking back to my computer, I input my information to set the appointment date and time for the consultation. *Good. Finally.* Once that's done, I close my laptop and stretch my arms up. It's about Saturday afternoon now, and I still have the rest of the day to do nothing. I think I want some fresh air. I should take a walk outside, and feel the sun on my skin.

Flashes of the men I've come across in my dreams go through my mind. *I'm always in the sun.* But that last dream had me in a storm. Weird.

After putting on some workout clothes, I look around my living room, grab my pepper spray, some ID, and my keys heading towards the door where I have a pair of sneakers waiting. The monotony of my movements in putting my sneakers on is relaxing. Maneuvering the keys in my hand, I exit my apartment door, making sure to look all around me in case Gary is out there lying in wait like the creep he is. Why is it that the strangers in my dreams make me feel more comfortable than one white guy who supposedly lives in my same apartment building? Is it me? Am I overthinking it?

Quickly exiting my hallway, I head for the stairwell that takes me down two flights until I reach the ground level. The apartment complex does come with a work out area for the residents, paid by our association dues, but it's a bit stifling to me. Fresh air is always best, plus you get different scenery along the way during the exercise — win-win.

Deciding to go a few blocks around my home, I start towards the direction of my workplace. I'm not running there exactly, but turning right on the block before it. My body is warming up nicely and I can feel my muscles loosening. The fact that you can now buy work out pants that have pockets for your things without it jumping and jiggling as you jog is amazing. Whoever thought of that, really needs an award. Once I'm halfway around my route, I'm working up a good sweat and my body feels a boost, probably from the adrenaline. I feel really good. I'm doing things — getting things done. I got the eye consultation on Friday and it's only Saturday. I still have Sunday all to myself.

While thinking about all the things I can accomplish tomorrow, I accidentally run into a hard chest, making me bounce back a bit. I was able to right myself without falling to the ground, bending over to catch my breath. When I look up, I see baby blue ocean eyes. *Shit.*

"Sorry about that, I must have not been paying enough attention."

That is seriously my bad. But the weight of the little pepper spray in my pants gives me a little comfort. No perfume so I can't mistake the two today.

"It's okay. Seems we were both trying to catch some exercise in the sun. We can ... run together, if you'd like?"

My red flag radar is alarming inside my head, but I try to keep a smile on my face. Seems Gary boy hasn't given up just quite yet, despite having introduced his balls to my knees the other night. Maybe he was just as drunk that night too? The smile currently on his face tells me otherwise. Is this his version of trying to flirt? Negatory, my man. How many times has that line actually worked for you?

"Thanks for the offer, but I'm about done with my route. Just walking home at this point. You go ahead and finish your run, don't let me stop you." Take the hint, buddy.

"Or… you can run, and I'll give chase."

Oh, my fucking God. This is kind of cheesy and creepy at the same time.

I start fast-walking away before things get weird. I mean, we're out in the open and in public. I don't think he's that stupid to try anything with all these possible witnesses nearby, right? Judging by my paranoia with each step I take, my mind is telling me otherwise. I made it home without seeing any sign of Gary following me as he insinuated, thank goodness.

Ugh. Isn't it funny how fast walking feels like more of a work out than jogging? Lord, by the time I walk into my apartment, my calves were killing me and I almost didn't make it through the threshold of the doorway. Pain or no pain, I never forget to lock up behind me. Once secured, I basically crawl to my couch and just flopped over the armrest breathing like I just completed a marathon — a five block marathon. *That's kind of pathetic. I should start watching what I eat.*

When my breathing slows down enough, I hit the shower and wash the day's activities away. I cannot believe Gary was running outside at the *exact* same time, on the *exact* same route. That is way more than a coincidence. This guy just can't take the hint, crazy fucker. His smile, though, tells me he thinks he's got game when it's coming off weird and creepy.

The water relaxes me again, making me stand under it longer than I should just to take in the warmth it provides. Rolling my neck around, I finally make myself turn off the water and get out. Once dried and wrapped in a towel, I go to check on my plants to make sure none of them are dying. Seeing as a five block jog and fast walk almost killed me, I need to make sure I eat well.

I love my plants. They look really healthy and happy. I should have probably been a Botanist instead of working an office job but life isn't always fair like that. Plus, how much does a Botanist make anyway? Returning to my room in my towel, I reach for my dresser to change into some comfortable clothes.

Ah, my comfort clothes, there you are. So soft, so nice, so welcoming. Now in my t-shirt and panties again, I stretch my body upwards until I feel my shoulders crack a bit. No one ever tells you about how your body begins to break down once you get older. Walking over to drop my towel off in my dirty clothes hamper, I come back to my dresser for my glasses and choker. The weight of the disk on my neck is the weirdest feeling of home. I never even feel this way when I go back home to India to visit my family.

I wonder how my parents are doing. They run a little store back in the homeland and my younger brother is now an adult, living his bachelor life. Their only major concern is how long I choose to remain single and when they can expect a grandchild.

Feeling kind of hungry, I make my way to my refrigerator to see what kind of leftovers I have in there. The cool air chills me when I open the door and I see a small pre-made container of grilled chicken and some vegetables. Choosing that for tonight's dinner, I bring it out and place it on the counter as I search through my cabinets for my uncooked rice. Taking the saran wrap off the cold dish, I pop it into the microwave while I multi-task with making rice on the stove in one of my little pots. The smell of the grilled chicken fills the kitchen and my mouth starts to water for the meal that's about to be devoured. It probably counts as a double portion, but I'll start watching what I eat the next meal.

It can be lonely sometimes eating at home by myself, but with men like Gary out there, it's no wonder I find myself in this predicament. Once my meal is done, I quickly wash my dishes and put it in the drying rack before sitting my butt down on the couch to catch some news. After about fifteen minutes, I am reminded of exactly why I don't like to watch the news. Everything is crazy out there. People dying left and right, economy is out of whack, politics this and politics that. *Good grief.* Shutting the TV off for the rest of the night, I walk back into my bedroom to see if there are any books I need to catch up on instead.

Fingering through my very small library of books at the foot of my bed, I select one I've read before. I love books about broken men and the women who drag them out of their self-imposed hell. What does that say about me? Shrugging my shoulders at no one, I tell myself it doesn't really matter, anyway. They're my guilty pleasures and no one has a say in what I choose to drown myself in.

Dropping backwards onto my bed, I start reading from the beginning, despite having read this particular book over three times already. I love going through the emotions and roller-coasters again. It's never like the first time, but close enough. I think I felt the book hit my face as my eyes became too heavy to open back up…

TWELVE

GARY

Removing the book from her face, I gaze upon the most serene expression. I can be a caring man. Placing her glasses onto her nightstand, I crawl over her sprawled body, making sure not to put my body weight on her just yet. I just want to savor this moment between us. She is the most beautiful woman I have ever seen, as well as the most unattainable. All the men in the office whisper about her when she walks by. But they're not going to do anything about it because they all know she's fucking mine, I made sure of it.

"Hey Jack, did you see what Juri is wearing today? Holy fucking shit does her ass look good in a pencil skirt. I'd hit that shit in a heartbeat."

"You and me both, Chris. Fuck, imagine tag teaming that shit. Fuckkk."

What started as mere anger, now boils into rage. These fuckers are talking about my woman like she's a damn piece of meat hanging off a hook to be devoured. If anyone is going to devour her, it's fucking me, and only me.

Bringing my mind back into the present, I lean in and sniff along the column of her neck. She smells of something floral, a little bit like lavender. She smells like my woman and it does nothing to calm my raging hard on. Unable to resist a taste, I lick up the same path I sniffed. God, she tastes divine. She must be in a really deep slumber because she only stirs the slightest before her breathing calms again. I love that about her.

I've had my fair share of one-night stands. I didn't think trying to woo a woman would be this much work. Maybe Juri is just playing hard to get.

Her shirt does nothing to hide her hard, dark nipples. *Fuck, I just need a taste. Just a small taste.* Slowly gliding the shirt up her torso, I almost cum in my pants when I am face to face with the very thing I hunger for. Her breasts were made for my mouth.

I need to hold it back. Keep myself together before I get caught. Sticking my tongue out, it grabs her nipple right into my waiting mouth and it's like fucking heaven. This obsession I have with her skin; it makes my chest hurt. I need to claim what's mine. Sucking harder, I hear her moan. *Yes, just like that. I know you like it. You're such a tease, Juri.*

I wouldn't want to leave the other without equal attention, and so my tongue trails a wet line across her chest to the other side. *Fuck, look how hard her nipple is for me.* Once I dull the ache a bit after having my fill of her breasts, I crawl back off of the bed. Dropping my pants down, I give my cock hard and fast strokes to the sight of her. *Soon, Juri. Soon.* Cumming all over my hands, I let out a hard sigh and go to her adjoining restroom to wash up my mess.

The carpet quiets my exit back out her window.

THIRTEEN

DUMA

The feral roar coming out of me shakes the wooden slats of my hut. The startled screams of the women and children nearby do nothing to calm me. I can hear the thundering footsteps of my warriors coming towards me, the sounds of their spears as they run. A rage inside of me burns and I feel the bloodlust coming behind my eyes, washing everything in my sights red with hunger for the kill. I left little Juri for only a moment to make another mat for our rest, and when I returned she was gone. Who would dare? She could not have gone far with her eyes. My mind tells me she was taken from me and the itch in my palms tells me I need blood now. I've never felt a rage like this in all my forty-nine cycles of life, not even when my female died during the war ten cycles past. It is said that age helps calm the soul — but not this warrior's soul. I feel it burning hotter than before. My Juri is not a warrior, she needs me and I have *failed* her.

My men gather behind me with their weapons pointed toward what they think is the threat.

"What has happened here?"

"Are we being attacked?"

"No one attacks Duma and lives. You all know this?"

My breathing is increasing and I feel some of them shift farther behind me.

"Then what is happening?"

The air inside my hut is getting thick, making my chest tighten and burn. I hunger for retribution.

"We need to remain silent until Duma tells us something."

My beast is raging but the leader in me is forcing myself to calm enough to speak to my men who eagerly await my next move. Taking a deep breath, I look at the warriors around me and make a decision.

"Our festivities end early, warriors. Something precious was taken from me and they must be found. We leave when the blessed suns crest the far lands."

Soon, little Juri. I will bring you back into my arms soon.

My men leave the hut and their voices can be heard gathering all the available warriors in the village. My mind is blinded by my need to shed blood in the name of Juri. The Chintkku tribe is now on the warpath under my lead. Every man in my way will be met with death until she is back where she belongs.

GAMBA

That Mata warrior has feet as swift as the raging waters he boats across.

Roaring at the skies, my feet followed their path through the trees but I was too late when I came upon the sands.

Slamming my spear down into the ground, my mind begins to think of what needs to be done to gain the advantage of this situation. The Mata warrior looks to be less seasoned than I am but his decision making is quick. His agility between the trees is impressive, but my forty-five cycles can still cut the skin from his bones when I get him — and I will, this I promise.

Gazing across the waters at their boat getting smaller and smaller in the distance, the brewing storm overhead only mirrors what I feel inside. The thirst for blood, the anger I feel, the hunger for killing the one who dares to take what I've claimed as mine.

"One misstep is all it takes. You better watch yourself and your people, warrior." My voice drowns out with the sound of roars from the skies. They too feel what I feel.

That Mata warrior has not only trekked across the boundaries into the Namwana tribal lands, but he has trekked it with a *prisoner*. For I know that female was not of his village. No. Our people will not stand for it — *I* will not stand for it.

The brightness of her fire inside calls to me. This was the reason for my wanderings this day. The Gods pulled me towards her without my knowing — and now that I've found her, I will not let another take her so easily. My mind is already racing with the different paths to take to bring her back safely to me. The call of the hunt — the call to *win*. The Gods have pulled my heart to her for a reason — a destiny yet unknown to me but I now know my purpose. As the skies continue to darkened and crack with the sound of anger, the light spears hail down to show me with its light that he has thrown the female over his ship into the waters.

Growling, my mind begins to drown in a red haze. "You will pay for this, warrior of the waters!" My beasts inside tenses at the call for blood in her name.

Grabbing the spear from the sands, I turn and run back towards the trees. I need to gather my men. Something must be done.

Ready yourself, Mata warriors, for war is coming to your island. And I will make that female mine.

CHIEMKO

What is happening? The waves anger, tossing our boat about and causing my Juri to become devoured by the waters. It was luck that brought me to her quickly — to be able to bring her back to life on the boat. The skies are filled with fury and it feels like tears of a mad God raining down from the heavens as, right before my eyes, my Juri melted away like the mist around us.

What is this? How can it be that in one moment she is solid and real, but the next she disappears like a dream upon waking? It was like the rain itself washed her soul into the air. Nothing makes sense. The anger that surges inside me rivals the storm and waves — the loss my heart feels.

"Why have you taken the only thing that was finally mine?"

The spears from the skies come down and light up the surroundings in anger. The anger belongs to me! Just as my Juri!

"What have I done to deserve this? She was to fill the void in my heart! You dare to give me a glimpse of heaven and yet pull me down to the depths of wanting death!"

The waters crash into the side of the boat, causing me to fall and splutter but it doesn't simmer the emotions running through me. I need to find her, I need to bring her back to me!

Shaking my head, I stand once more and cry out my roar into the heavens. How can the Gods and spirits make me wait for the one my heart yearns for, only to take her from me?

I will find you, my Juri. Even if I have to wash the mainlands to the ground with waves and war, starting with the Namwana.

FOURTEEN

Okay, that was the most erotic dream I have ever had. But unlike my other recent dreams, it was all fuzzy. It's strange, isn't it? When I was with Duma and Chiemko, my vision blurred the way it does without my glasses, but everything around me felt so real. This last dream, my head and not my eyes, felt fuzzy. When I came to, I found my shirt ridden up and my nipples peaked from the coolness of the room. I must have touched myself in my sleep because I found myself still wet between my legs from all the sensations I went through. *I really need to get laid. This has to be the problem.*

The sun's rays shine in through my bedroom window, letting me know it's another day. *Sunday.* My last day of the weekend before I have to return to the mundane of work life. Rolling over and stretching, I realize that I must have fallen asleep while reading last night. But where's my book? More importantly, where are my glasses?

Staring at my nightstand, my mind blanks for a few minutes. *Did I put that there?* This is exactly why I need to get that consultation for corrective eye surgery. This is scary stuff, waking up and not knowing where your 'extra set of eyes' are.

Alright, might as well get the day going. I usually like to meal prep for the work week, so that means grocery shopping. I'm very lucky to have been born during this era of Ubers. Getting onto the app on my phone, I set things up as I get ready to head out. Washing up my face, throwing my hair up in a messy bun, I go to my closest to find something comfortable for my shopping trip. Some jeans and a form fitting, slightly loose shirt should do. I like to wear a bralette most of my days off to let my girls' breathe a bit. My C cup fills it just enough to not spill over and not sag so far. When the shirt is slightly loose, you can't really tell, anyway. Unless it's a cold day and my nipples peek out.

Sandals are my shoe of choice as I lock up my front door and head down the two flights of stairs. We have an elevator on the other side of the apartment building, and I'd rather not run into Gary in case that's the side he lives on. I swear, despite what he's said, I have never seen him here in the five years I've lived in this apartment complex. Strange, but not because I know he's a crazy bastard. For all I know, he just moved in the building once he found out I lived here. A shiver goes down my spine at that thought. Patting the right front pocket of my jeans, the comfort of the pepper spray gives my heart a little rest. The weight of the choker on my neck brings me extra comfort too.

The Uber driver is an old Italian man who loves to talk and listen to his own voice. By the time we reach our destination, his story hasn't even ended yet. With an awkward goodbye thrown in during his continued storytelling, I get out of the car and make my way to the front of the store.

The gust of cold air that comes out after the double glass doors automatically open, feels really nice on my face. Like a fresh start. Grabbing a cart, I make my way to the produce aisle. I like a lot of vegetables with my meals, so the produce aisle is always my first destination. Plus, it makes me hurry my butt up when I know I have them sitting in my cart, losing its cool freshness.

After ten minutes, I find myself in the meat aisle, looking over the chicken pieces and their prices. Something inside of me tells me to look behind me, and when I do, I see none other than Gary shopping not too far away. He's not looking at me, but you'll never know. *What are the odds of him shopping on the exact same day, at the exact same time?* The moment I think this, Gary gets farther away and goes down another aisle. *Am I crazy?*

Finishing up grabbing what I need, I head to the register area to line up. While in line, I get on my Uber app to make sure the car gets here by the time I'm done. I don't want to wait around too long with these groceries.

"Fancy seeing you here, Juri."

My spidey sense is going crazy. That's Gary's voice, there's no doubt about it.

Schooling my features, I turn to look at him with a pleasant smile. "Oh, Gary! I should say the same about you! Is this your usual store?" *If you say yes, I will never come here again.*

"Nah, just the one I happened to choose today. How are you doing? Are you ready to get back to work on Monday?"

So, we're pretending small talk, hey?

"I'm doing alright. You know how Monday's can be. I'll talk to you later, it looks like I'm up." A small wave, a fake smile, and I'm pushing my cart to the register, putting my groceries on the conveyor belt.

The Uber has perfect timing, because I've only been standing outside for about one to two minutes before it arrives. *Good, I don't have to talk to Gary if he comes out of the doors.* The Uber guy, a younger Hispanic man, helps me with the bags as I get myself into the backseat. Once the door shuts, I let out a breath of relief.

Gosh, this elevator guy is really getting on my nerves a bit. He's stalking, and I know it. But now I'm getting kind of mad at how blatant he's being about it.

My anger dissipates a little bit by the time we arrive back at my apartment complex. A lot of my vegetables fit into only a couple of bags, which is good because my arms and shoulders are strong enough to carry everything I have up the flights of stairs.

With no sign of Gary around , I quickly unlock my front door and lock it back up once I'm inside. I really hope we don't run into each other on Monday, but from his questioning at the store, I think that is exactly his plan.

The meal prep goes smoothly like it always does, my body just performing muscle memory at this point. Five years at this job with the same hours five days a week. What are my aspirations? Am I going to be Anderson's assistant for the rest of my days, basically doing all the paper pushing for him so he can sit back there in his office sleeping? But where would I go? The convenience of the job from my apartment is what really keeps me rooted. It's a walking distance. Saves me a lot of money. But now there's this Gary issue. Should I let *one* guy chase me out of the contentment of my life thus far? What if he just follows me wherever I end up moving to? Then what would the point of all the change be?

As these thoughts flitter through my head one after another, I didn't even realize I've completely finished meal prepping for five full work days. I totally forgot that I am going to put in for a day off this Friday for the eye consultation. Oh well, I guess that will just be left overs for a night where I don't feel like cooking.

Looking at the digital clock on my stove, I see that it's already three in the afternoon. Where has the time gone? Since these crazy dreams started, I feel like time is slipping through my fingers. Making sure all the meal containers are stacked neatly in my refrigerator, I walk back to the bathroom for a shower. The feel of Gary near me gives me a creepy crawly feeling on my skin. I need to wash it off.

The steam in my bathroom fogs up the mirror as I step out of my shower. Wiping it down with the palm of my hand, I stare at my reflection. These past couple of days cat napping has helped a lot with the bags under my eyes. My tanner skin tends to make them very prominent when they do appear. Something seems different about me, though. *Are my eyes lighter today?* It must be a reflection of the lighting in the bathroom. Feeling satisfied, I get ready for the night in my usual wear and secure the choker back where it belongs. My glasses have become a sort of second thought. I hope after the consultation; my glasses will not be an extra thought I need to have anymore. It's quite annoying.

My mind tells me I should continue the book I started. Flopping down on my fluffy bed, I grab the book off of my nightstand and read it while I'm lying on my stomach. Maybe this will help me stay awake instead of having the book fall on my face.

FIFTEEN

DUMA

My men from my home village have gathered. We are fifty strong in this camp and there are other village camps scattered nearby on the west plains. I will need to march and gather the warriors from each camp on our way to the east. The warrior count from last cycle have us Chintkku tribe at about nine hundred, but I do not know how many new warriors have come into season since then.

The war drums tell them of my calling. It is time.

Along our path to gather warriors, we came upon a Namwana scout, hiding in a tree. In our search around the area, we saw that there was only one, much to our dismay and bloodlust.

Onto our second Chintkku village to the east of this one, we drag the scout with us and now have the warrior held in one of the huts on the outskirts. It is important we keep him away from the women and children at the heart of this camp in case he escapes. Some of the warriors can be seen walking towards our prisoner's hut behind me with weapons in their hands but no one says a word or asks any questions. The villagers know better.

His cries can be heard echoing into the plains, making the birds fly off their branches in which they rest judging by the sounds of their wings beating outside of the hut. My sharpened bone knife carves the skin off his first two fingers as I continue to ask him the same question time and time again.

"What have you done with my Juri? My female who has eyes that hail from light spears in the skies?"

"Ahhh!"

"If you answer me, this will end for you quickly."

"Ahhh!"

"If you do not, you will feel the wrath of the Chintkku tribe. I am not known to be a patient man, warrior. Head my warning."

"Ahhh!" His blood-curdling screams continue to echo through the village as the women gather their children deeper into their huts, occupying them with other things to distract them from the torture I'm gladly giving him. We should have replaced a cover on the doorway but my need to find answers clouded my judgement. The kids cannot see what we do inside, but the cloth has been removed from the doorway to bring in fresh air to chase away the smell of urine that has saturated the ground.

I bare my teeth in his face like the golden leer as the warrior continues to mumble through the blood in his mouth that he knows not of what I speak. *He lies.* I bite his cheek hard enough to tear the flesh from his face, spitting it out on the ground beside him. My bloodstained smile should remind him again that I am not one to be taken as a fool.

His third finger is placed on the tree stump found in the middle of this hut. He struggles but my grip remains strong. I call for Jomo who has accompanied me with this torture and hand him my biggest bone knife. My eyes blaze into his with fury, and I need not tell him what I wish for him to do.

This is the way of the Chintkku. We win at *all costs*.

The shift of wind in the swing of his blade has the Namwana warrior choking on his own blood, some dripping down the hole in the side of his face. He does not need his middle finger to hunt if he stays alive. He will last this night. I will not stop until my little Juri is back in the safety of my hut — in my arms. My mind roars with the fears I have over her survival. How will she fare with her eyes? *By the blessed suns, please lead me to her!*

The ache in my heart tightens, the monster inside of me hungers for justice, and I cannot handle the feeling anymore. Grabbing the larger knife from Jomo's hand, I cut off the warrior's head in one swoop. I tire of these games. His head rolls onto the ground, but it does not satisfy my hunger for blood one bit, despite it splattered all over my chest and Domo's arms. All I am is more angry that I could not find where my Juri is. As his blood starts to pool on the ground creating a deeper blood mud, I turn my face to Jomo.

"Jomo, place his head on the outskirts of this camp with one of our spears. The Namwana have been warned. Come back the moment you are done, for the warpath has only started."

Jomo, one of my younger seasoned warriors, nods his head and jogs out of the hut to look for an abandoned spear to post his head as warning for our closest enemy tribe. This day has not fared any better than the last, but we have yet to gather all our warriors before we head East towards Namwana lands. If a scout has been sent to the west towards our territory, who knows what other things they have in store for us?

GAMBA

Our tribe has started to gather from the surrounding camps to the East. We are currently seven hundred strong and twenty of our warriors have set to the shores to start making boats. Some scouts were sent to the West in case trouble comes from many directions. But our current war lies with the Matalo'toa tribe beyond the waters. In order to beat them, we must become like them and fight on their preferred hunting grounds — the raging waves in the storms to come. I've gathered the warriors and drawn my strategies on the ground so that we all understand the moves we need to carefully make in order to win. Most of the warriors have trained under me when they came into season, so it was easy to explain everything in detail without too many misunderstandings from the younger men.

The skies have not ceased in its anger and tears since my female was taken from my sights. She was someone important; I felt it. She clawed at my insides with her warrior spirit, the fierceness that shone in her eyes that reminded me of light spears. I was led to that place, in that moment, by the blessed suns. That warrior I fought on the ledge will feel the wrath of a Namwana warrior. How dare he throw an innocent, unattached female over his boat in the middle of a storm? *My female.* He may not have known my hunter's eyes caught his actions, but he will know soon enough.

Walking past my men, along the shores that border our tribe, I see that four boats have already been made, able to carry five of our warriors each. We must make sure our strategy will let us get the foremost hand to win before they even see us coming. Long-range weapons and the preparation for close combat have been drilled into the mind of every warrior willing to face the waters. While one set of warriors carve boats, the other set are sparring in preparation. We rotate until it is time to set out towards the island.

CHIEMKO

My heart feels like it's been ripped out of its chest. How can the Gods' tear me down so many times in this lifetime? My parents, the separation I feel from my people, the loss of my heart's desire, *my Juri*. Am I meant to drown in these waters, to finish off what I know they are planning to do? The Gods' are toying with me until their final blow. How can my Juri slip through my hands right in front of my very eyes? How is this possible? It can only be the workings of a higher power.

I cry out another roar into the storm, expressing my anger with the Gods' decisions.

The waves move with the angry skies and wind. Many times, I almost lose my own footing if I was not holding onto the piece that ties our sails, but the years of being a warrior of the water have made my mind swift. As my boat arrives back on the island of my people, I jump out in the raging waters, straining my muscles and relishing the pain in my muscles as I drag my boat in against the waves onto the shore. The festivities have been done for some time now and I feel a tightness in my chest in what I have to do. From bringing joy to bringing this kind of news.

The warriors must be gathered once more because it is not only the storm and tears of the skies coming, it is war. I feel it.

SIXTEEN

JURI

Monday goes by in a blur. It's always like this, usually. Trying to catch up on paperwork, trying to avoid Anderson and trying to discreetly get into the elevator at odd hours to avoid elevator boy Gary. Well, that last part is new, but it feels like it's something I've been doing a lot lately since that fateful night by my apartment door. He can be relentless with his weird flirting.

The day has ended and after leaving thirty minutes later than usual; I head down to the lobby, changing out my office heels for flats. A warm hand comes over my shoulder while I'm bent over putting on the last shoe. The hairs on the back of my neck rise because I know exactly who this is. Damn, even thirty minutes later, he still catches me? Is this some sort of fucking game to him? That even sounds creepy in my head.

Cutting my eyes to the right of me, I see that I am not alone in the lobby at least. *Good.* The front desk person can be a witness to anything that happens.

"Hey Juri, glad I caught you. Did you want to have coffee sometime, maybe tomorrow?"

I already gave you a knee to the balls, though. "I'm sorry, Gary, I need to get home. I don't think it would be a good idea to date a coworker."

He leans in even closer to whisper against my ear. "I'd hate to have to spike your drink anyway. You look beautiful today, by the way."

Mental red flags are waving erratically in front of my eyes. *Time to go, Juri!*

Using the strength in my shoulders, I slip out from his grip and start fast walking out the door back onto the streets. The trek to my apartment is quick — no weird person running into me this time. My head still feels tight and my heart is still beating out of my chest. I take the elevator this time when I reach my apartment complex to change up my route. My mind is getting frantic as I fish my keys out to open my door, looking left and right in case I'm being closely followed. Once I make it in, I lock the door, throw my bag on the floor, and put my hand over my heart to calm it. *What is wrong with this guy? Now he's getting more brazen in public. Shit.* Once I calm my racing heart down, I continue like normal.

After Netflix and chilling solo to help get my mind off of things, I go to the bathroom to start a bath for once instead of just a quick shower. Throwing my clothes on the ground, I get my hair up into a bun, gently placing my choker and glasses next to each other on the sink.

The bath water cooled much too fast for my liking after laying in it for only a short period of time. I was starting to doze off a bit, laying inside of the bath relaxing. Trying not to slosh water over the side of the tub, I carefully pull the drain and wait for the water to go down. The room is warm enough from the initial steam that I don't feel like I'm freezing by the time I take slow steps out onto the bath mat. Drying myself and covering up with the towel, I put my choker and glasses back on before I walk back into my bedroom.

After getting my clothes on for the night, I sit on the side of my bed and just think about everything that's happened today. If I do decide to make any drastic changes like move, it will have to wait until I get that corrective eye surgery. I feel vulnerable as it is, and I don't need one more thing to give me a disadvantage. I hope the cost isn't too high when I get to that consultation this Friday. I told Anderson, and emailed HR, about requesting my day off. HR approved right away, but I had to put my foot down with Anderson. That man wants to run a slave ship even though he does nothing all day long.

When my hair is almost dry, I climb onto it and lay my head down sideways on the pillow, my body on my stomach. Hopefully tomorrow will be a better day than today.

SEVENTEEN

JURI

I feel like I only closed my eyes for five minutes, but when I come to, something is off. I can't move and it's because my arms are tied up. My legs are free and I twist my neck backward to try and see what is going on — see how I ended up this way and what's tying me. It looks like a thick rope that's been used. My arms are tied in sections down from my upper arm to my wrists, and it somehow connects to my shoulders as well.

I'm about to turn my body when warm flesh, that is not mine, snuggles up behind me. A hand caresses down my bare hips and my mind freaks out. *Bare hips? I'm fucking naked.*

"Good morning, beautiful." Is that Gary's voice? *He is out of his fucking mind!*

His teeth are nipping at my shoulders that are pulled back from the position of it being tied up. I can feel him tug on my ropes to bring me closer to his body — his very warm, and very naked body. This is getting worse by the second. His hands are roaming all over me like he has the permission to. It's making me shiver in unease at what he has in store for me.

But he must take the shivers as something else, because some of his fingers have come around and found my pussy. I'm dry as a desert and he can feel it. Since half of my body is basically tied up, he easily turns me over onto my back. The position the ties have me in makes my chest jut out to the ceiling like a damn offering. He takes one of my breasts into his mouth with confidence, like he's done this before…

My mind flashes back to the day I woke up with my shirt ridden up. *Fuck, it was him, wasn't it?* He was in my house before doing who knows what to my body. I'm not the lightest sleeper, and it seems this fact puts me at another disadvantage. *Dammit.* I wasn't sore between my legs, so there's that.

He's devouring both breasts like a desperate man, one that probably hasn't gotten laid in a while. What he's doing right now feels good, but I know it shouldn't. This doesn't make any sense. He can have anyone he wants. There are plenty of other women in our building, so why me? Is it because I keep turning him down? I don't see a solution to the problem at hand, just a lose-lose situation.

I scream a little when he twists the nipple that's not currently in his mouth with such force that I know it will be bruised and tender. With a pop of his mouth off the other nipple, his fingers go to do the same thing. *Fucking hell!*

His eyes are dilated, and he's neither smiling nor making any sort of face that tells me what he's thinking. It's blank. This makes it even scarier. When I feel him moving down my body, I clamp my legs shut. *No.*

Caught in his blue-eyed stare, his face doesn't react at all when his left arm pulls something and my right leg is forced open. Shit, I didn't realize there was a rope tied to my ankle too. He ties the other end of the rope on the closest bed post near my head, preventing me from closing my right leg. His hand forces the other leg open with his strength and he gives a slow lick from the bottom of my pussy all the way up to my clit. It feels good but I don't want it to feel good right now. Guess he's making his own wetness since nothing he's doing to me up to this point is getting me off.

He continues his ministrations with the help of his other hand now, the one not holding my left leg down. My body tenses up when he pokes and prods my opening with one of his fingers. I am still so utterly dry with this man that I internally wince. *Please don't make it hurt.* He shoves another finger anyway, and I do physically wince in pain from the intrusion. Nothing I say to him will make him stop. The ropes and pre-planning already tell me as much. He's waited too long for this to hear no again. *Shit, for all I know the word no turns him on.*

He licks and suckles on my clit for a while and I'm lulled into a false sense of security. I'm taken by surprise when he takes a hard bite down causing me to cry out in pain. My clit is throbbing and his continuous licking isn't helping anything, just makes it feel ten times worse.

His tongue stops and I let out a deep breath of relief. I've had my eyes closed since he started going down on me, not wanting to see the sight in front of me — of Gary taking advantage of my body. Maybe closing my eyes wasn't such a great idea since I scream in pain again, when I feel him whipping my pussy with something thick and hard. My eyes fly open to catch him swinging his arm down again for another whipping with the same type of rope he has me tied up in. But instead of just straight rope, there are a couple of knots at the end of the one in his hands.

My skin feels hot from each impact, the echo of each hit lingering long after the rope has already finished its punishment. My mound feels bruised. My hips, my inner thighs. He's relentless. I can't even tell if he's enjoying it or if he's just punishing me. His stoic face remains the same, except now he's breathing harder from the exertion of his swings. All the clenching my pussy is doing in anticipation of each swing and throbbing of welts has inadvertently made my pussy wet. *I can't believe this. Am I secretly a glutton for punishment?*

I'm a sobbing mess right now from all the pain I'm feeling, all from different random places, but it doesn't stop him one bit. Gary drops the makeshift whip in his hand onto the bed next to us, quickly climbs on top of me, bites down on one of my nipples and shoves into my pussy with one quick thrust. He's too much, the intrusion too big without enough of a prep. Whatever wetness I had, I wasn't wet enough for the invasion. It's a searing pain, the topping on the cake to all the other pain he's inflicted. The biting of my nipple doesn't deter what I'm feeling between my legs at all.

The pace of his thrusting is brutal, and his firm grip on my one leg that isn't tied, is bruising. I feel like my hip joint is going to pop out of socket any time now. Each pound pushes me up on the bed, the slap of his hips against mine creating a different sensation on top of everything else. He's going on forever; don't men usually only take a few minutes? *Good grief, everything hurts!*

"Juri, you feel so good. You didn't like it when I was nice."

He was being nice before? Why does his praise do something to me? Shaking my head, I dislodge all the crazy thoughts trying to slither into my mind.

After what feels like forever, I hear him groan and his thrusts become erratic, losing its rhythm. I'm glad I just got another dose of the three-month birth control shot a few weeks back. Thirty years old, single Indian woman in an apartment — did I make myself too easy a victim? Did I have a label on top of my head that said easy statistic? My eyes water even more just thinking about how I will be able to explain this to my parents who are in India living their lives blissfully unaware of what's happening to their only daughter right now.

Gary stops thrusting finally, leans down against me and starts talking into my ear like we are having a couple's intimate moment. I'm so confused by this back-and-forth personality.

"I knew you liked it hard. I tried nice, and you hated it. You don't want a nice guy, do you Juri?" What is he talking about? "You want one that can control you and make you do what you want to do on the inside but are afraid to voice out loud. I can do that for you, Juri. I'd do anything for you." These kinds of sweet words shouldn't be coming out of the mouth of the man that just did what he did. "I can make you take my cum in all your holes, never leave you wanting. I can be whatever you need me to be."

Fuck. The sound of his voice — he truly believes everything he's saying.

What do you say to someone who is out of their mind? You can't call them crazy because it might make them crazier. I shut my eyes and feel more tears fall down my face. But this guy right here, he never stops — nothing deters him at all. He licks up my tears like it's the beverage he's been waiting for. The end result.

His lips travel across my face so gently, I'm not sure what to think.

A hand goes around my neck suddenly and my eyes open in shock. The squeeze is tight and I can't get any air in making my mouth gape open. Gary takes advantage and drops his spit into my mouth right before he takes it into his in some psychotic version of a loving kiss. His teeth bite my lips until I can taste my own blood and his tongue is probing inside my mouth while I'm still trying to catch precious air. I guess it wasn't enough because both of his hands are around my neck while he takes what he wants from my lips and mouth with his. One squeezing, the other caressing the curve between my neck and shoulder — hot and cold, dark and light. My eyes, once blurred by tears, are now starting to get dark around the corners. I'm struggling as much as I can, but his weight on top of me is too heavy for me to make any significant movements.

The blackness finally closes in and takes not only my sight, but my breath away.

142

EIGHTEEN

DUMA

We've come to the fifth village in our tribe.

Dum drum. Dum dum dum drum. Dum drum. Dum.

The men continue to beat the war drums as we walk through. Warriors come out of their huts with weapons in hand and follow behind the army we lead through.

Dum drum. Dum dum dum drum. Dum drum. Dum.

It is the third rise of the suns over the crest of the far plains since the march started. I am nowhere closer to finding my little Juri. The rage inside of me has not simmered, and I have left many heads on spears in my war path.

Dum drum. Dum dum dum drum. Dum drum. Dum.

The heads of the scouts of the Namwana tribe are increasing west towards us. My suspicions must be true; it has to be them who took my little Juri from me. Or else, why do they need so many eyes and ears on our side of the plains, so far from their homeland?

Dum drum. Dum dum dum drum. Dum drum. Dum.

Tea-kettl-da-caw!

A simulated bird call carries on the wind towards my ears, the call of one of the Chintkku scouts — he has found something. I feel the need for blood inside of me rising.

"Chiku!"

"Yes, warchief!"

Tea-kettl-da-caw!

We glance at each other once, my hand signaling for him to follow me towards the sound. With a nod, we begin to trek in the direction on foot. Our bodies have been honed for long distance travel and our skin has been thickened by the constant suns beating against it. Jogging eastward towards a next call being hailed, I see our scout in the distance by the black feather on top of his head piece. Both arms are banded with the grass we make our beds from, to help hide him behind the land and trees. We are almost to the elder cave by the river. What has he found?

There are more trees here because they are refreshed by the water of the river. When Chiku and I finally make it to where he stands on top of the cave mouth, he points his spear towards something lying at his foot. My heart races and I feel the blessed Sun telling me to hurry.

Leaping over and onto rocks, grabbing the closest tree trunk to make my climb onto the cave's ascending ledge, my eyes zero in on the sight before me. It is little Juri, I know it from the color of her skin and from the beautiful mane that spills over her face. She has no covering, and she is tied up by something I have never seen before.

I feel the need to kill. Someone has hurt her. Picking her up gently into my arms, her head falls back like life has been stolen. Placing my ear down next to her nose, I feel the slight shift of air to her breath coming out. *She is still alive then.* Who could do this to one so vulnerable? What monster could attack a helpless female who cannot fend for herself? *They will pay, I will make sure of it.*

Cradling her in my arms like a babe, I tell my scout to continue his duties. Chiku walks by my side as we slowly make our way back to the fifth village. I will not let little Juri leave my sight or side again.

The trek back is slower than the jog to the elder's cave. I need to keep my walk steady in case little Juri is hurt in places I cannot yet see. The most important thing is that she is back under my protection — where she belongs.

The Chintkku people have named me their war chief because of my age and bloodline. I do not care for names, but I will do right by my people, by whatever means necessary. It is how one survives these lands.

The hut they left for me in this village is on the outskirts, as I've requested. The females of this camp were nice enough to bring three mats for us, two for Juri to tend to her wounds. None of us warriors were sure of how to unravel the ropes, making my anger boil again, so I just took my sharpest blade to cut them all off. The injuries on her body make me want to rage war the very moment I saw them. The signs of injury from whips were easy to understand. The bite marks were something else. They look like bites from a people, and not a creature. There were not any extra torn skin from the fangs usually found in the beasts of the plains. And if it is done by a people, who's people?

My mind wars with going out and killing everything in my path and staying by Juri's side to help bring her spirit back into her body. She has only stirred with movement a few times; her bottom lip is also coated in blood.

The village women have tended to her skin with water and rags, enough to clear most of the dirt and blood away. My mind is in a state of confusion at what I am to do but the tug in my chest forces me to stay by her side until she wakes.

What war have you come from, little Juri?

JURI

My body hurts and everything feels so hot. A hand caresses my face and I flinch in fear. *Please Gary, just let me rest, you've done enough.* The hand stops for a moment before attempting to continue the movement again. On instinct, I grab at the wrist, still with my eyes firmly closed. I don't want to see his face, what lust he has for me. The skin under my palm, though, sparks a memory. The raised healed welts, in patterns — skin like it's been warmed by the sun.

I open my eyes to find a face close to mine, a face that makes me cry all over again. Like a dark knight, my heart is elated to see Duma. I need to feel safety again; I need him closer to me. I feel so broken right now.

Moving into sitting, I wrap both of my arms around his shoulder and hold him as tight as I can as I let out all the demons that haunt my mind through the tears flowing down his broad shoulder. My body is shuddering from the tension, the fear of being unable to move while tied up in the comfort of my own home.

Am I that easy of a victim?

Duma picks up the rest of my body and makes me straddle him while he's sitting cross-legged on the ground, just holding me. The feel of his warrior marks brings me a sense of peace because I know my eyes are not fooling me. I don't need my glasses to know I'm safe in Duma's arms. It's only after my tears subside that I realize my rise in body temperature is from our flesh pressed against each other. I'm naked as the day I was born. But I feel recently cleaned, some parts of my skin are still damp. Or is it the sweat from being back in this place — this place reminds me so much of the African plains with multiple suns.

Each breath in and out from him pushes my own chest — forcing it to sync with his steady rhythm. He's so solid and steady, does anything bring him fear? I need to take in his strength, his steadiness at this moment. I need to let it soak into my skin and push my own fears away, after all, it's already said and done and Gary is not here right now.

I must have fallen asleep in his arms because the next time I wake up, I'm back on the grass mat. I'm not one to stay stupid for long though, I know now that this isn't a dream. Duma feels too real. This pain from the welts left on my body feels too real. When I roll onto my side to get myself up into sitting, I hear a scratch outside the hut walls. I remember seeing Duma do that before we entered that crazy old man's hut for the first time. It must be their version of a door knock. I watch as Duma has to bend over before he is able to enter the doorway that's covered by cloth. I forget how tall Duma's presence is, literally and figuratively. Sadly, he's still blurry from where he's standing, which means I don't have my glasses again.

I feel more vulnerable than I did the first time, but safe in Duma's presence all at once. There are scars I carry on the inside now from what Gary did to me, as well as the disadvantage of my vision. When Duma comes to sit in front of me, he stares into my eyes. I find that he's someone I can allow myself to be vulnerable with. But what happens when I end up back home — back to Gary? I don't have him there with me to chase these fears away. I feel myself tear up again because so much is out of my control, and it's a horrible feeling to be so helpless.

His warm hands enclose around my face and I can't bring myself to open my eyes to look at him. I don't want him to see the broken girl inside. I know I can get through this, I just need some time to find myself again, to find that inner strength I always harbored being an independent woman living alone in the city. How did life stray so far, so wrong? What did I do to deserve this?

I feel him rub his nose against mine and a small smile creeps up on my lips. He's so gentle with me. A stark contrast to Gary. I need comfort. I need to take back some sort of control. Leaning up a little more, I press my lips to his. He's still — a little too still. Do they not kiss here? My face flushes from embarrassment as I pull back slowly. But suddenly, I feel his warm hand behind my head pull me to bring my lips back to his. The piercing in his nostrils tickles my upper lip, but it reminds me that it's just Duma — piercings, warrior marks, eyes as sharp as a hunter, skin kissed and darkened by two suns. I will always know it's him, even with my eyes closed.

My hands roam his neck, down to his shoulders where the tell-tale signs of raised welts from his warrior marks begin. He smells of earth, sun and dust. A man who spends his time in the elements and comes back stronger for it. I need to take his warrior spirit inside of me; I need it; *I need his strength.*

Licking the seam of his lips, Duma groans against my mouth and gives in to the request. For a man who does not know what a kiss is, he is very willing to submit to me and my wants. When our tongues touch, it feels like my heart has found peace. This is where I am supposed to be, with Duma. He is a fast learner and his kiss grows more domineering by the minute — a battle to see who will win the lip match we've started. I should have known better than to challenge a warrior.

When his body leans into mine, pressing me against the mat, I let him. I want to erase all the memories and feelings my body still echoes from what happened back home. I can feel my nipples tracing the ridges of his muscles and some of his warrior marks with my squirming. It makes me hot and makes my nipples tight. My hands roam down his solid arms and I come across dual bands he has on his biceps. *I'll have to ask about the significance of these later.* One of his hands caresses my sides with such feather light touches. I can feel the coarse callus of his palms and fingers, hands that have worked much and probably wielded many weapons during his years. The thought gets me hot — being under someone so dangerous yet is so careful with me. When my legs slowly travel up his calves and thighs, Duma presses himself into me even more, bringing all his weight down against me finally.

I feel cocooned in warmth and protection. Our mouths haven't stopped their exploration and my hands seem to have found a mind of their own as they travel down his corded back, his warrior markings, down to his tight ass. *Holy shit.* That loin cloth of his that's shifting between us, has no damn back to it. *Good grief.*

My legs come around him fully at his waist and I pull him against my body even more. My bruises and welts hurt, but the warmth of Duma's sun-kissed skin dulls the ache. There's only one ache that won't go away, and it's flooding in wetness at the moment.

His cock is as hard as a steel pipe from the moment his body came against mine. I can feel his wetness making a smear on my inner thighs and it makes me wiggle and glide against him some more, hoping he'll just "accidentally" slip in.

But his cock is longer than I anticipated and the head is past my pussy opening. We're going to have to adjust our height differences a bit here. Taking my lips off his and putting some pressure on his shoulders to let him know I need him a little lower, I gasp when his lips softly take my nipple into his mouth. *Okay, that works too.* I'm far from being a virgin, but there's just something about the way Duma worships my body with his mouth that makes me feel like one.

His loincloth has moved to the side on its own, and his cock is sliding against my overly wet core. *I can't take this.* The flames are rising too high, my body wanting to combust with the need that's growing within me. The hardness of his cock to the softness of his caresses and kisses — the contradiction kills me. This giant warrior of a man and the ability to control his strength, I've never been so turned on in my life.

"Little Juri, I do not want to hurt you. You've been hurt enough."

I can feel the vibration of his words against my neck as his nose rubs against my sensitive skin there. Can a woman melt any more with that declaration? I need him to erase my pains, I need him to catch my fall. *I need his strength.*

"I need you to take me, Duma. I can't make it without you." My whispered words against his scalp must have tipped him over the edge because he shoves his cock into me right after the request, making me gasp at his sheer size. I feel so damn full. I feel myself stretching to accommodate his girth, but he's just so big.

He's breathing hard into the crook of my neck and is hissing. "Juri, you are so small. I am not all the way in yet, and I feel like you will push me back out."

"Then conquer me, Duma, get all the way inside." He does just what I say on the next thrust and I feel the breath get kicked out of my lungs.

Holy shit, this man is huge. It feels like he's hitting my damn ribcage. But I'm also so wet and feel so needy for it. I need him to take over and just ravish me like I know he can — he's a damn warrior.

When my hips start moving and my abs flex against him, Duma lifts his head to look me straight in the eye while he starts slow thrusts. *This just will not do.* I pull him closer to me by the back of his neck until our foreheads are touching. Staring right at him in a challenge, I tell him "take me like the warrior I know you are Duma, take me hard and don't stop until you're done."

His lips curl into a snarl and he starts ramming his cock into me full force. Right in front of my eyes, Duma has turned from man to beast, all unleashed fury. His grunts sound more like animalistic snarls and it makes me want him even more. Extending his arms straight against the mat, he throws one of my legs over his shoulder and uses it to leverage to get even deeper inside of me. The sounds of our flesh slapping each other against and the sound of our combined wetness is turning up the temperature in this hut.

The friction we both create together is causing me to chase my own pleasure as my hips lift up to meet every one of his thrusts.

With a roar, Duma spills into me with warm jets, making me want to explode but I haven't quite reached my own climax yet. When he pulls out of me so suddenly, it makes me gasp as he moves down my body again and starts to eat me out. *Holy guacamole.* His tongue is savage, and it's like he's attacking my pussy with the force of a hunter felling his prey. Duma has a big tongue, and that thing is everywhere. He is definitely using the skills he's learned from our previous kiss by kissing my lips down there the same way — with growing domination.

But he's missing the most crucial point. I gently grab his head and guide him where I need to go, and he follows without any resistance. He's suckling and lavishing such aggressive attention to my clit that when he groans against me, the vibration from the timbre of his voice shoots me straight to a climax I did not see coming. It's blinding and I have to pull my digging claws from his neck and shoulders to put my hands against my temples as I scream from the intensity. My hips are thrusting on their own into his face, and he doesn't seem to mind one bit. In fact, his big palms grab my asscheeks to bring my pussy even closer to his face as he laps up the combination of both our juices being flooded out with my recent orgasm.

This man is ravenous. Once the waves of my orgasm come down, Duma is still going at it. Then his tongue starts to lick across all my welts inside of my thighs and I want to cry. The way this man takes care of my body, with such gentleness despite his size. He is the opposite of Gary and everything I needed at this moment.

NINETEEN

Washing in Juri's restroom feels like home. I've come here so much, I leave a part of me behind. Laughing to myself at my own inside joke, I dry my hands on her towel and lift it up to my nose to inhale.

She's become a part of me, the very smell of her burned into my mind so deeply I can taste her like a phantom dish in my mouth. Soon. Soon she'll understand that we belong together — that she's always belonged to me. Placing her towel back where it belongs, I adjust myself once more before leaving the room. How does she create such a hunger within me?

The moment I enter the bedroom, I know something is different. I left Juri for only a second as I used the restroom. My mind goes through a myriad of emotions — first anger, then denial and finally my chest bubbles with laughter. Could I have misjudged her? Does she secretly have the ability to untie herself and escape my grasp? Oh, Juri, how you entertain me so. I laugh out loud once more as I think about how far we've come in our relationship. I'm the kind of man who deserves to have the woman I don't deserve.

And Juri is the only one for me.

Alright Juri, challenge accepted. I'll play your little cat-and-mouse game.

GAMBA

There is something not right.

"Kellan! Has Abo returned?"

Kellan looks around and begins to question some of the warriors nearby who are coated in dust. Each one shakes their head.

"No one has seen Abo yet."

"Thank you, Kellan. Join the warriors by the well to get things ready."

With a nod, he runs towards the heart of our village. Plans have been set forth, each group have their own tasks to complete.

My mind wanders as I stare out into the far lands we must scour. Every time my scouts are sent to the west, none of them return. I have hand chosen them all and they are great hunters who have the ability to hide themselves well during the hunt. Many beasts have been felled this way. Have they been captured or run across trouble? If so, why has word not come back from the other scouts I've sent north?

There is a sounding of the antedeer horn carried across the wind, telling me the last warrior I sent to scout two moons ago has returned.

"Jahi! What do you have for me? What has come of our other scouts to the west?" His fast strides bring him closer with each step he takes. I can see the bow slung across his shoulder and arrow bag behind him. The red feather on his headband lets us know he is a scout from the Namwana tribe, in case one of my newly seasoned warriors shoots their weapons before seeing their faces.

"Gamba, I need to tell you…"

I let him catch his breath for a moment for I know the plains can be hot and far-reaching. The dust that coats him tells me that he has gone farther than many of our other scouts in the past. The color of the dust is not the usual found around here.

"Gamba, I came back as fast as the wind and feet would carry me. To the west, close to some of the Chintkku camps, there is a line of spears thrown into the ground with the heads of our other scouts. The birds and creatures have not eaten all of their flesh yet, so I was able to recognize their faces. They are of our people."

My nostrils flare and my eyes burn with fury but I must keep my thoughts controlled — strategy must be changed according to what Jahi is telling me. This is not good news at all. My mind is quickly going through all the tactics and strategies that our people can use to come out on top of this new challenge issued by these barbaric actions. Not only are we preparing for war with the Matalo'toa tribe, it seems war from the Chintkku is coming to *us*.

"Kellan! Call the warriors who are not building boats, we have much to discuss. War is coming, and it is time we end this once and for all."

CHIEMKO

Jumping off the boat, I quickly pull it to shore and run towards the village.

"Chiemko! What is happening? Why are you running? What news?"

"Call all the warriors. Plans have to be made."

"What news from the waters? What shall I tell them?"

"Hemi, tell the men we need to prepare for war?"

"War?"

"Go, now!"

Hemi nods and turns with swift feet across the sands. I watch as one then two men spread the news across the island.

I feel it, the skies have warned me with their storms and tears. I need to find my Juri. Something in my heart is telling me she is somewhere on the mainland and that is exactly where I plan to conquer first. Tactics tell me that the tribes to the east, having speciality with their bows and arrows, isn't the first place we should arrange to travel to first. Perhaps there will be a path between the Chintkku and Namwana we can take to bring surprise.

With each footstep towards my hut, I watch as the women run to prepare weapons for their men, packing food and other necessities for the trip across the waters. We are a good people, we work well and I must make sure it stays that way. War cannot come to us, we must get the first leg and bring it to them on their own lands.

My mind continues to run with all the information I have gathered in all my years, information passed from our elders to us as we became of season to join in on warrior hunts. Even though the Chintkku are known for their bloodlust, we have no other choice. We must take our chances with the middle path on the mainland before we can move our people to the east against the Namwana tribe, who are known for their skills in long range weaponry.

With our combined skills in the waters, and hand-to-hand, we will have better chances giving the Namwana a surprise attack from a direction they did not see coming — surround them. It is better to deal our hand-to-hand with any scouts that may be from the west than to get our numbers taken out before we arrive to the east. The Namwana tribe will decrease our numbers with their skills in bows and long range spear throws if we come from a direction they expect.

My men gather around my hut as I continue to think through what we must do.

"Chiemko. Is it true? There is war?"

"Laki. War will always come. It is only a question of when." Looking into each of the eyes of my warriors, I find determined faces — the faces of those who know what this trip might bring: death.

"Mata warriors! The Gods have spoken. War must be brought to our enemies before they can be brought to us. We must protect our women and children. We must cross the waters and make sure every person we come across knows the fear of a Mata warrior."

"Aruh!"

"We boat across and find the middle path. The trees will be our advantage on our arrival."

"Chiemko!"

Turning my head towards the call of my name, I watch as some of the older warriors come towards us. What is going on? Has something happened to the women?

"Malosi! What news?"

The old warrior leads a few of the others who have recently spent their time defending the island while we are out on hunt.

"Chiemko. We give you our numbers. If war is to happen, you will need more than the men you have here."

"Malosi is right. We can lend you our skill, if only to make it easier on the younger warriors."

"Malosi, Tala. There will be nothing you can do to make it easier. This is—"

"Chiemko! Do you think we do not know of battles? Have you forgotten the one your own parents have died in?"

Growling at the mention of the memory, I try to bite my tongue in front of him. He knows well how I feel about that!

"Alright, you old fools. If you wish to join us in this bloodshed, so be it." Turning back to address the rest of my men who have been silently watching us speak, I stare into each other their eyes with the intensity of the rolling emotions I have inside.

Though my heart aches for the sacrifice of the older warriors, I know it must be done in order to secure our advantage. We are few against the warriors of the west and east, only five hundred strong, but our ability to quickly adapt to different combat styles will give us an advantage.

"We divide into groups. I need one elder warrior with each group to begin sparring. We need to make sure our skills are up and we need to understand each other's fighting style in order to gain advantage over the other tribes."

"Chiemko, there are not enough elder warriors to go around."

Turning to one of the newly seasoned men, I bare my teeth at him. "Then I suggest you find more and fix the problem. We are going to war. Whether you wish to make sure of your survival is up to you, but I suggest you start thinking of answers before you speak to me."

"Men! We must prepare the best we can before bloodshed is brought to our shores. Make your way to your families. The young who want to help will gather the boats. We have one war boat that has not been used since the days of old, but it will be necessary to bring her to life again. Its sails remain strong from the hides of the largest creatures found in these waters."

"Yes, Chief!"

"Yes, Chief!"

"Yes, Chief."

The men sound out my title one by one. How Many days have I longed for another way to lead my people — to lead them into something joyous. But it seems the Gods have led me down the path of bloodshed instead.

I watch as my men split up and do what they must do. Some gather their weapons and begin their training while others have gone to gather the people for assistance in other ways. One of the seasoned elder warriors looks my way with much in his eyes but says nothing as he turns to grab a weapon. The women can be seen helping to collect food stores and crafting extra weapons in case the waters carry predators on our journey and we lose some of our tools striking them down.

We are a good people — strong together. It is with a small feeling of guilt that I must take their men from them again but it is necessary. The decisions of a leader is never an easy one.

It will take a few spans for us to prepare. The moon will lose half its light before we journey across the waters and bring war to the mainland.

TWENTY

DUMA

My time spent with my little Juri has made me a new man. I am no longer unattached and I am not ashamed to show it to my men. Her mating marks on my neck show them enough as I walk ahead of the line of warriors I have collected for this warpath.

Dum drum. Dum dum dum drum. Dum drum. Dum.

The drums are pounding into our hearts to amp up the blood thirst we already feel. The Chintkku tribe is known for their bloodlust because our bloodlines make us go berserk in war.

Dum drum. Dum dum dum drum. Dum drum. Dum.

We become blinded by our red haze that takes over our minds. It is an advantage that has benefited us during wartimes. The numbers we lose to war are a lot less than the numbers lost from the other tribes. We are proud of this as people.

Dum drum. Dum dum dum drum. Dum drum. Dum.

Juri's love and passion only spurs my rage to *win*. Baring my teeth, I address the warriors before me.

"The day has arrived, my brothers, we must make our warpath seen beyond the eastern suns cresting the land. The Namwana tribe will feel our hate against the wrong they have brought upon us and will not see our wrath coming until it is too late. We will walk through the plains like the face of death and deal blood that needs to be let to secure our path to our victory!"

"To Guergalo!" *To war!*

"To Guergalo!" *To war!*

My men roar with agreement, banging their spears against their wooden shields, creating the sound of a land storm as I walk back across the front of my warriors again.

I growl and roar out, "Gamja! To Guergalo!" *Yes! To war!* The men repeat the chant over and over as the war drums beat into our hearts.

Dum drum. Dum dum dum drum. Dum drum. Dum.

The stomping of their feet brings thunder through the grounds to match the warring grey skies. With this camp, we have become seven hundred strong. The rest will be left to defend the women and children of the tribe. Word has spread to divide the remaining soldiers among the five camps.

Looking at the heads and bodies before me, I am confident this day will bring us victory. We will win and bring honor to our tribe. With my spear held high towards the sky, all the warriors let out a war cry that will carry on the winds.

After gathering my men to build the sounds of war with their drums across the village, some have been tasked to begin standing outside of our village as well. My heart beats loudly with anticipation of battle as my legs carry me back to my hut. My blood calls to hers, wanting her touches, her smiles to see me off to war. When I reach the hut, I push aside the cloth without scratching, wanting to surprise her of my return.

"Ahhhrrggh!" The creatures of the skies fly as my own roar pierces my ears.

I go back to check on Juri only to find that she has been taken from me again. Footsteps around me become drowned out by the blood flowing near my ears. I'm shaking my head to rid me of the distraction. Juri. They took my Juri!

"What—"

"Abeji! Stay away from Duma when he's—"

My beast rages, making me grab the closest warrior to the hut by the neck. Dragging him inside, my hands squeeze more than they should as he sputters and kicks.

"What have you done with her?"

He continues to sputter and it only enrages me more.

"My. Female. She is gone."

His eyes are rolling and I am angry at the fact that his life is so easily taken. Warriors of mine need to survive the most grueling of tortures. What happens when they get captured by the other tribes? Biting the air in front of his face, I watch as blood blooms on the whites of his eyes.

Grabbing the bone knife on the ground from the last torture, I quickly bring both of my arms up and over my head to impale his chest. My beast inside thirsts for blood as I rip open the bones of his chest cavity and rip out his heart with my bare hands. The blood collecting onto the floor makes for a slick ground as I stand back to my full height and roar at the heart before me.

"Arrrhhhgg!" My chest tightens, the pain welcomed.

The heart in my hands begins to slow its rhythm. Staring at it with disgust, it does nothing to bring my female back. Tossing it aside, I exit the hut with eyes that hunt for my next prey.

Questioning everyone in the camp with my bloodied hands, I can now only assume one of the Namwana scouts snuck in when I wasn't looking.

"Is there Namwana hiding here?"

"N-no, Warchief."

"How then does a female leave this village without any warrior's notice!"

"Fe—"

Grabbing his neck to stop him from speaking, I growl in his face and toss him against the other men. How dare they? They will feel my anger. I *will* find out who did this. Kwame follows behind me in my rampage and my feet stomp around the village to look into the huts only leaving me unsatisfied when I still cannot find her.

Lifting my hand, I point at the closest male. "Bring me all the warriors who were near my hut when Juri was brought into the village! The women as well." With a nod, my assigned warrior goes to complete the task I have given him.

I am going to kill anyone who has touched my Juri, even if they are of my people. Who would dare?! I bend down to enter the doorway of the hut that now holds the dead warrior and my nostrils flare in anticipation of the bloodshed to come my way.

"Duma, you must let the bloodlust calm before you make this decision." Growling, I turn to face our sight seeker. "We trust the honor you hold and we follow you as a people. Do not let your feelings cloud your mind as a leader." Turning my head back to the blood before me, I stay quiet even though my beast inside rages. "The trust of the people can become a fragile thing with too much bloodshed inside our own camp." Kwame and his sense, it angers me as I stare at the still heart on the ground before me.

My mind is in pain; it is hurting for my loss of Juri — again. I cannot be in two places at the same time, I must lead my people to war. What if she is found once more in a beaten state? A growl slips from my lips as the thought crosses my mind. My mind tells me that Kwame has offered wise words to many of the war chiefs of old. Breathing hard through my nose, I try to calm the storm raging inside of me.

A scratch on the outside of the hut lets me know my warrior has completed his task. Five of the newly seasoned warriors that come from this camp, walk slowly and quietly into the hut. Staring at the men before me, I can feel the fear that comes off of their skin. It is a skill grown as a hunter to smell it on prey. Taking a deep breath in as I walk in front of them. I do not smell her floral scent on any of the warriors in front of me. No, these men did not take my Juri. Kwame is right. Any further blood-shed I perform in this hut would cause my people to lose the trust they have in my leading of the people.

"You can leave." The men quickly do as I say as I walk back towards Kwame. He nods his head in approval of my decision. Grabbing the pots by the wall of the hut, I dip my hand in and bring back red painted hands on top of the bloodstains that were already there. Smearing the war paint on my face, I do the same with the pot that contains the white. Turning to Kwame, I bare my fangs.

"We leave at the next rising of the sun over the eastern lands. Namwana blood will be spilled in sacrifice to the blessed suns. I will bring my Juri back home to me."

TWENTY-ONE

I'm still in an after sex glow as I stretch my body like a cat who's been napping in the sun too long. The kinks in my body working out and the popping of my bones feel good. When I open my eyes and rub out the grogginess, looking around, I notice I am back in my own room. How does this keep happening? I'm not as caught by surprise anymore, though. I don't have control of anything and I've accepted that, but I already miss Duma's warmth. I can't stand the 'real world', not one where Gary exists. Grabbing my glasses from my nightstand, I look around and find that I am alone in my room.

Leaning over my bed to grab my phone that's still plugged in, it tells me that I need to get ready for my Tuesday's day of work in the next four hours. These dreams — I find that I don't really want to wake up from them anymore. Not when reality tells me it's worse than the life I'm living in these dreams. Duma's touch and the phantom feeling of his cock inside of me still pulses. I can feel the sensation of his erection inside my pussy making me wet from the memory of our lovemaking. He's the biggest dick I've ever had in me. It erases the physical memory of Gary.

How do I face this man when I go back to work? Do I pretend nothing happened between us? Do I report him to HR? How can I do that exactly when the crap happened in my home with no signs of forced entry? He's got me in a catch twenty-two and I hate it.

After my quick shower, I put my choker and glasses back on, proceeding through my daily routine like the other day did not happen.

Is this how it is for rape victims? You feel so detached, yet you are forced to play the role of a regular woman in the world that has let you down. Put on a pretty face, let the world you are still the same while you are dying inside slowly the more smiles you put up.

Tuesday's work day goes by in a blur the same way Monday's did. I'm glad for it. I can't concentrate on Anderson's relentless flirtations during my attempts to be a good personal assistant at the desk and Gary's insinuation that we are a thing after what happened between us. He even managed to slip me a written note somehow into my cubicle, like we're in grade school.

If I followed you home, would you keep me?

This disillusioned bastard thinks he's living the fairy tale of his dreams as I'm dying with every creepy pick up line and flowery word that comes out of his mouth in public. *Am I being overly dramatic? I don't think I am.* The memory of the last time he caught me in the lobby again, comes to my mind.

Someone grabs my hand as I'm putting on my flats. Looking up, I see Gary kissing the back of it just before he says, "There must be something wrong with my eyesight. I just can't take them off you." What is wrong with this guy?

What the hell do you say to that? Who will believe me about what happened with a guy that looks as endearing as Gary? Typical cute white boy in the office that all the girls usually lust after. They would believe him over me any day, and that's a damn depressing thought.

The nights I spend in my bedroom never lead me back to Duma and his arms. I don't know how to get back. The next few days go by in a blur again, or maybe I'm just working in zombie mode, but soon enough Friday approaches.

Sitting in the lobby of the Lasik eye surgery office for a consultation, I am mindlessly scouring the magazines they have at the desk until my name gets called.

"Miss Juri Chakrabarti, you're up next. The doctor is ready to see you. Let's step to the back, shall we?"

Getting up from the seat in the lounge, I follow the nurse to the back room.

"Alright, we are going to just write down the numbers for your current eyesight. Then check the health of your eyes."

"Okay."

She performs some eye exams in different rooms, and paperwork being placed in a file. The nurse finally leads me to an office to wait for the doctor's face-to-face consultation meeting.

I'm getting kind of nervous. What if they say I don't qualify? My eyes are pretty bad. There's a knock before the doctor comes inside wearing a typical white lab coat. A man who looks to be in his thirties from some sort of European descent. Once he takes a seat behind the fancy wooden desk in the room, he proceeds.

"Miss Chakrabarti, it is a pleasure meeting you. My name is Dr. Morales. Looking over your file and eye exams, I would definitely say you qualify for corrective eye surgery. Your prescription is higher than our usual, but I think it would still benefit you. There is a chance that you will not be able to see 20/20, but the result will be much better than where you are right now."

Okay, that doesn't sound so bad. Anything is better than how I am without glasses at this point, I agree. "Okay, so how much will it be?"

"Our prices vary based on the severity of the client's initial eye prescription. That being said, we are looking at about five thousand dollars for both eyes." *Oh, sweet lord.*

I'm going to have to think about this. That's almost my entire savings. Thinking about all the times I found myself in danger and vulnerable because of my eyesight, I tell myself it's now or never. I'll build the savings back up. "Okay. When can I schedule an appointment?"

"Oh good. If you go out to the reception desk in the lobby, she will be able to help you." He rises up to offer me his hand to secure the deal. Shaking it firmly, I square my shoulders and walk out the office. It has to be done. I need more control over my life. I don't want my eyes to hold me back or put me in a situation I could have prevented.

The front desk lady was very nice and was able to set an appointment for me tomorrow morning. Taking a deep breath, I walk out of the office feeling a little lighter knowing I will have one more burden off my shoulders soon.

GARY

There she is, walking to her car. She looks like she made a decision. The last time I was in her apartment, I saw the date circled on her calendar. A little snooping in her computer and search history led me to this plaza. Seems Juri wants to correct her vision. Good, then she can see everything we do together without having to rely on her glasses. I know she's doing this for us. I've been lying low, giving her a break. I read somewhere that a man shouldn't come on too strong. I also want her to anticipate the times we come together. She wasn't happy with our last encounter. *I fucked up.* I was just trying something new — something I thought she'd like. *I'll have to make it up to her.* Who knew convincing a woman to love you would be so damn hard? *Juri is worth it.*

I'll have to think of something else we can do together, a different way of making love so that she will be able to enjoy herself with me. New couple sexual exploration and all that. I'm getting excited just thinking about all the things we can do and try out. I'm not going to let a little mishap stand in the way of our relationship. Juri gets into her car and I close my eyes, letting the memories of the recent events unfold before them again.

"Hey Chris, what are you doing tonight? Do you want to go out for some drinks?"

"Yeah man, I'm always down for alcohol."

"Cool, how about you come on over to my place around seven. We get a little buzzed first before we hit up some bars or clubs. Your choice."

"Fuck yes, I need to get my dick wet. Seeing Juri walk around makes my dick hurt, straining my pants. That reminds me, have you seen Jack lately?" I'm about to cut this fucker down, right here in this office, if he doesn't shut the fuck up about my girl.

"I heard he took a couple weeks off."

"Ah okay, that makes sense. I'll see you tonight."

As seven o'clock approaches, I check over my basement to make sure everything is where it should be. This fucker thinks to look at my woman, whacking off his cock to her in the janitor's closet every time she walks by. My blood just boils thinking about it.

The doorbell rings and I quickly smooth down my hair after running up the stairs. When I calm my breaths, I plaster on a fake smile before opening the door.

"Hey Chris! Glad you could make it. Let's go down to the basement so I can show you what kind of alcohol I have."

"Fuck, you have a whole collection? Damn, I can't wait to see that shit." Greedy bastard.

Letting Chris lead in the front, I open the basement door for him and without turning on the light; I shove him through the doorway. Even people who are good for nothing have the capacity of bringing a smile to your face. For instance, when you push them down the stairs. The sounds of his body tumbling creates a beat. The crunch on the ground accompanied by his moans makes me smile even more, but we're not done yet. Oh now, it's only just begun.

Turning on the light and walking down slowly, I see a pool of blood forming under him. Red is such a striking color.

Tying Chris' arms by the chains hanging from my basement rafters, I pull the chair I have down here closer to him. This fucker thinks he can look at my Juri and get away with it. He can just fucking join his buddy Jack in hell.

Sitting in my chair, I lean in closer and unbuckle his pants. Grabbing my bag of tools I brought along with me by the foot of my chair, I grab my small gasoline powered chain saw and start it up. The angry growl of the motor makes me smile even wider. As the blood splatters on my walls and all over my face, the only thought that runs through my head is Juri.

Is it sick, this love I have for her? She's everything to me. I'd gladly bathe everything in red if she asked me to. I'm getting hard just thinking about it. I'm going to have to try harder and make it up to her. Our last date didn't go exactly as I planned. Well, it did, but the results did not come out as I planned. I just want to make her feel good — with me, her man.

I can make her love me the way I love her. I just need to try harder.

TWENTY-TWO

GAMBA

I have rounded my men into two groups. The strategy we will use is to send our warriors to the west to head off the Chin-tkku tribe that has already started on the warpath. Our scout was able to come back and tell us of the sounds of their war drums coming eastward towards our village. The other group will remain here to protect our women and children. We will also be the force to drive away the Matalo'toa if they come to our shores. It is best to have warriors ready on all sides.

I am sending Jahi and Kellan with the warriors to the west. I trust they will lead the men well. Jahi has excellent eyes that let him see his prey quickly. Kellan will be his sprinter on the ground to relay messages to the rest of the warriors.

Kaikura will stay at the village with me. His skills with the spear will assist us in any of the hand to hand fighting we must do if the Mata warriors arrive.

As Jahi and Kellan turn to head out to the front of the warriors, about to lead the men away from the village, we hear war drums in the distance carrying in the wind. The ground shakes under our feet in a constant rhythm of footsteps, the way the beasts do when running together, and we know the Chintkku are close.

Go swiftly with the wind, my brothers.

"Kaikura. We leave now."

Spee-spee-chik. Kaikura calls our men and signals the beginning of the march. They quickly gather with their bows and their spears around us. My men and I stand at the ready, facing the west. The suns are starting to fall and the war drums can be heard mixed with our battle horn. The tension in the air can be felt through all of us. There is blood lust in the wind and it carries the scent of the dead. In the skies, we see wings of black darkness flying in circles in the distance. The sparcra feast on the dead. Their flight tells us the fight is not as far as we would like from our village.

My blood is pumping behind my ears and there is something inside of me telling me to head to the west to join my other men. Is this a sign from the Gods?

"Kaikura! Find five warriors who are light on their feet, we are to join Jahi and Kellan. *Now!*" My warrior has been trained well and swiftly moves to do as I say without question. When my five swiftest men gather around me, I pass the village protection duty to one of the newly seasoned warriors who stand nearby.

"Kufuo. You will lead this group. Be swift!"

"Yes, Gamba." He quickly turns to the rest of the men and starts to give them orders. Good.

Looking at the five around me, I give them the strategy. "My brothers! You and I will come from the upper pass overlooking where the beasts roam. We take the high ground and ready our weapons. The Chintkku will not see us coming from above where the sparcra flies. It is this surprise that will give us an advantage in the battle."

My men nod in understanding and we run north to the pass. The trees there will help hide us and our positions.

When we make it beyond the trees to the edge of the pass, I signal my warriors to lie low. The battle can be seen below to the west of us, and there are many dead from both tribes. Swiftly moving my eyes across the lower lands, it feels as though the Chintkku still outnumber us.

I signal to one of the warriors close to me who holds a bow. "You and I will be shooting our arrows down there. If you see the war chief, do not hesitate to take aim, my brother. He will be the way to winning this battle."

The Chintkku wooden shields easily let our eyes see which of our men are fighting the other tribe. When shields go down in preparation for the thrust of their spears, the red and white faces marked in war paint create a sight to be found in the darkest of dreams as they roar in their bloodlust. They move like demons, with quick thrusts of spears piercing through the bodies of our people. If their hand weapons are caught in bones, unable to be pulled back out, they use their shields to cut arms and necks, spurting blood over their war painted faces as well as bathing their shields red in warning for the next warrior.

My eyes zone in on one warrior who towers above the rest with skin as dark as a death dealer. His spear is like a part of his arm as he thrusts into the bodies of our warriors one after another and pulls it back out with their insides stuck around the head of the spear. This must be what the elders call berserk, for he looks more beast than man, one about to devour the insides of our people as he bathes the lands in blood.

Standing myself up, I take my bow and raise my aim. This is the way, it must be him. This is how we control the battle. I take a deep breath in and out, feeling the direction of the breeze, making my ears cut out the sounds of war. My fingers let the string loose and the sound of my arrow cuts through the battle cries and cries of pain below.

My aim is true when the war chief lets out a roar, but what I did not expect is for him to turn his sights around to spot me up on the pass. His hand breaks the end feathers and pulls the arrow out of his body from behind his shoulder — his teeth bared in challenge my way. I did not anticipate the bloodlust giving him extra strength.

"Men, we go down the pass now! Our spot has been seen and the war chief is coming. Spears!"

My five warriors let out a battle cry as we run the rest of the way down the pass and join the battle below. The cries and calls of the sparcra can be heard above us.

TWENTY-THREE

JURI

My nerves are a mess getting ready this morning. *This is it. Goodbye glasses.* Amy agreed to hang out with me today at the apartment after the surgery. She's also giving me a ride to and from the plaza.

"It will be alright. There are plenty of people who've had this done. I hear it's a walk in-walk out type of ordeal. You'll be back to work on Monday without a hitch." I hope she's right. It's nice to hear her reassurances.

Amy waits out in the lobby as I'm taken to one of the back rooms where the laser machines are held.

"Okay, we're going to have you lay down on this table and stay as still as you can. You might smell some smoke and hear the laser shooting, but it will be alright. You'll start seeing the world in HD soon." The nurse is very nice, and it calms me a bit.

The doctor comes in and gives me another calming speech while he maneuvers the laser to point at my eyes. A few zaps in each eye. The smell of something cooking reaches my nostrils, and he tells me we're done. *Wow, I really should have done this a long time ago.* It was much simpler than I thought.

The nurse hands me a care kit that includes shields for my eyes, eye drops and a packet of FYI notes. A number is also written on the packet in case I have any further questions during my recovery.

Amy leads me by the hand out the door and despite the shield on my eyes, the sun looks extra bright. Is this what it's like in HD? Have I been living in a world of dull color all this time?

"Amy, would you be able to stay until Sunday with me, just in case?"

"Of course!"

The drive back home was a smooth one and I don't feel any different. We decided to take the elevator to my apartment instead of the stairs for good measure. Plus, it faces away from the sun at this time of day.

I spent the rest of the day relaxing and sleeping from the pills they gave me. Amy can raid my refrigerator all she wants. I made sure to pre-make plenty of meals in preparation for this weekend's recovery.

By Sunday evening, I'm feeling pretty good. The packet states that I should start wearing sunglasses to protect my eyes until they heal a bit more.

"You sure you don't need me to stay?"

"I'm feeling pretty good. The surgery was pretty simple. As long as I use my eyedrops, nothing bad should happen. Plus they always have their hotline if I have any questions."

Amy gives me a look and I'm just elated that I can clearly see the look on her face.

"Alright, Juri. If you say so. But you have my number if you need me, okay?"

"Got it. Thanks for everything Amy."

"Of course! What are the three amigos for?"

"I really appreciate you, girl."

"I'll appreciate you even more when you get back to work so Anderson can stop hovering between the two of us left in the office."

We both laugh at that because Anderson will be Anderson — it doesn't matter how many or how little women are in front of him. You can't stop a guy from being who he is.

"Here. Take some food before you go. It's the least I could do."

"You and your crazy salads. But they do taste good, so don't mind if I do."

"Don't worry about the container."

"You sure you're not one of those crazy people who count every container and lid they have and make a spreadsheet?"

Laughing out loud, I also laugh internally at the fact that the tears forming is probably helping to lubricate my eyeballs as well.

Walking Amy to the door, we say our goodbyes. I make sure to lock it securely behind her exit. Now it's just me and the bed again. I don't know how one can get tired from sleeping all the time, but that's exactly how I feel at this very moment. It's not like I have anywhere to go today, so I let myself succumb to the sleep that's creeping in.

GARY

She's had a long weekend and I'm glad Amy is finally gone. I couldn't even come in to take care of my woman with her around. How am I supposed to be able to show her how caring I can be? Juri fell asleep again. She must not be one hundred percent yet. *I'll make her feel better.* Slowly opening the window to her bedroom I was able to unlock earlier, I creep to her bedside. She's so beautiful when she sleeps. I don't want to mess up her eyes, so I rummage around her dresser looking for something I can cover her eyes with. Noticing some lace panties, I stuff a couple in my pocket before finally finding a soft dark scarf. *This should work perfectly.*

Walking slowly towards her, I gently wrap the scarf around her eyes tightly enough to remain secure. Juri is such a deep sleeper, it makes me hard knowing the games we play together end up with her waking up to my surprises. *All for her.*

Leaning down and reaching the ground, I go to grab the rope I hid under her bed. Wrapping both of her wrists up, I make sure to secure it to the closest bed post. Tonight is all about Juri. I'm going to make her feel good. I noticed she was dry during our last session. But that's how couples learn, right? They learn and explore together. I'm going to make it up to her.

Easing her legs apart, I start a slow lick up her pussy. She tastes so good and I've missed her, I've missed her smell. I told myself to go slow, but soon I find that I'm feasting on her pussy with gusto. Her sluggish movements and moans just encourage me to eat her even more, stick my tongue in her a little deeper. She's starting to get wet and my dick is starting to weep. But tonight is only going to be about her, I'm just going to have to beat one out in the shower later.

I don't want to leave her clit out of the love and so I start to suckle and tug it with my lips. Her breath is hitching, and she's still asleep. This is too fun. Her juices are starting to slide out and wet the inside of her thighs and ass. My fingers easily slide into her wet pussy as I continue to assault her clit with my tongue and lips. I can feel her thighs wanting to close, pushing against my grip. Opening my eyes to look at her, I see she's still asleep and so I let her legs do what they want. When they wrap around my head, I can feel her pussy starting a slow clenching movement around my fingers. I think she's close. It makes me want to stick my dick in her, but I need to show her how much she means to me by holding my urges back. *I can be what she needs.*

A gasp comes out of her mouth as her legs squeeze my head from both sides, the pressure warm and welcoming. Her hips thrust into my face and I use the opportunity to move my hands to grab her ass to hold her in place while I enjoy all her pussy juices flowing out of her. *She fucking taste so damn good.*

"Oh my god."

Best way to wake your woman up. I mentally pat myself on the back.

"Juri…" I can't say much since my tongue is busy licking up what her pussy is putting out for me. I feel like giving myself a pat on the back.

"Gary? Oh my fucking god."

I hum into her pussy and her hips start thrusting again.

"What are you doing? Get off of me!" What? I thought I was doing a good job.

Giving her clit one last suckle, I climb up her body to give her nipples some attention. I'll soften her up to me. She's just a little surprised, that's all.

"I missed you, Juri. You've been on my mind all day."

My mouth licks and sucks one nipple while my hand plays with the other one. Gentle is the name of the game today since it seems that's what makes her wet for me. She's trying to stifle her moans — so modest. Paying her other nipple the same love with my mouth, I can feel her body starting to squirm under me.

When I've had my fill, I climb up higher and take the passionate kiss I'm owed for all my hard work. She clamps her mouth shut and resists at first, but I'm able to coax something out of her as I kiss her jaw and the column of her neck gently. My finger travels back to her clit, making slow circular motions. On her next gasp, I put my mouth on hers, making sure I sneak my tongue inside before she knows what hit her. Seems my fingers down there are the perfect distraction because she slowly returns my kiss with hesitation.

"I'd do anything for you Juri..." Goddamn this woman makes my heart hurt. *I fucking need her.*

While my thumb plays with her clit, I stick my forefinger and middle finger inside her hot wet pussy. She moans into my mouth and is distracted enough to finally give me the passionate kiss she owes me. My chest tightens. *I knew she loved me* — I just needed to remind her how good we are together. How good I can make her feel. When I feel her pussy clenching, I know she's getting close again. I take my fingers out and she whimpers. *That's it.* I need her to crave me, crave my touches the way I crave her so damn much.

Moving back down her body, I start eating her pussy again. Fuck, I can't get enough of her. I'm a damn lucky bastard. My cock is hard as steel. I can't handle it. I slip one of my hands down my pants and start stroking as my lips and tongue worship this woman before me. Her legs are tightening around my head again, making me grip my cock even harder, giving it furious and angry strokes. It makes me even hotter knowing I do that to her, making her lose control. *That's my girl.*

"Fuck, what do you do to me Juri? I'm like a lovesick fool that can't keep it in his pants." I can't get enough of this woman —

my woman. Her increased wetness on my tongue tells me she wants this just as much as I do.

When my own climax hits me, spurting out all over my fist, I groan into her pussy. The vibrations from my mouth must push her over the edge because she moans too while thrusting her pussy deeper into my face and I happily oblige by licking up her juices.

Over the next few minutes, Juri must have passed out because her breathing becomes even again and her legs go slack. She's so fucking beautiful when she's sleeping. Shit, my cock is stirring again just thinking about it.

Moving towards her bathroom, I wash up my mess as best as I can. Untying her hands and blindfold, I give her one last kiss on the nose before placing my items back in their spots, walking out her window and closing it shut.

TWENTY-FOUR

JURI

Another work week goes by and I am left so confused. Confused over how I feel about Gary. He took advantage and abused my body the first time. The second time felt like he was worshiping my pussy until I passed out, whispering sweet things to me. What am I supposed to do with this information? My mind can't make a decision whether I should hate him, or appreciate his tongue worshiping. And the little love notes he keeps slipping onto my desk?

"You have the sweetest smile when you're asleep."

That shit is creepy and cute at the same time. Dating and finding your significant other should not be this complicated. I mean, is that what we're doing? I haven't seen Duma since our last sexual encounter, and now this thing with Gary. *Am I really entertaining Gary?* I'm so confused.

Coming down the elevator from work, it's Friday, and I had to decline an invitation for another assistant's night out because I have a follow-up appointment with the laser eye clinic to check on the results of my surgery.

The Uber picks me up in front of my work building and soon enough I'm back at the plaza.

"Miss Chakrabarti, please come with me." The nurse takes me back to the same room that held the eye exam equipment from the first day. After placing my forehead against the machine, she checks my eyes then tells me to sit back. Turning off the light, the eye test on the wall lights up and she asks me to repeat different lines just like at the optometrist's office. I know I miss a few, but she doesn't say a word and writes something down in my file.

"Well, Miss Chakrabarti, it seems the correction surgery was able to give you about 20/30 vision. Which isn't bad at all. You were predicted to have a much different number — something with lower correction."

"So, what does that mean exactly?"

"It means you can do normal things like move around a room. Drive and recognize the neighborhood you find yourself in. Read books in a moderate light, though I suggest you do the best you can to give your eyes the least amount of stress at this point. You can even probably recognize faces when you are out and about in a crowd."

Okay, that doesn't sound so bad at all. I couldn't do any of those things before the surgery, so this is amazing news.

"Will my eyes change over time?" I need to know. I need to prepare myself for any chance of disappointment, just in case.

"Most likely not dramatically. Though we do find our clients having a drastic change when they hit the age of forty-five, this is due to the natural aging process. You should have many good years of life without glasses."

"Thank you so much!" She gives me a smile and tells me that they need to set up future follow-up appointments every so often just to make sure there's nothing to be concerned about.

My mood is elated as the Uber drops me off in the front of my apartment building. I decided to brave the two flights of stairs today. I feel on top of the world. When I make it to the last step, I see a bouquet of flowers in front of my door. I'm not sure how I feel about this because I know exactly who it's from.

When I reach it, I bend down to pick it up. There's a white and silver card right in the middle of the bouquet. Pulling it off, I read the note.

I had a wonderful time together. Can't wait to see you again.

Creepy and sweet at the same time. This is becoming Gary's theme. He's acting like we've been dating and all our circumstances were nothing but consensual sexual encounters. I mean, it felt good towards the end of our last one, but that's not the point. *What is the point?* I'm so confused. How can something so wrong, feel so right? My mind says he's crazy, but my pussy is kind of excited for more attention.

Opening my apartment door and making sure to lock it, I look for a vase in my cabinets. Finding one quickly, I place the flowers in them and just stare. Shaking my head at everything that's happened to my life thus far, I walk towards my bedroom to complete my nightly routine.

TWENTY-FIVE

DUMA

The group of Namwana we encountered towards the east before the pass took some effort for my men to overpower, but I knew we would. We were coming down on the group like a golden leer coming down upon a set of antedeer until an unexpected few happened upon us from a distance with long-range weapons. But win, we did — not without losses from our people as well.

The lands are bathed in red under our feet as we regroup ourselves and look down at the prisoners we've collected from this fight. The warrior who shot the arrow into my shoulder is among them and I can feel my need to rip his heart out and offer it to the blessed sun as a sacrifice, not without taking a bite out of it to receive his prowess into my own body. My monster inside is growing, and the battle has only given it a taste of what it wants.

"War chief, what will you have us do?"

Kill them all, place their heads on spears for the sparcra, and return their bodies to their village. But Kwame's voice is inside of my mind, telling me to calm my emotions.

"We take these five Namwana warriors and bring them back as prisoners to our village. Jomo, you will tie their hands and be on watch from the front, have Chiku follow behind the last prisoner." Watching Jomo move to do as I command, I stare into the eyes of the warrior that shot his arrow into me. His eyes are fierce, brave — the lack of fear coming off him tells me of his seasons in battle.

Looking at my men, I count the numbers we still have. "My brothers, we must regroup our warriors before the next warpath to their village, bring our numbers back up." My eyes veer towards the Namwana warrior again, on his knees before me. "And this time when we bring our drums of war east again, we will end it."

All my surviving warriors cry, "Ahoo! Ahoo! Gamja! To Guergalo!" *Salute! To war!* Beating their weapons against their shields. The sparcra in the skies cry out with us as we turn to head back west to the camp.

TWENTY-SIX

GARY

She accepted my flowers. This is progress. I knew it would work. You see, she loves me. But since our last date was about her, I think she owes me. This time it will be about me. It's only fair.

The weight of her body on the bed depresses the mattress above me, letting me know she's completed her nightly routine. I'll just wait here a bit longer until she falls asleep, then we can play. Stroking my cock passes the time, I can't allow myself to cum just yet. After what feels like ten minutes have passed, I roll from under the bed slowly and thank the apartments again for carpeted flooring, giving me a smooth exit. Too bad she didn't see it.

Standing over her form, I can't stand how beautiful she is. The way her smooth soft tan skin glistens with the lotion she applies, the way her eyes send a jolt straight to your dick. I bet every man she walks by feels the same thing I do and it burns me up inside just knowing that. She's mine.

It seems all the time we've spent together has quickened my hands when it comes to this shibari rope stuff. *All in the name of love.* I hum a tune while my hands stay busy with the ropes.

I decided that today we will try a full upper body bondage. I want her in a comfortable position after all. The rope I have in my hands already feels heavy and ready to be used. A gentle glide there, some caresses, a knot here, making sure to pull the rope a bit taught and I've accomplished the first step. Her body looks beautiful this way. The rope goes across her torso and arms in three sections and down the center. Her back creates a lovely criss-cross pattern in design. This is getting me hard, admiring the things I do for her. Both of her legs are still free, free to wrap around my head if she likes. Pretty thoughtful, if I must say so myself.

There I go again. Today is supposed to be about me. She's going to have to make my cock happy today, the way I made her pussy weep in happiness on our last date.

I'm already conveniently naked, so all I have to do is get on the bed with her. In my haste to tie her up, I guess I left her shirt on, that's alright, I just need her panties off for today. Moving them slowly down her legs, I toss them aside as I inhale the floral scent of her skin from her ankles up to her thighs. She makes my mouth water and my dick leak precum. Goddamn.

Just one lick wouldn't hurt. My tongue starts playing with her pussy and Juri is wriggling in her sleep. It gets wetter the more I stick my tongue inside. I'm getting lost in pleasuring her again, I need to keep on track. With a few sucks and nibbles of her clit, I'm climbing over her body. I'm disappointed her beautiful breasts aren't on display for my mouth, but it will just have to be for another day.

Rubbing the length of my cock on her wet core, I can hear her breaths change with her eyes still closed. Her eyes, her eyes. She's captured me and slayed me. I can't stay away from her.

I've noticed her eyes have become much lighter these days, I wonder if it is from her corrective eye surgery.

Making sure the head of my cock bumps into her clit with every stroke, I slowly bring my body weight down on hers so her wriggling will stop. Who am I kidding? I just want to feel her soft body against mine. The tease of my cock is amping me up when suddenly those piercing eyes open and stare right at me with her mouth hanging open. Is it open in surprise? Is it lust? Staring right back at her, I see that her eyes look like a mixture of light brown on the outside with hints of grey taking over the inside today. Just fucking beautiful. I give her a grin; it seems I've made my Juri speechless. Good.

Flexing my abs back a little more, I slide right into her hot, wet pussy. Her eyes roll back and I'm frantic to make her feel more for me. Thrusting like a man on a mission, I force her legs with my hand to wrap around my hips. Better yet, let's just throw one of these legs right over my shoulder so she opens up to me even wider. That's it.

As I start to ram her harder, the mattress starts to bounce us against each other, making our skin to skin slapping even harder. Fuck yes. My mind is in a haze and all I can think about is the tensing of my abs and the tension in my balls, when I cum inside of her furiously. Shit, it feels like fucking heaven and the spurts of my cum just make me fuck her even harder until it ends.

Out of breath from our little adventure, I lay my head against her neck and close my eyes. Damn, the things she does to me. My heart feels tight and warm, like it's about to explode. I have no control over it and for some reason; it doesn't scare me. It just makes me want to crawl deeper into her, to be surrounded by this feeling that's washing over me.

"I fucking love you Juri. You were mine the moment you walked into my life." My hair moves with the exhale she lets out. I know she loves me. If not, I can love us enough for the both of us.

I keep my dick inside of her because I can't make myself disconnect just yet. I need to feel our combined juices, our souls connecting just a little longer. The warmth of her breaths and her body pull me into the darkness as I let my body relax and succumb to sleep.

TWENTY-SEVEN

CHIEMKO

Our boats for war are ready before the time we thought it would take. Gathering the men on the island, we divide older warriors with newly seasoned ones on each boat. The old will provide enough wisdom to the ones who are only just joining us in their first battle. I count six boats and our bigger war boat that can carry many times the men our normal boats would. One hundred warriors have been chosen to stay behind to protect the people of the island. The four hundred will leave by waters today. Each chosen way finder takes the front of the boats as lead.

Once the women secure our extra weapons onto our boats, the warriors who remain take the task to push our boats into the coming waves. I can feel it inside of me, something is coming. The string that the Gods have tied me to Juri is pulling again, leading me towards her. She is here, and my heart roars against the crashing waves that keep me from her.

"Issa, we must speed our paths along the waves! The Gods are calling me to the mainland. Paddles!"

The sun is at its highest right now. It will be some time before we reach the closest shore — time I feel we do not have. As we come closer to the waves that push us back towards the island, I know we have entered the area that will soon bring us closer to the wave that takes us to the opposite shore.

"Paddle into the current!"

Soon the gugull birds are seen ahead, we know that land is coming and the rhythm of the waves brings us closer and faster to land.

The waves push us against the sands with a *thud*. I am the first to jump out and pull our boat to shore, the rest of my men do the same behind me. It's at this very moment, my movements stop. My men say nothing as they continue to bring all the boats to shore. I *feel* it, something is telling me to run. Following where the God's lead me, I move with swift feet around the trees that scatter before me. My heart is beating loudly in my chest and behind my ears, the wind whipping at my cheeks and the blood pumping makes my eyes sharpen and the tightness in my chest makes me grab one of the knives secured at my waist.

Around the next handful of tree trunks, I see something. *No.* My eyes focus on the bodies lying on the ground. The strings that pull at my chest tell me it is Juri, but there is another body on top of hers — a male body with skin as light as the sands. My feet continue to bring me closer and closer, dodging the plants around us and the larger rocks in my way. The moment I am of leaping distance, I jump onto the male and choke his neck with my free arm. My knife pierces his skin, letting the bloom of blood trickle down onto Juri's still form. The beast inside of me is hungry for vengeance.

Pulling him off of my Juri, we wrestle on the ground for domi-nance. The sharp rocks and branches only ground me as my eyes see red and my insides hunger for blood. Elbowing his throat, his neck snaps back but he rolls and shoots his foot out against my side. The small distance he creates is enough for him to stand up and circle me while I do the same to him. The blade is still in my hand as I lunge. He jumps out of the way a few times but trips on something the last time, letting my knife slice his skin at another short distance. Jumping on top of him again, I pin his neck down with my arm — the blade close enough to kill him if I so choose. I am too enraged to care how much this sand beast before me takes from my blade because the sight I came upon in this cluster of trees makes me want to offer this male as a sacrifice to the waters and creatures that lurk there.

"You dare to touch what is mine?" My roar is right by his ear and I see him bare his teeth at me in challenge.

His eyes reflect the waters we just left. Is he a creature of the water spirits then? He is quick with his movements, his fighting style is something I have not seen. This gives him the advantage as he takes me by surprise and escapes the hold I had on him. But he does not flee, no. He stands proud like a warrior who knows this moment might mean his last day alive. The smile on his face tells me he is more than happy to take me with him if it means his end. I accept the challenge he issues with his eyes. We circle each other, lunging, until one of us finally grabs the other by the middle and throws the enemy to the ground. His fists are as hard as his head as we both take hits to our bodies. Hooking my legs around his, I overtake him once more, gaining the upper position in the hand-to-hand battle.

Taking his life when I have him in my grasp is too easy. We will battle as warriors do — with honor and to the death in front of my people. Slamming his head on the ground to slow him, I stand and shake out my arms. I hear swift footsteps around us and I know my men have this male surrounded, watching and waiting for my command.

"Issa! See to my Juri! This male has dishonored himself and will be made to pay in blood."

I can see Issa bringing out his hunting knife, calling to others to free my Juri from the ropes that tie around her body. What monster is he to do this to a female?

The male before me hails from lands I have not traveled to. His hair is the color of bleached sunlight and his eyes are one with the waters we have just crossed. It is no matter, for this will be his last kiss of life, he will die by my hands this day. Looking at his body, I see that he has no covering or weapons. I am a man of honor and so I whistle to one of my men, telling them what I need with a hand signal. They quickly understand what is happening and one of them throws their knife at the male's foot, making it stick up from the ground.

A moan to the left of me tells me that Juri is alive and well and coming awake. "What's going on? Chiemko?"

"I will defend your honor, my Juri. This male will pay for the dishonor he has brought upon you. I will bring you his heart as a sacrifice."

"Gary? Oh my god."

So the male has a name, he is called Gary. Strange — not a common calling. My mind begins to try and understand what's happening without taking my eyes off the enemy.

"Gary, your end comes today." I lunge at him and he quickly grabs the knife off the ground and rolls away.

So, a good fight this will be, then. I am glad for it.

Moving to the left, I quickly do a trick of foot, and lunge to the right to take his body down to the ground. This Gary is as slippery as the creatures that slither on the beaches. After a few moments of trying to take one another into a bottom position, I begin to notice his patterns. He uses a lot of knees and heels for his fighting style and I quickly adjust to block it.

The fists he lands on my face only call to my enraged monster inside, making me smile wider in his face. My hand shoots out and my body twists, locking his neck in my arm while my knife enters his side. Baring his teeth again in challenge, I did not catch the knife he had also put into *my* side. What Gary does not know is that there is another knife held in my thigh bands. Throwing my fist into his face to stun him, I grab the other knife and bring it up for more force in anticipation of cutting his head off.

"Nooo! Chiemko!"

Juri? I turn my head to look at her face to see what has saddened her when Gary uses the heel of both his feet to throw me off of his body, landing mine onto the ground. Some air is stolen from inside of me when I land, but I quickly jump back to standing with my knife ready for any more sneak attacks.

"Come and get me, fucker."

"Chiemko! He — he came from my lands! Please, stop! This is unnecessary."

Her lands? I do not believe it. They are as opposite as the suns and moons.

"What would you have me do, my Juri? The God's led me to you and I find you have been battle worn on the ground, tied up like meat to be brought to feast! This dishonorable male does not deserve your mercy."

My men around us chant with me, telling me they feel the same need to fight for her honor. Many of them ready their knives in their hands. The foot stomping and call of the inner beast comes out of my people as we decide what to do with this Gary.

"ARuh. ARuh. ARuh!"

The vibration of the ground makes my eyes focus on my prey in front of me.

"He deserves no mercy!"

"Dishonor to women!"

The vibration of the ground runs up my legs and makes my inner beast coil to ready for attack…

"Chiemko, finish him!"

"ARuh. ARuh. ARuh!"

My head feels tight and the need to spill blood is becoming too much for me to stand so still.

"I can finish him for you!"

The trail of blood coming from his neck calls to me, the need to take my knife out from his side that still sits there as we stare each other down in challenge. A primitive call to battle once more. His eyes light up with fire as he smiles, a mouth stained with blood.

"No! Please!"

My Juri's voice tastes of fear, and it stops my bloodlust for this male before me. In my mind's eye, I have already sacrificed his blood to the lands, but Juri's voice stops my hands from doing just that.

"Why do you fear for this Gary, my Juri? Have you attached yourself to him? You are mine!" I beat my fist onto my chest so she sees I am serious. *She is mine.*

"Chiemko, have mercy, please."

Her pleas fall heavy on my heart and I cannot deny her. Her eyes pull me in the way they did the first time and I find that my ache to be close to her is over powering my need to kill the male from her lands.

"Issa, take him prisoner. He will not leave our sides until my Juri decides what she wants us to do with him. Our war path is not finished, we must move the men towards the middle path between the east and west to move towards the Namwana tribe."

My men move quickly to do exactly as I say. Issa, grabs this Gary and pulls him away from my sights. The other men continue to move forward towards our planned path — all the boats having reached the shores by now.

"…War?"

Her face is one of surprise.

Staring at her eyes that remind me of light spears that come down from a crying sky, I give my men time to do what I have tasked them. Issa walks over to me and places my bloodied knife back in my hands — the one from Gary's side.

Issa gathers some of the newly seasoned warriors and tasks them with tying up the male called Gary by the hands. He will be brought with us along this war path. We cannot have an unseen enemy from behind. It is best to keep him close while we move.

"Yes, my Juri. War is here and we will be the surprise they will not see coming."

TWENTY-EIGHT

GAMBA

"You are beneath me, Namwana warrior. My beast tells me to cut your head off but my mind tells me you will be of more use to me alive."

Laughing out loud, I watch as the warchief bares his teeth at me in challenge. My eyes never leave his and I watch as his eyes never leave mine. Predators are all the same in our instincts, it seems. Oh, I accept his challenge but he knows the position I am in as his prisoner and he would not be found fighting like a coward with a prisoner of war.

A battle between warriors must be done with honor.

"Take him to the outer huts. Find one of the empty ones."

"Yes, Warchief."

The warriors grab me off my knees and roughly push me to walk. Warchief Duma needs to sleep with one eye open in case I feel like paying him another visit with an arrow.

We walk for a few moments and the smell of blood rises in the area. One of the hut's cloth is open but none of the villagers here enter. It seems my luck is in the hut right beside it as the warriors kick me, making me trip inside and dropping to the ground. I have been separated from my other men on purpose. It seems the war chief, Duma, is still upset over the arrow I sent into his shoulder.

Moving myself up to sitting, I look around my new place of captivity. The sounds of warriors coming and going can be heard right outside the walls. The sound of women and children are farther in the distance — a smart tactic to keep them away from the enemy.

Time moves forward and no one comes in. My throat begins to dry from the warmth of the sun heating the inside of the hut. But my pride refuses to let me ask for water. These bloodthirsty people have probably seen their share of dead bodies if the smell in the next hut is anything to go by.

Jahi's news of our scouts with their heads on spikes run through my mind and I growl. The Chintkku will pay when I make it back to my lands.

My mind is running through the different tactics of counter attack when I realize I have been sitting on the ground in this hut for two sun rises — the heat and rays spill between the wood sides, telling me so.

The shadows that cover the sunlight tell me that there are warriors who constantly surround my hut, circling it. The war chief is a smart male. The Chintkku left my hands tied with rope but my feet free. *So not too smart.* With the right strategy, I may be able to slip into the shadows of the night and regroup our warriors back in the east.

"Duma, you must find her. You are tied to her destiny. With eyes of light spears, it is her! She will end the wars."

My ears sharpen.

This old man's voice, I have not heard before. But there is only one person I know that has eyes of light spears that hail from the skies. It is Juri he speaks of. Duma is looking for her. Why? She is in grave danger then — for it is not only the Chintkku but also the Matalo'toa that have had her in their grasp. I am unsure of how she fares after her fall into the water, but I do not doubt the Mata warrior at least has her body with him on his island.

I must find her first, save her from these barbarians.

My mind runs with all the ways I can make my escape from this camp. I look through the space between the wood slats and see that the suns have fallen from the skies again.

Footsteps come closer and I quickly move back into a sitting position in the middle of the hut.

"You remain alive. I'm surprised by our Warchief's decision when so many of your men are sitting out for the sparcra to eat."

One of the newly-seasoned warriors, by the look of him, throws me a stick of dried meat before he leaves again. He doesn't care for my answer. It is good to know that they plan on keeping me alive for now. After finishing the small meat stick, heavy footsteps come towards my hut once more. He clouds the doorway in darkness with skin as black as death. Even up close he looks as if he has come to steal my soul.

I do not want him to know what I am thinking and so I sit here with a smile on my face. It is not safe to rile the beast, but it might give me an opening to leave this camp.

"Namwana, where do you keep my Juri? I know it is one of your scouts that has stolen my female from me and I will bathe the lands in Namwana blood before I let anything else happen to her."

His Juri?

Did not that Mata warrior call her by the same name? I planned for her to be under my protection after warring with the Mata islanders. The Chintkku is a thorn that came unseen during my strategy. I thought I had more time. Bringing myself to stand so that he can feel my position of challenge, I bare my teeth. The warrior before me still stands above my head, but it does not stop my inner beast from coming out to fight.

"You know not what you speak, war chief. I found a Mata warrior who had stolen her away. She was under my protection the moment I saw her in his gasps, and she will belong to *me* when I find her."

"You dare lie to me, Namwana!"

His roar shakes the wooden walls of the hut, but it does not stop me from sneering at him. *I dare?* She is *mine* when I find her. I felt it inside of me when my eyes landed on hers, the color of angry skies. It is the will of the Gods that she be mine.

As quick as a beast of nightmares, the war chief cuts my stomach with his knife, but my reflexes let me jump back with enough distance to not let him spill my insides out. I can feel the warmth of my blood flowing down and each breath brings searing pain, but I cannot let a predator see my weakness. Standing tall, I stare into his eyes with my fury.

The war chief is not one to back down so easily and so when he comes at me again, I jump to the ground and roll past his feet with a quick sweep of mine to knock him down from his position. One of his knees hit the ground but his other leg shoots out as well and hits me right where his blade kissed me. The blood makes his foot slide, weakening the kick.

Placing my tied hands on the ground, I bring my feet under me to give me enough power for this tactic I am about to use against him.

The war chief does not lunge at me right away, but stares his predator's eyes at me and my new position. He stands to his full form and circles me slowly. The moment he is beyond my hunter's eye range, he pretends to swing his knife hand down to distract me and instead brings his other fist up to my chin, making me fly back onto my back. The hit my back makes on the dirt pushes air out of my lungs.

In a black blur, the war chief jumps on top of me and swings his knife towards my chest. My beast screams at me from the inside to move from a prey's position, and I throw my tied hands up against his knife. The moment my ropes cut free, I roll my upper body to the side. *Thud.* The sound of the knife hitting the ground makes me grin in satisfaction, but not without a shallow cut along my arm. My smile falls when I feel the war chief's large hands around my neck, squeezing.

"Duma! This is not the way! We need him alive to find the one who hails from the skies! She must fulfill the stories of old! She must end our wars!"

It's that old man's voice again, the one I heard outside of my prisoner's hut.

With a beast's growl, the war chief throws my head onto the hard ground, making it bounce, before getting up off my body. I cough as I try to take in breath and life back into me, still pretending to have my hands tied by hiding it from their eyes.

Both the war chief and the old man leave the hut and I lay on the ground for a little longer. The sounds of footsteps and shifting shadows from outside of my hut tell me the warriors have continued to walk around my hut. There must be a fire made in the village, for the shadows now move in all directions this time.

Now that my hands are free, I just need to think of a strategy to escape without letting the warriors around my hut see me.

TWENTY-NINE

GARY

I don't know what the fuck is happening, but I need to get my mind around this shit quickly. A cloth skirt was tossed to me before we started marching through the path of the trees up ahead. The leader of this rag-tag bunch seems to think Juri belongs to him. I'm going to kill the fucker before I let him touch her. *She's mine.*

Seems Juri has been here before, to respond so quickly and with his name at that. It kind of pisses me off how comfortable she is with his name. There must be an island across the waters, because these guys have that look about them. We are walking deeper and deeper towards the trees and into the land we appeared on. These guys look like Samoan/Polynesian, but not. There's something a little more raw, more primitive about them. Their leader's ability to adapt fighting styles is impressive.

My mind quickly takes in all the information I can gather. The guys responsible for keeping an eye on me look younger than the majority of the group. They must be new recruits. Some of the warriors are older but they keep themselves to the back while the ones in their prime lead the front. A few of them occasionally fall back to mix in with the ones back here with me. They're keeping an extra eye on me from all sides, but they can't do it forever.

The fucker up ahead will pay for trying to kill me off. Just watching the way he walks beside my girl makes me fist my hands back and forth. I've fought plenty growing up, surviving around my deadbeat drunk father. My mother escaped the best way she could — protecting me until her dying breath. Flashes of my father beating her to a bloody pulp cross my mind and my body temperature rises. I couldn't save her then but damn if I let anything but me take care of Juri. I'm not the best guy around, even a blind man can see that. I'm not sorry for how I turned out either. With adulthood came responsibilities, and I adapted the way I needed to in order to perform menial tasks behind the computer monitor. I hated the choices I had to make, the life I had to live until Juri walked into it. She became the beacon of all my desires, my purpose. The one I'd kill for.

In many ways, I finally understand the intensity of emotion my father must have gone through with my mother. But unlike my father, I'm going to keep Juri by my side and alive. It doesn't matter if she tires of me, she's stuck with me until we both die.

This warrior leader is standing in my way. I'm outnumbered, but the moment I get a chance, I'm going to steal my girl back. Maybe slit his throat just for the hell of it and watch Juri cling to me for comfort.

She won't miss him long. I'll make sure to keep her happy and satisfied. I don't know where the hell we are but I'm sure we can survive together.

CHIEMKO

We will need to make camp halfway to our destination. From fighting the waves to walking across the mainland under the heat of the suns, we must be at full energy when we make it to the east, to face the Namwana at full strength.

After marching for what feels like a good while, I look at Juri who walks beside me to make sure she will be strong enough to make it to our camp grounds when we come upon it. The women of the island had packed, not just weapons, but clothes and extra material to dress wounds. Juri was small enough that we were able to use some of the material to cover her up where she asked to be. She used what was left of her sliced top covering to make a smaller one that ties around her body. The skin on her stomach is bare to the sun, and it makes my mouth water. She is a vision. Her soft body calls to me, my beast inside pants with want.

"My Juri, how do you feel? Will you still be able to walk until we find camp?"

When she brings her eyes to face me, it feels like a light spear has struck my heart and my chest physically burns. My yearning has settled the moment she was near me again, but now something else is growing inside of me and I am not sure of what it is. She doesn't respond, instead choosing to stare at me while I stare at her. Her eyes, there is something different about them. It is in the way her eyes focus on me. Her eyes are becoming like that of a hunter, zeroing in on prey.

"Thank you Chiemko. Yes, I am doing alright. The warm ground helps me keep going. I don't understand what is going on. What's happened since I left?"

Left? She speaks as if she took a walk on the shore to get away from company. It is more like he disappeared like the dark clouds when the skies clear and stop crying onto the land.

"My Juri, you did not leave. You disappeared." Her eyes sharpen and my previous thoughts cross my mind again. "It just makes my insides feel right to say that you were sent from the Gods for *me*. It is their will for you to be mine." Her eyes widen as I step closer to her, needing to feel her again. "My heart has been pulled to you since you left. It was what led me to find you today — to save you from the one they call Gary."

My top lip lifts a little thinking of that Gary. He would have died by my hands if my Juri did not stop me.

"Yeah, I don't know what's going on with that, but I don't think he means harm to me." Her eyes shift and my eyes narrow. "I'm not sure how I should feel."

Feel?

"You should not *feel* anything! You are mine, Juri! My heart wept for you when I could not hold you — when I lost you. I am not letting you go *again*."

I need to make her understand.

Stopping her small retreat, I grab her body under her arms and lift her to meet my face. When my lips crash onto hers, my heart soars and beats like there is a war inside of *me*. Her arms come around my neck in an embrace and I know she feels the same. The warmth of her skin against mine makes me burn. She just needed a push to be shown she does not need to hide anymore. When her tongue starts trying to invade my lips though, I become weak to her request and let her in.

This strange practice must be done by her people. By the blessed suns, the things she is doing to me with her lips and tongue can make a grown warrior get weak in the knees in surrender. I'm lost in her embrace — her very being consumes me and wants to become one.

The yells and calls from my men stop our movements, bringing us back into the current moment. With my Juri still in my arms, I turn us both to see the one they call Gary on the ground with Issa on top of him, choking him into submission. Issa has his knee between his shoulders, his arm is on the back of Gary's neck to hold him down, with a knife held at the side pointed towards his skin.

"Keep your hands off of her! She's *mine*! I will kill you!"

He has a warrior's spirit, but it is *he* who is wrong. She is *mine*. Gently, I let my Juri down back to the ground on her feet.

"Bind his mouth."

"Yes, Chief."

I do not wish to hear him spit his lies to my ears.

"Get off me!"

"Kaipo! Grab his arms!"

"Ahhrrrggh!"

"...Chiemko."

"The command has been given, Juri. Do not use that tone with me."

"...But—"

Turning to her, I lean right at her face and watch as the blacks of her eyes change size. She sees me as a hunter does. Staring into her eyes, I see her fire but I also see her confused emotion rolling inside. "The command has been given, my Juri. The Chief has spoken."

She inhales sharply and I straighten and turn away from her to address my people. "We walk, warriors, until we find cover between the trees and make camp. It is only a few more steps up ahead, beyond these low plants."

The men, seeing that we are close to stopping, start marching faster. When we make it to the destination, we all sit down and rest on the rocks scattered around us.

"All those who are newly seasoned, start the fires."

The few men near me move quickly.

"Elder warriors, I ask that you gather the food stores the women have packed for us."

The older warriors begin to stand up slowly.

"Issa, keep the one they call Gary on the opposite side of my Juri. He needs to remain closer to the direction of the shores rather than the path to the east."

"Yes, Chief."

Finding a low-hanging, strong branch, I throw a large skin over it and tie the ends far enough to make a small covering for Juri. Walking towards the food storage we brought with us, I grab a small bag to give my female rest and to help her get her energy back.

"My Juri, rest here while I help the warriors set up their sleep spaces. I will come back to you as soon as I am done."

She watches me but does not respond. Juri goes inside the shade of the tent and it comforts me to know I have provided it for her. I signal to a couple of the warriors nearby.

"Keep a watchful eye on my female. I am going to help some of the elders make camp as fast as we can. We need to rest up before our warpath continues."

"I will help as well."

"Keep the newly seasoned warriors close by. We do not want them wandering too far and bringing trouble to camp."

"Yes, Chief."

"Chiemko." Her soft voice is low but my ears catch it, making me turn. "Will you stay by me? I don't want to be alone right now."

"You need not have any worries, my Juri. My men are nearby and I will return as soon as I can after I help my people settle in."

"Okay."

I am torn between duty and want. As chief of my people, I cannot lead them to failure. We must win this war. Then, and only then will I be able to bring my Juri home safely with me. She can have all my attention then.

With the additional warriors we've brought, camp is set up quickly.

"Why are you here?"

Turning to Issa, I look him over. Who is he to question me about this decision to march for battle? He should have made his thoughts known before we left the island.

"Don't look at me like that, Chiemko. That's not what I am speaking of. Why are you here when your woman is over there?"

He tips his head in her direction and my initial anger turns into something else. I need to make sure the camp is set up and that she is safe.

"The camp is safe."

Snapping my eyes to Issa, I begin to wonder if he has extra talents I do not know about. But with the thought already planted in my mind, I place a hand on his shoulder and nod my head before turning to leave.

She sits there, in silence, watching me the closer and closer I get.

"Protect this tent. Do not let anyone pass until I say so."

The few younger warriors around me look at each other before saying, "Yes, Chief."

"Chiemko?"

I do not let her change my mind with anything that might come out of her mouth. Grabbing her, I bring her onto my lap as I sit down in the tent with her. The warriors have their backs to the tent, blocking anyone from seeing inside.

My lips slam on hers to continue what we've started. The warmth of her body against mine makes my hunger inside grow tenfold. My hands roam her back all the way down to her bottom and my fingers are already seeking the heat I find there.

"Chiemko." Her soft whispers against my lips provide me with the perfect opportunity to slip my tongue inside causing her to moan in response.

The sound ignites the beast inside of me and with a few quick movements, I'm able to push aside both our coverings. My cock is as stiff as the boards that wash up on our shores, the shaft sliding against her wet center, letting me know she wants this just as much as I do.

"My Juri, you destroy me with just a touch." Pulling down her top covering, my lips close over her exposed breast.

Her hands reach between us and the heat that engulfs me makes me choke and hiss all at once. It is nothing I've ever felt. If there is a heaven where the Gods reside, it must be like this.

"You're so big."

Groaning into her neck in response to her soft whispers against my ear, Juri continues to ride me until my mind wants to shatter with the brink of pleasure and insanity. The tightness of my abs makes me grimace while my hands grab onto her hips and begin to grind against her ferociously.

Nipping against the smooth crook of her neck, I subdue my growls as my cock releases it's pleasure inside my Juri — a union made by the Gods. This is where I'm meant to be, in her arms just like this.

THIRTY

JURI

I don't know what's going on between Chiemko and I, but with everything that has gone down since all the crazy began, I am just seizing the moment now. Just like with my decision for corrective eye surgery. I waited so long, and for what? I could have had so many more years of being able to see — to become more confident in myself. It's the same with this situation.

The young warriors were kind enough not to make me feel awkward about what happened in the tent with Chiemko. They even gave me some extra fabrics and water when I asked them for it. I cleaned up as best as I could much to Chiemko's dismay. He gave me a sour look when I told him what it was for. I stuck my tongue out at him and it lightened his mood just a bit.

Watching Chiemko work from inside of the tent, I admire his need to honor his duties. He's a leader of his people, I see that now. Everyone looks up to him for direction and for calm on this march. I can't help but feel still a little out of sorts right now. I'm not a stupid woman, I know what's happening to me are not dreams. There's too much evidence against the fact. Everything feels too real. Chiemko's kiss was too real. My mind goes back to Duma and my heart constricts a little. I wonder what he thinks has been happening this whole time? How do you explain something you barely understand yourself?

I'm not even sure if I'll see Duma again. This place — this land is much more vast than I first realized. From two tribes on the mainland to a whole island across the waters. Who else will I come across? My mind's cogwheels have been turning from the moment I was brought back here — with Gary of all people. That's another reason why my mind has finally been convinced of this assumption. I think I'm being teleported to another place — an alternate Africa in an alternate earth with two suns. There are way too many similar things for it to be anything else. The people look too similar to the people of the same region back home. It is what it is and I'm going to have to roll with the punches in order to survive.

One thing that did take me by surprise was the fact that someone else could teleport with me. Is it something inside of us? Is it something else altogether? Could it be because he was touching me at the time of my travel that we both ended up traveling together? Well, that doesn't matter now because he's here and he's already causing trouble. All this stuff about me being his? These men — it's too much. I'm sitting here, crossed-legged in the shade, trying to decide how I feel about all of them. Is it wrong of me to feel something for more than one person?

I can't help but care for Chiemko. He's been trying to protect me since the day we met. I could see the heartbreak and raw pain in his eyes when he thought I left him on purpose — his vulnerability practically pouring out of his soul through his eyes. He does have some inner turmoil going on and it comes out as rage especially when he challenged Gary to a fight. He is an unrestrained beast, beautiful in motion, a body meant to kill and take down prey. Oh yes, I was watching it all with morbid fascination.

That brings me back to the thought of my eyes. Thank goodness I had it done, I can finally see everyone around me and know who I'm dealing with. Chiemko's been staring into my eyes more frequently because I think he knows there's something different about me.

Leaves are rustling but I barely hear it — until it rustles again in a non organic way. The sound is coming closer from behind my makeshift skin tent and my mental red flags go up. Is someone back there? Looking out the front of the tent, I see that all of the warriors are still setting camp and moving stuff around. It's probably one of Chiemko's guys. Maybe he's gathering some fire wood or something behind me. These islanders look very similar to the Samoans of Earth, it's amazing that they're not from there. I bet if any one of them were to teleport there, no one would be the wiser. Except for the fact that these guys are much more feral than the men back home. The thought of feral brings back the memories of Chiemko and Gary tousling on the ground like two creatures about to devour each other.

I'm lost in my mental musings of half naked men fighting when suddenly, one side of the tent flap is opened and lifted letting the bright sun in and temporarily blinding me. A hand covers my mouth before I can even let out a gasp and someone much larger than me grabs me from behind, removing me from the tent. His height difference means my feet don't even reach the ground to cause any sort of physical resistance. There are warrior marks on him, I can feel it rubbing against my back — the raised ridges on the skin. It's not Duma though, because I would know his body anywhere. This warrior is much thinner, much smaller, where Duma is a beast of a man.

His footsteps are quiet and quick and before I know it, I don't see the camp anymore. A few moments later, I hear a roar in the distance from where we left.

Chiemko.

My captor's footsteps quicken to a sprint and I try to kick and squirm out of his grasp but he's much too strong. Tiring of the idea of trying to escape, I stop moving to save my energy for when we arrive wherever he's taking me.

The scenery changes slightly the farther we get. The trees become sparse, the land becoming drier. There's dust getting kicked up and the color of the ground begins to change subtly as well. I'm getting tired of my body getting jostled but it doesn't seem like this guy is going to let me down any time soon. Well that's on him because I'm not the lightest person around. Hopefully, he doesn't drop me along the way.

Once we are far enough from the Mata camp by his standards, my captor lets go of my mouth and I can finally take a good breath in and out. It takes a few more moments of him jogging with me in his arms before he slows to let me walk beside him instead of being carried like a rag doll. Nothing is said between us. I'm not sure if I have anything to say because I already know he's one of Duma's men. It only leads me to believe that our destination will be his village then.

The sight of a cluster of huts approaching in the distance has my captor slowing enough for me to comfortably catch up. *Duma must be there.* A sort of bird call goes out, startling me. I think it's coming from this guy next to me. *How does he even make that noise?* The same bird call comes back from someone in the village and soon, a very imposing sight is stampeding towards us. It's Duma, and he looks like a raging black bull from hell with the intensity of his gaze on me. My heart, though, my heart says it's home.

"Duma!"

At the sound of my voice, he runs faster and the guy beside me starts to separate himself as fast as he can in another direction. I'd be scared too if I didn't know how soft he could be when he wanted to.

I was expecting to be rammed into like a mack truck by his speed and size, but when he finally gets to me, he picks me up high in his arms and buries his head in my chest. *Wow, can a beast of a man truly be this vulnerable?* His arms are banding around me tightly, like he's afraid I'll run away. *My poor Duma.* Hugging him back, I rest my head on top of his and just savor the emotions bouncing between us. This moment makes my heart hurt. I didn't mean to cause so much pain with these men.

I don't want him to lose face in front of his warriors who are all lined up at the edge of the camp watching this display, so I pick up his face with my hands and put our foreheads together in an affectionate gesture. I need to look into his eyes, to see his emotions. He doesn't give me the chance though because the moment his head is up, he gives me a fierce kiss that I wasn't expecting but appreciate. *I missed him too.*

I'm lost in everything that is Duma, the warmth of his embrace and the strength that surrounds me. Our mouths and suddenly our tongues are dancing and dueling. The heat between our bodies is turning into something uncontrollable. How does he do this to me? How does he make me let go so completely? Our lips slow down into a steady rhythm, my heart finally beginning to slow with it. He lets my body slide down his with our lips still locked — it seems we're making up for lost time, wanting to drag this reunion out longer.

Duma is the first man to make me feel this protected, and I missed the feeling. Gary leaves me confused. Chiemko makes me hurt on the inside for him.

When he pulls back to end the kiss with small pecks, he gives me a really big and blinding smile. It's like the weight on his shoulders has finally lifted. *My poor Duma.*

He grabs my hand and pulls me towards the camp. His grip is firm and warm. When we meet the line of warriors in the front, they part like the red sea for him. *Wow, this is new.* There are two to three huts that are noticeably separated from the rest of the village. I'll have to ask about that later. I wonder if one of them is his? Duma leads me to a bigger hut that is closer to the heart of this camp that I don't recognize. I'm also noticing that this isn't the camp I came to before from what I can remember through the blur of my vision. The scattering of the huts is almost in a different pattern. Everything looks a little bit different, but some things look the same.

"Blessed suns! You have found her! Your destiny starts Duma. You must lead her in her path."

Kwame, the old guy from Duma's original village is here too, it seems. Turning my head to look where the voice came from, I see him walking towards us and he still looks like I remembered. His long dreadlocks are wrapped around his head like a makeshift turban. His scraggly grey beard can almost rival the ones found on that band ZZ Top. His body is thinner than the other guys, with some rib bones protruding out. His eyes are the color of dark brown clay. But today, there is a smile beneath the beard and his eyes sparkle with crow's feet wrinkling at the side of his eyes.

"Kwame, little Juri needs rest. We will figure out this destiny you speak of soon enough."

The old man's eyes squint and wrinkle even more from his laughter. *What am I missing here? Why is he laughing?*

When Duma pulls me into the hut he was supposedly leading me towards he lets the cloth over the door fall down completely, shielding us from the villagers. When the hut is completely covered and our privacy is guaranteed, he's on me like a panther. His mouth is devouring my mouth with an intensity I did not see with our reunion kiss. His low growl between our lips sends shivers down my spine in anticipation as he leads me farther and farther into the hut and onto a mat on the other side. I'm lowered to the ground without a word and when his body presses on top of mine, I relish in his warrior marks scraping my skin. His hands reach between us and I feel him moving his loin-cloth aside. His cock is hot and hard as a steel pipe as he rubs it against my pussy.

I shouldn't want this so badly right now, but I do.

My hands caress his shoulders and neck as his soft lips nibble along my jaw, the wound my hand grazes over makes me hot for this warrior on top of me. I decide it's time to seize the day again when my hand snakes between us and grasp his shaft firmly, forcing it to rub against my clit harder, spreading my wetness around. His warm groan against my ear turns me on even more than I already am. Duma lets me have my way with him without any protest. His hips are actually encouraging me with my explorations, eager for more. When I feel myself getting wetter and wetter with my ministrations of his cock on me, I lick the shoulder that's by my face and nip at his skin. It makes him tense up his abs and the head of his cock slips into me. *Oh dear.* I've almost forgotten how big he is. The tease makes me feel so good and the stretch makes me hunger for more of what he can give me.

Exhaling against his skin, Duma slowly rocks into me. How he goes from desperately wanting to touch me to holding himself back is driving me nuts. Moving my hips up to meet his, he reads my body language and pushes his cock into me further. I'm panting and I don't think he's more than halfway in.

"Duma…"

"You feel as hot as the blazing suns, Juri."

He pulls out and pushes in again slowly. Dammit! He needs to just push it in! Wrapping my legs around him in encouragement, Duma pulls back until it's only the head of his cock in me again and then slams home, making us both let out a strangled groan.

His voice is a low rumble, the vibrations of all the noises he's making against my skin and adding to the overall sensation of him surrounding me. Now that he's in to the hilt, the sex becomes frenzied like time is running out and the end of the world is coming. His hips slap my inner thighs creating a little pain that only amplifies my sensitivity. The way he's leaned over me tightly, the welts and marks on his skin graze my clit with every thrust and it sends me over the edge. I can feel my pussy squeezing him on and off while I wrap my legs around him tighter, keeping him close to me. His arms go above my head against the ground, using the leverage he has to push his cock deeper into me, digging my ass into the mat. I swear he's hitting me in places he shouldn't but I can't find it in myself to tell him to stop.

His dick starts to grow a little more, and it makes my pussy feel extra full. With a few more hard, deep thrusts, Duma brings his head down to groan into my ear as hot jets of his cum overflow inside of me. *Who is this wanton woman?* Then again, who can say no to a man like Duma? *I have no regrets.*

We lay there in the afterglow, holding onto each other. The sweat on our skin makes us glide a little bit with our hard breathing but doesn't stop us from our caresses and embrace. I missed him; I missed his strength, his power, the way he makes me feel protected. I love the way his big body cocoons me.

His hips continue to grind in slow and steady movements. His hand comes down between us and starts to rub our juices around my clit and then to my inner thigh. The haze of the lust is starting to dissipate and my mind brings up a question that I've been wondering about since my kidnapping.

"Duma, why did your man steal me away to bring me here?"

He raises his head at that statement and looks me straight in the eyes with a stern expression that's starting to cloud over with something.

"Juri, you were taken from me. No one steals the war chief's female. You are *mine*. They had no right to take you from me."

They? Take?

After a few moments, I think I understand now.

"Duma, no one took me." His sharp gaze tells me he believes otherwise. "I have to explain something to you, and it may sound crazy, but please listen." His hands stop playing with us and I cradle his face between mine. "I'm not from this world of yours. I'm from another place, far away. Something happens to me that I can't control. It usually happens when I am asleep so I can't explain what it looks like, but one moment I'm with you—" I make sure to caress his face to keep his focus on what I'm trying to explain. "—and the next, I wake up in my bed back home. I didn't leave you. And no one took me."

He's staring, unblinkingly. His eyes look between mine, back and forth. He's searching for something but he's not asking me verbally what he's searching for.

"Why are you looking at me like that? Say something."

"I do not smell or feel lies coming off you. But what you tell me does not sound real, little Juri. My mind is trying and I cannot understand it."

I don't know how else to explain it to him. I mean, I thought *I* was going crazy, and that this was all a dream until I finally lifted the veil of denial off. How much harder would it be for a man like him to hear all this otherworldly stuff happening? I mean, I haven't even run to a city yet in all my visits here.

"But your eyes, they are different. The color is still of light spears, but they are sharper." He's so astute that it amazes me. "You are not as you were when I last saw you. You see me clearly, this I know."

I can feel my eyes burn from the tears forming. I've always seen him clearly, I've always known who my Duma is — be it through the braille of his skin or my sight on his face. My eyes must change color when I am in this world. That's the only explanation I can think of with this constant light spear reference — which I assume is their reference to lightning. I have noticed my eyes getting lighter every time I am back home, and at first I thought it was just a trick of the lighting in my restroom.

I give a small smile to ease his mind, and bring a hand up to caress his cheek. His eyes soften and I know I've reassured him. Change can be hard, especially with what's happening between us.

Maybe the more I explain, the more he will be comfortable with the idea of me being from another world. "When I found myself back home, I made sure to go find…a medicine man, to help me fix my eyes. They are better now. Not as sharp as your hunter's eyes, but I can see you clearly Duma. *I see you.*"

Duma buries a kiss inside the palm of my hand that is holding his face. It is such a small gesture but shoots straight into my heart. This beast of a man has given himself to me irrevocably, baring his vulnerabilities before me, and I do not mind it one bit. In fact, I kind of revel in it.

"I have hunted and seized part of the other tribe in your name, little Juri. When I could not find you, my beast roamed the lands and killed everything in its path. It wanted you home, just as I did."

Wait. What do you mean killed everything in its path?

I grab his face again and bring it up to face me again. "Duma, what did you do? Speak clearly. Who did you kill… in my name?" *I should brace myself for his answer.*

He removes himself from our afterglow embrace and sits up while still staring at me, with no sign of remorse. When he next speaks, the sound of his voice has changed from the Duma who's been lying with me to the Duma, the leader of this tribe.

"The Namwana have sent many scouts towards my lands. I thought they had taken you from me, my Juri. Stolen a treasure I have only just found. It was as if they tore my heart straight out of the bones in my chest."

He beats his chest with his fist as emphasis. His lips curl, showing his gritted teeth.

"They had to know that poking the beast would bring war upon their lands. I am war chief of the Chintkku, we do not show weakness. The first battle is done, and we have lost many warriors on both sides in the bloodshed. But now I have five of their warriors here until we march the warpath again."

I gasp. Has it really gotten this far since I've left?

"It will be finished. There will no longer be a chance for them to get that close to my village again, even if it is not they who took you from me."

This is the war chief speaking. This persona clouds over Duma's demeanor and shrouds him in darkness like the grim reaper. A man who deals death.

Crawling over to where he sits, I bring both my hands up to his face to calm him down. He stares into my eyes and I can still see the embers behind them, readying to grow into flames at a moment's notice.

Alright Juri, you're going to have to say something to smooth things over.

"Duma, I am proud of you for being a great war chief to your people. But the bloodshed must stop now — now that you have me back. It was not them. Who do you have here? Let me go see them so that we can sort this all out. It was all simply a misunderstanding." I give him a kiss on the lips to seal his anger in for just a little longer in case he hates my idea.

The sigh he lets out is a long one. One from a man who has seen too much, done too much, lost too much. *My poor Duma.* That is quite a burden to bear on his own. He closes his eyes before he responds with something I wasn't expecting.

"I cannot stop what has already begun, little Juri. It will be finished. We leave by tomorrow's sun rise over the eastern lands. You will not see our prisoners."

With that, he stands up and leaves me in the hut without looking back.

THIRTY-ONE

I'm kind of ticked off, but I know I shouldn't be. This isn't my world. The rules here are far different from the rules of Earth and living in the city. These men are all warriors and this is probably just how they deal with things — through blood and death. Showing weakness might mean death for them because only the strongest survive.

I get it. I really do.

But these rules are not for me. I'm not trying to be stupid but something has to be done to stop this war from happening. I know Duma would protect me. And from what I've seen so far, all the warriors under him follow the same idea: respect the war chief — respect his woman. So I'm going to do this on my own. *Operation solo mission.* I'm going to find these prisoners and let them go. If war is coming regardless, might as well level the playing field for everyone. Is that bad of me? I need to find out what their version of everything is first when I meet them.

Chiemko mentioned bringing his warpath towards the east, to the Namwana village. Duma mentioned the Namwana too.

Sounds to me like the Namwana has two against one. I don't know if there are any other tribes out there besides the ones I keep hearing about.

It has to be those two huts that were slightly separated from the village on our way in. Where else could they be held? Surely, you wouldn't want a prisoner in the heart of the village where an escape could do a lot of damage? I assume the women and children are there, in the heart of the camp being protected by their people. Duma has gone off to do whatever it is war chiefs do. Once I dress myself back in the clothes that Chiemko fashioned for me before, I exit the hut. The moment they hear me, the three to four warriors nearby turn my direction.

Crap.

"Hi, yeah, I'm just going to go… pee somewhere really quick. Um — farther out, that way it's not too close to the camp." With a little wave and quick steps, I'm walk-jogging away before anyone suspects anything. If I am lucky, I'll make it to my destination without much trouble. Duma has a jealous streak and has forbidden all his warriors from touching me from the way everyone's acting. Although, now that I think about it, that scout that stole me away from Chiemko's tent is still alive, I think — I hope.

Trying to discreetly walk by the villagers, I keep to the shadows between huts instead of walking too much out in the open. Everyone around me seems busy preparing for the upcoming battle. Some men are sparring, while others are gathering supplies. Spears and shields are being carried around in different directions. This helps a lot with camouflaging what I am trying to do. Tip toeing around like a ninja, I make it pretty far without catching anyone's unwanted attention. *Forget Botany, I should have been a spy.*

I come up on the first hut that's on the outside of the camp. Some warriors are walking in loose circles around the perimeter. The moment one of them goes to the side to relieve himself, I sneak into the hut quickly and make sure to put the cloth back down the way I found it. Letting out a quiet breath, I turn around to find a warrior right up against me. *Woah.* I didn't hear him move at all. Looking up into his face, my memory is sparked with the person that stares back at me.

"I know you."

He smiles a sinister smile right before putting one hand over my mouth and giving the universal 'keep quiet' signal. Nodding my head in understanding, he slowly removes his hand and brings his face to my neck where he starts sniffing me. *What in the world?* Shoving him a good arm distance away, his hands hold on to my arms in a firm grasp.

"I knew you would come back to me. The Gods willed it." *What now?* "I saw it in your eyes when that Mata warrior took you."

What is with everyone who thinks everyone else is stealing me away from them?

"Look—"

"Come, we must keep quiet. When the suns crests back down the eastern lands, that is when we must escape. I have planned it; it will not fail. I will bring you to the safety of the Namwana tribe."

Guess he was planning his escape well before I came along. But I need to fix this mess we're in and fix it quickly before it escalates.

"I wasn't stolen away. This has all been a big misunderstanding."

"Shh. The warriors that circle are returning."

Lowering my voice, I continue to try and explain the situation. "Maybe if you just talked to your people, I can talk to Duma—"

His hand covers my mouth again and he pulls me into a tight embrace.

"You do not speak of the death dealer's name. He will hear you and it will make our escape impossible."

Death dealer? My goodness, Duma has created quite a reputation for himself. Shaking my head to let him know I won't say anything to Duma, he slowly removes his hand — but doesn't remove me from his embrace.

His face lifts in a cocky grin and I don't know what to make of it. Shouldn't he be scared that he's a prisoner here? What is there to smile about? If we're going to keep talking like this, I'm going to have to address him somehow. Did he ever mention his name? It feels so long ago, I can't remember at all.

"I don't remember your name."

He chuckles. It's the strangest response. I can feel my face scrunching in confusion.

"Gamba of the Namwana."

That's right. I wonder if he's a leader too? Before I can ask, he answers my thoughts for me.

"I lead my men in war tactics, but the Chintkku came on strong like the beasts of death before anyone was ready for it. The war chief's war path started long before we even had them in our thoughts and plans."

Oh, Duma.

Red against his skin catches my eye. "You're bleeding."

He almost coos his response and it makes my eyes snap back to his. What is up with this guy?

"It is nothing. The war chief was angry over his loss of you. He spoke of one stealing his female, but he did not know that you are not his." There's that smile again. What is he trying to say? "Come, it is almost time."

He's pulling me by the arm now towards the back of the hut. I'm almost tripping over nothing with how fast he's moving. His foot begins to scrape the dirt on the ground and one of the wooden planks moves. *This guy.* I don't remember the huts having wooden planks. But then again, I don't think this was the original village Duma is from. Shaking my head to dislodge thoughts over trivial matters, I ground myself back in the moment.

"I can't go with you, but I can help you escape. I'm going to stay here with Duma." I don't need him getting pissed again. He's a big guy — one that just so happens to lead a lot of angry looking people.

"Duma? The war chief? Have you lost your mind? That beast is as bloodthirsty as they come! He is the one who took down almost half of my first group of warriors, bathing the lands in blood."

I wince a little at this. I know Duma can be a bit much and it's my fault. He's really not that bad of a guy.

"It was a mistake. Everyone is just making a big mistake; we need to stop this fighting." Pushing him away from me, I try to encourage him in the direction he was taking. "You go and tell your people to stop the war with Duma. There is also a war path coming your way from the islanders."

Obviously, my attempts aren't getting anywhere. All of these men are stubbornly on the paths they've chosen. Gamba quickly turns around and grabs my hand again.

"Oh Juri, I know. And I plan to win. The Chintkku was just a surprise of timing. I had planned to win both sides." He's already turned and is tugging me along. "Now come, so that I may protect you from these barbaric people."

Now, now. Don't go name calling. Sounds to me he is just as blood-thirsty as everyone else in this damn place.

Pulling against me, I try to make him see reason. "I can't! Duma will annihilate your entire village if he knew you left with me."

That sinister smile is back on his face and I'm not sure what he's thinking. Is that crazy smile for me?

"He can try. I hope he comes."

Is he really that confident in winning against Duma? Stopping his removal of the second wooden slat he had loosened with his foot, Gamba abruptly turns to me and quickly leans down to steal a kiss from my lips. *Woah, now. Where did this all come from? I don't know you like that, buddy.*

I'm a little stunned for a few seconds and he takes that exact moment to grab me and swiftly remove us from the hut through the opening he made, then placing me beside him. *Bastard.* That must have been his plan all along. We make it out of the hut but the sound of footsteps are not far away. We're going to get caught, I just know it!

Footsteps come closer and closer, Gamba pushes us flat against the back of the hut with his arm and I hold my breath. How did I get myself into this? I just wanted to warn him and free him, not go on a damn escapade with the guy! The footsteps are only a few feet away when suddenly, it turns around and goes back the way it came. A harsh exhale escapes me, but I don't think it was enough to draw attention from the warrior that was patrolling the hut. Gamba grabs my hand again and pulls me along so fast I almost fall on my face. What the hell? Dammit, I'm already in it with him now so I remain as quiet as I can. No point in both of us dying when someone finds us and we have to fight our way out.

If Duma finds I'm gone again, everyone is dead anyway. I can't have that on my conscience. But Duma is already on the warpath to kill everyone as we speak, even if I stay. What am I to do?

My internal conflict of thoughts must have been slowing him down because suddenly Gamba throws my body over both his shoulders like a piece of deer he's bringing home. *These guys!* I'm getting jostled with his increase of speed and some of the wind is getting knocked out of me with his steps. How can he still run with this kind of energy, with my weight on top of him and with bleeding wounds? The guys from this place must be used to this escaping all the bloodbaths. That's not an encouraging thought whatsoever.

Once we're far enough from Duma's camp, I slap Gamba in the back to make him slow down and listen. "Dammit Gamba! You will get your people killed!"

Trying to whisper while getting jostled over someone's shoulder is kind of hard. Gamba only chuckles under his breath and he continues his path of escape between trees and bushes he must know like the back of his hand because there is no hesitation in his steps at all. I don't recognize any of the tree patterns or the land out this way. I hope we don't get stuck in the middle of nowhere and get captured again anyway. What a waste that would be.

Gamba continues on without another word. It's getting dark fast by the time the entire village is out of our sights. His speed begins to slow to a jog, and he's not bothering to hide as much between the trees and shrubbery. Where does this guy get the energy? Must be in the water.

The thought of water makes me think of my other guys. I hope Chiemko and Gary are okay.

Finally, he stops and is leaning down behind a cave wall, sliding my body back into the upright position. My head becomes a little dizzy from the change in position and I end up inadvertently leaning against him in an embrace to try and stop the world from spinning. He steadies me with his hands waiting for me to blink a few times. Gamba then grabs one of my hands and starts walking us towards what looks to be a river.

"We will stop when we reach the last group of trees beyond this river."

My eyes scan around us. There's trees everywhere in different scatterings. Which one is he talking about?

The stream that flows before us is shallow enough for us to wade through safely. The coolness against my feet is refreshing and helps to clear my mind a bit. Before we fully exit the other side, Gamba leans down and cups his hands in the water for a drink. *Smart. We need to hydrate.* Who knows how far we really have left to go? So I do the same, not knowing when the next time water will be available. The coolness feels so good going down my throat. These lands can get really hot in the daytime with two suns beating down. Being outside at night, I look up at the sky and see that there are also two moons. *Just so very odd.*

Gamba takes another drink and turns to walk out the other side. Following Gamba's lead, I walk behind him until he finds a place to stop. There are tall trees around us just enough to keep us covered but not enough to make us trapped. I'm not sure what he has planned. He looks around quietly and moves away from me to start dragging branches and pieces of broken shrubbery to hide our corner a bit more.

Sitting down cross legged, I stare at the sky and wonder if Duma is looking for me now — what Chiemko is doing and if Gary is still alive. Everything is happening so fast, and nothing makes sense, but things are moving forward and the only thing I can do at this point is control my decisions from this moment forward as well. How can I help this situation without making it worse? Everyone is at war with one another. All over a misunderstanding? How does that make sense? No — everyone seems to already have old beef with each other even before I came around. But am I the catalyst of what's happening now?

The best thing to do is find a mediator and sit everyone down to clear the air. That's how business meetings go when no one can agree, right? These guys are more intense though — solutions are found through physical fights and bloodshed. I need to find a way to make these guys see reason. The only common denominator I can see here is…me.

Was that why I was sent here? Is it me? How does a single Indian woman living in the city do anything to stop warriors from killing each other? What skills can I possibly bring to the table? So far, I've been taken advantage of, taken care of, kidnapped, and worshipped. Watching Gamba continue whatever he's doing, the sight of his muscles glistening under the two moons make me wonder what else is in store for me. What do I do when we reach his village? Will it be another situation where I'm stolen away again, only adding to the animosity between the tribes?

Lifting my heads to the skies, I think of how Chiemko always talks about the will of the gods here. Is there someone out there I can speak to? Someone I can ask for answers? What am I supposed to do?

Once Gamba feels our cover is enough, he lays down on the ground next to me and joins me in looking up at the sky. It's quiet between us, the initial sense of urgency gone leaving only the calm and silence of the night.

I wonder how my family's doing. I wonder if Anderson is giving the girls' a break at the office. *Pfft. I already know that answer to that one.*

"Lay down with me Juri, we will be okay this night. We are not far from the Namwana tribe lands. I will keep you safe."

I turn to look at him and see a little smirk cross his face. This guy and his smirks. He's a cocky one, isn't he? Laying there with his wounds like it doesn't bother him one bit. Unable to think of a good response, I let my eyes wander over his features now that I can see him clearly. There is a little bit of facial hair that has grown out since the last time I saw him, probably from his imprisonment with the Chintkku. His dreadlocks are long and tied up on top of his head. He must be enjoying my perusal because his eyes are closed like he's asleep, but I know he's not.

"You can look as much as you want Juri, but it will be better if you lay down next to me, then you can touch."

Oh boy, his cocky smirk is even bigger now. I need to keep things on track, find out what I can do about this upcoming war.

"Gamba, why do the tribes war with each other? What started it? Why do you guys hate each other so much?" *Let's get to the bottom of this.*

"I will tell you everything you want to know Juri, but you must lay down with me."

Sneaky little thing, isn't he? I should rest anyway. Who knows what awaits me in his tribe? Every time I think I'm going to rest for a little bit, something or someone proves me wrong. Slowly laying myself down and keeping a good foot distance between us, I clasp my hands over my stomach and stare at the sky. Gamba stretches his arms up in a slow yawn and I'm lost looking at the stars, trying to see if we have the same constellations when he rolls his whole body on top of me.

Slick.

"What are you doing Gamba?" He should not be this attractive. It gives him an unfair advantage.

He gives me another smirk before running his nose over the bridge of mine while staring into my eyes. It's such a sweet gesture from him that I relax a little. In this quiet moment we have, I take a good look at him with my improved vision. His skin tone is much lighter than Duma's but slightly darker than Chiemko's. It is amazing how one area of land can have so many different types of tribes with such contrasting features.

His eyes dart to my lips before he steals a kiss from me, and I'm taken by surprise. I shouldn't be — the bastard. He doesn't even know me! Trying to push his chest off of me, Gamba steals another kiss as his hands firmly grip mine and slowly bring them over my head in a show of dominance. This shouldn't make me feel so flustered.

"I like that fire in your eyes. It makes me feel like a light spear will take me down right here, and I am willing to let it into my body even if it means death."

I'm still annoyed and getting even more flustered by his brazen personality. *Ugh, what is with the men in this place?* I take that back; Gary is just as bad. He fits right in. It seems like I attract a certain type.

"You need to get off me, Gamba."

"And what will you do for me if I do as you ask?"

Not knee you in the balls.

"Will you honor me, Juri? I choose you for my female. I have not claimed one before. But the Gods had me wait for you to fall into my path. When I saw your eyes and the spark inside of them, I knew you were mine. The Gods chose well for me."

I didn't see that coming. Where are all these sweet words coming from? My breathing is picking up a little bit. Damn if I don't feel flattered. Duma, Gary, Chiemko and now Gamba. I feel guilty for all of this attention and yet I don't. I am a young woman who has her whole life ahead of her. Life should be my oyster. That decision to correct my vision gave me a confidence boost I didn't know I was lacking.

Fuck it, you only live once and this isn't even earth, so no one is going to judge my decisions, right? His cocky attitude and smile are just too enticing right now. The sparkle of mirth in his eyes has me curious to get to know more about him.

"What will you do for me, Gamba, if I agree to become your female? Hmm?" Let's play this game a little. Maybe I can make some good out of it. He still has my hands locked over my head, keeping me at his mercy. A warrior of the Namwana tribe — an escaped prisoner of war — now has me as *his* prisoner. That thought shouldn't be so hot, but it is.

"What do you wish of me, Juri?"

He rubs his nose slowly against mine again. He is very good at this game, it seems. I wonder how many women he's pulled this on? But he said he hasn't claimed a female before. But it doesn't mean he hasn't fucked around either.

"I need you guys to stop the bloodshed." Is my breathing picking up? Why did that come out so breathy?

He chuckles. "War is already here." He rubs his nose along my jaw and it's distracting my thoughts.

"Isn't there anything we can do to stop it?"

His eyes roam over my face and land on my lips again. My breath hitches a little, knowing he would be cocky enough to just take what he wants. Why does that thought turn me on?

"What would you do to be free?"

Another stolen kiss. It's so feather light, I almost don't know what to make of it.

"What do you mean?" His kisses become heavy and travel down my neck and onto my clavicle. I feel goosebumps rising in his wake. He's too damn good at this seduction game. Wasn't I supposed to be the one seducing him to get some answers?

He asks me the same question again. "What would you do to be free?"

"Whatever I have to do."

Gamba takes that answer as his invitation. Putting both of my wrists in one of his hands, his other hand is now freeing my breast from its confinement. When the cool air hits it, my nipples peak. Gamba brings it into his warm mouth and the contrast of temperature has me trying to clench my thighs. But since the bastard is on top of me, all they can really do is grip his body to me, encouraging him to rub against me.

Letting my hands go, he covers the crook of my neck instead with his palm, making me think of Gary's choking sessions. But Gamba's way is much more seductive. A firm dominant hand but not squeezing. When he moves his mouth to my other nipple, my hips inadvertently make a slow grind against him out of my control. Staring at the stars hanging over us, I'm lost in the moment. Cradling his head to me, my body telling him I need more. I like this newfound me. She's just as hungry as he is.

But I shouldn't make it that easy for him, right?

His nose runs downward along my stomach and my legs bend up to push him off me.

He rolls to the side with a soft chuckle but doesn't make a move to come back.

I'm a little annoyed with his response to my rejection that I turn away from him and try to relax the tension he's brought to my body. We need to rest and see what the next day brings. I don't even know how long their days are here.

Fingering my choker, my eyes begin to get heavy with every exhale. The coolness of the night feels nice against my skin, helping to cool the heat that was building between us earlier. When my mind feels like it's in limbo between dreams and wakefulness, I startle myself awake with a gasp and sit up abruptly.

Shaking the grogginess out of me, I rub my eyes and take a deep breath in and out. What if I teleport again? I can't leave these guys right now, not when we're so close to coming to a head. I feel a small headache coming on from forcing myself awake. This isn't going to do either. How am I supposed to function on no sleep?

Maybe I'm jumping to conclusions. I don't even know how any of this works. You're being stupid, Juri. Ugh. My inner voice is probably right. I am being stupid. Laying back down, I try to relax myself again. Staring at the sparse blades of short grass in front of me, I begin to count them all in an attempt to put myself back to sleep. My eyes become heavy and I'm getting pulled into the darkness again when I feel something heavy and warm wrap around me from behind.

THIRTY-TWO

I awake to kisses on my shoulders and someone nuzzling the back of my neck. Sadly for him, I'm not that much of a morning person. Shoving him off me, I roll away and stretch my limbs. I can hear Gamba chuckling nearby and I ignore it.

Whatever.

When I finally get the kinks out of me, I sit up and roll my neck. Sleeping on the hard ground is not as easy as it looks on TV. How do people go camping all the time?

When I turn to look at Gamba, he's doing little jumps like he's ready to take on the day. How disgusting. I can still see the river we crossed earlier and the thought of washing my face to wake me up sounds like a good plan.

Standing up, I begin to walk in that direction when someone slams from behind me and picks me up by the midsection, making me squeal.

"Dammit, Gamba! Put me down!"

"Is that a lover's name you give me?"

Is this bastard serious right now?

He kisses my shoulder again and begins to walk us both towards the river. He doesn't drop me like I anticipate but instead, bends me over with his body and grinds his hip against me. This horn dog is going to have to control his urges because there are more pressing matters to attend to.

Pushing him off me, he laughs as I lean into the water and cup my hands to splash my face. God, that feels good. I start to splash against some of the skin I have exposed just to clean myself a bit. It's been quiet around me the whole time. When I turn to see where Gamba is, I get an eyeful of ass full of muscle as he bends over to wash himself the same way I am.

My mouth is hanging open and I'm trying to string some thoughts together but I'm utterly distracted by the way his calves and thigh muscles move when every bend he performs. He really shouldn't be that attractive. But all these guys living out in the elements have given them a body fat percentage that gym rats would die for.

I'm still bent over with my hands cupped, the water having already seeped through my fingers when Gamba turns around to face me. Where the hell did his bottom covering go? And why does his cock look so much bigger than it felt against me last night? The covering must have been hiding him well because holy hell, I cannot take my eyes off him.

"We can rest a little more before starting our day."

His voice breaks my reverie, but his twitching cock brings my eyes back down. *Naughty, Juri. His eyes are up there.*

Clearing my throat, I turn my face back to the water and pretend to wash my arms. "No, we can start moving. We've rested enough."

He laughs and I can hear the splash of him exiting the water. My face feels so beet red that I can't believe I was caught oogling him like that. I'm no better than Anderson.

I take that back.

There is no way in hell *any* woman in their right mind could take their eyes away from *that specimen of a male.*

By the time my embarrassment of the moment dies down and I make my way back to our rest spot, Gamba has already redressed in his loin cloth. Thank goodness.

"We move east."

"Okay."

The walk is slow, unlike last night where we were running for our lives away from Duma's camp. It's quiet between us, the only sound that can be heard are the beasts nearby and the birds that fly up ahead at times.

"Sparcra."

"What?"

"The creatures that distract you in the skies. They are sparcra. They feast on the dead."

Gulping at that explanation, my eyes remain forward for the rest of the way.

We pass a small cluster of trees and jagged rocks when Gamba speaks again. "You need not fear, my Juri. I am a warrior of the Namwana. I will protect you."

So everyone keeps saying. What are they all protecting me from? Each other? This reminds me that I need to find a way to get these guys to sit down together and just hash things out.

"Why do you all hate each other so much?"

"The Chintkku is hated by everyone."

"That doesn't explain anything, Gamba. It doesn't even touch on the fact that you hate the islanders as well."

Gamba scoffs but keeps facing ahead as he continues to walk. Must be a sore spot. But I need someone to tell me something.

"We have not gotten along since the days of old and the old wars."

"Seems you guys are always fighting. Who started it? What was the reason why it all started to begin with?"

"The tales around the tribe fire goes back too far for it to be the full truth. Every child has heard the stories of how the Gods created the people."

That's it? That's all he's going to tell me? Hitting him with the back of my hand, I catch his crooked smile looking back at me. The jerk knew exactly what he was doing teasing me like that.

We dodge some low hanging branches and start going around some of the tighter grouping of trees before us. For a place that simulates Africa, the pattern of grouping foliage here makes absolutely no sense.

I hear a hiss from beside me and shriek, jumping against Gamba who breaks a branch off and stabs the snake-like creature right through it's scales. It writhes erratically and I shiver in disgust, burying my face into his chest. His arm quickly shoves the snake and stick away before coming back and enclosing me in an embrace.

I mumble against his chest like I have to explain myself. "I don't like snakes."

His chuckle vibrates through me and I want to pinch him for laughing at me. Jerk.

"No one likes creatures that move on their bellies."

Creatures. There's more than one kind here? Ugh. Pushing out of his arms, I pretend to dust myself off and start walking our path again.

"I can carry you if you fear more on our path, Juri. All you have to do is ask me nicely."

I turn to give him an exasperated look. Really?

He laughs and we continue our trek side by side. I swear this guy said we weren't far from his village. Why is this taking so long?

"It is said the world came from darkness."

"Darkness."

"The father of skies and the mother of the ground found themselves in love but could not be together. Somehow they found a way to go to the other side but it did not turn out the way it should have."

I'm invested. It sounds like a story of star crossed lovers and I'm a sucker for romance. "What do you mean? What happened?"

"Father of the skies found a way to reach the ground and mother of the ground found a way to reach the skies. What they did not understand was that they were now caught on the other side and still separated from one another."

Oh no. That's horrible.

"This is why the sky has two suns and two moons. It is the echo of their travels left behind once they returned to where they belonged. A reminder of their longing to be together."

"But that doesn't explain—"

"My Juri, do you wish to hear the tale you asked for?"

"Well, yes, bu—"

Gamba lifts me behind the knees and carries me across some really jagged rocks. My arms wind around his neck in surprise, bringing my face right beside his. He stops walking and we stare at each other in awkward silence. Well, awkward for me. Or maybe that's the butterflies I currently feel in my stomach. There's a sexual tension sparking between us and I can see the laughter in his eyes even though his expression remains calm. When Gamba dips his head down, I close my eyes in anticipation of him stealing another kiss from me but it doesn't happen. Instead, he softly rubs his nose up and down the bridge of mine and plants a kiss on the tip.

He's killing me with how good he is at this game.

I exhale as he puts me back down and we continue walking on foot.

"We rest here."

This place looks familiar. This cliff.

"Is this—"

"Yes, my Juri. Sit down beside me so I can tell you the rest of the tale."

I do as he says and criss cross my legs. We look over the ledge and it's so much different from what I remember. The last time I was here, I was afraid to fall to my death. But in this position, it's actually quite peaceful to overlook the land below. Some of those non zebra things are grazing about, completing the whole scenery.

"The gods gave father of the skies and mother of the ground children."

Wait, so earth and sky weren't gods to begin with? That's so interesting.

Gamba looks at me like he's waiting for questions. When they don't come he turns to look out over the cliff once more and continues his tale.

"The gods gave them the form of people so that they may make many children and live happily. They made many children but their time in this form caused the earth and the sky to anger with their absence. So the gods had to send them back where they belong, leaving the children to grow alone in the form of people."

"That's...kind of sad."

"It is the way of life. It was never meant to be fair, Juri. Do not forget this. The children grew and made their own families. But during their time here, their souls also grew to learn new emotions. Without the guide of their mother and father to help them, some emotions became all consuming and some became vulnerabilities and weaknesses for others to prey on."

I think I know where this story is headed.

"Hate and rage became out of control. The sense of envy and lust fanning the fires to grow into a live thing. Wars between brothers and sisters, children and their parents — no one was spared during these times. It is what the elders refer to as the wars of old."

My chest hurts just thinking about children who were left to fend for themselves and the fact that they had to grow up raising themselves.

"The gods intrude into lives when they want and stay away when they wish to be entertained."

"Death is never an entertainment."

He turns to me and there's something in his eyes that I can't name, but it draws me in.

"Blood covered the lands and over time life was made anew. With death also came life. But the lives left behind were scattered. Blood ties no longer holding meaning. The Chintkku is the only tribe known to have blood ties to the first children made by the skies and ground."

"So you're telling me that your hatred for each other just never died since the beginning of time?" How does this make any sense whatsoever? Looking back on the history of our world, I begin to rethink things. How many countries have had wars that date back to biblical times? What Gamba is telling me isn't anything new under the sun — or in this case, under two suns and two moons.

"The tales by the fires go on saying that tribes were born, holding onto the tales told by their elders."

And that's that? That's it? My mind is spinning with this new information. I'm unsure of what to make of it — I'm unsure of what I can really do to stop a hatred that runs so deep that it's been passed down from generation to generation through tales around the fire.

"Gamba."

He stares at me and waits. There's such a longing in his eyes that it takes my breath away. I've lost my train of thought and my words die in my throat. His hand slowly reaches out like he's afraid he'll break me and it makes me choke up even more. What happened to the cocky bastard I've been hanging out with these past few days? The prisoner of war that wouldn't accept defeat and found his escape so easily under the nose of a warchief that is known to kill everything in his path?

When his warm, calloused hands palm my face so gently, the walls I've built up around him begin to crumble a little. I'm reminded of the beginning of his tale. When the earth and sky just wanted to be together, but nothing they did worked. It took the meddling of the gods to finally give them what they both longed for.

Is this what's happening between us right now? The meddling of the gods in his world? Is what he's been telling me true? Have I been placed before all these men for a reason? Is this why I feel so drawn to all of them? His next words take my breath away. Despite hearing them once before, it holds such a different impact now.

"Will you honor me, Juri? I have chosen you for my female. The Gods may have played their hand in this but it is my own heart that chooses. I have not claimed one before but I never had reason to. You call to me, my Juri — to something buried deep inside of me. It is something I never knew existed until the Gods put you on my path."

Gamba is like two people living inside one body. One personality is the total polar opposite of the other. I'm getting whiplash and getting butterflies in my stomach again all at the same time.

When he steals a kiss from me this time, I don't resist. Instead, I let myself go. We cannot control everything that happens to us but we can make small decisions right now when moments like these present themselves. And damn if Gamba hasn't snuck under my skin.

His hands roam the back of my head, threading my hair and bringing me closer to him. Somehow I end up on top of him with my breast pressing against his chest, the closeness feeling so right in the moment unlike the other times when I wanted to push him away.

He flips us over and grinds his hips down on me, the loin cloth blocking everything I want to feel between us. His hands roam my sides and pull my top down, exposing my breast to the air. His fingers explore as his mouth continues to create a path of fire down the crook of my neck. When his tongue comes out to lick along my clavicle, I gasp at the sensation of the warm air cooling the wet spot.

"Juri..."

Oh, the gruffness of his voice does something to me — gives me a tingle right between the legs. His hands are pushing my coverings up and caressing my thighs so deliciously. When his hips grind down again, I grind up against him too. My legs are rubbing against him and feeling the flex of his muscles as he moves on top of me. His hands go down between us to push his loin cloth to the side and I can finally feel the heat of his hard cock against my wet folds. How did he work me up this fast?

When his shaft glides against my juices and the tip of his cock hits my clit, I automatically open up and wrap my legs around him. I'm curious to see what this Namwana warrior has in store for me. The scruff of his beard tickles the skin of my shoulder and my abs tense up from the sensation. I'm not the skinniest woman, but none of these men seem to mind my softer body. In fact, they all seem to love it with the way they caress me reverently. When his nose grazes over my jaw, I hold my breath then let out a long exhale. He whispers against my face with words that make me flush.

"Your smell calls to me. The smell of my female."

I whimper at the loss of his cock sliding between my legs but then gasp when he crawls down my body and takes my clit into his mouth. He gives me a hard suck and my back bows up with it. One of his hands holds me down by the waist and the other opens my leg farther. His tongue starts to explore my folds, and it's such a languid feeling. His slow strokes make me crave more intensity but at the same time want to enjoy his leisurely pace, reminding me that I'm not in control anymore.

I can feel how wet I am when his lips and tongue leave my pussy to lave the inside of my thighs. I didn't expect the light nips of teeth along with it and the little shots of small pain increases my lust. Climbing back up my body like a panther, Gamba stares into my eyes with his signature cocky grin, caging my head with his arms outstretched against the ground. I can feel his hard length slapping against my clit. Damn, who knew I'd be turned on by that stupid smile of his? He moves his hips back and forth a few times, getting the head of his cock wet before he buries himself inside of me to the hilt. His thrusts are slow coming out and hard going back in. Needing something to hold on to, I grab onto his arms by my head and just stare right back at him. These guys are like beasts with their constant eye contact to issue a challenge. I don't dare to look away, accepting all he has to give me. His thrusts become faster but it's not enough to chase the pleasure I'm just beginning to feel. I don't know how different this would have turned out if I didn't become this more confident woman. Gamba doesn't seem like the others — it's like he's waiting for my own beast to come out and play with his.

If that is the case, then challenge accepted.

Using all the strength I have, I flip Gamba over onto his back and take control with my knees on the ground straddling him. Placing both of my hands on his chest, I stare straight into his eyes as I ride him at a faster pace, chasing my own climax. *Sometimes you need to win the small battles before you can win the war.* Gamba gives me a wide toothy grin, like he's baring his teeth at me with a slight lip curl. It spurs me on and I ride him harder. The friction we are creating between us drives me mad. The pleasure from this new angle is clouding me in pure lust. Forcing his hands on my hips, I continue my rhythm with one hand on his chest and the other rubbing my clit in circular motions. *Yeah, I'm learning to be greedy and I'm not ashamed one bit.* The extra wetness that comes out of me makes our hip grinds slide and I can feel myself getting close.

"Oh God."

The hands on my hips get tighter and start forcing my movements down harder. Moving my feet flat under me to give me more leverage, I let myself go and ride with abandon. I'm climbing — the sensation becoming a bit overwhelming with how close I am. One of my hands pinches my nipples and my climax hits me hard. I try to stifle the scream I want to let out by biting my bottom lip because I know we're technically still on the run and out in the open. Forcing my screams back down my throat makes this moment even hotter, and the waves of my orgasm continue as I keep riding his hard cock.

Gamba has other ideas as he flips us over and starts ramming into me into the ground at a speed that tells me he's chasing his own finish. It hurts so damn good that I can barely keep my eyes open. He bites down on my shoulder to stifle his own groan, and I can feel the girth of his cock swelling before he cums inside of me. The pulsations give me another small wave of pleasure, making me moan out loud. He gives me a cocky smile in response and I want to slap it off him. *Asshole. Way to ruin the moment.*

He must read my thoughts because he leans in and gives me the slowest kiss that chases all my thoughts of kneeing him in the balls away. Gamba lays his head on my shoulder and my hands caress his back as we both soak in the breeze that comes by. We lay there in our afterglow quietly for a few more moments while I feel Gamba licking his bite mark with reverence.

THIRTY-THREE

We ended up staying the night by the cliff. Gamba's reasoning was that it was a place that brought him peace, and he needed a clear mind for his return to this tribal lands. With an early start, we make it back to his village before the sun fully crests over the far distance.

"Gamba!"

"He's returned!"

"He's alive!"

"Chief!"

We have yet to fully reach the village when Gamba gets a very warm welcome from his people. In contrast, everyone is staring at me strangely. I try to give them a friendly smile to show them I'm of no threat. It doesn't deter the stares, especially from the women. Mostly, they are staring at the exact spot Gamba bit me on the shoulder. It must mean something significant, or maybe he bruised me really badly.

That can't be it because the other guys in the village all look at me from afar while only the women are not afraid to be close to me. Narrowing my eyes at Gamba, who's still greeting everyone, my mind starts to put things together. He didn't tell me he marked me in an animalistic show of possession. It's the only thing that makes sense with how the other males around me are acting once they see the mark. I give Gamba a side eye once more and he just smiles at me with no remorse. *The bastard.*

His demeanor changes as he turns around and addresses his people. "Gather our warriors, young and old! War is coming!"

His booming voice gets everyone into motion. I've never seen this side of him before. Then again, I've only seen him when he's alone.

Turning in my direction, Gamba pulls me towards what looks like a water well in the middle of his village with a pulley system over it. Using the pulley to bring the bucket of water up, Gamba starts to wash his face with the wooden ladle sitting on the edge of the well. With a sideways glance, he lifts his head a little bit towards the bucket, probably to let me know I should wash up a bit too.

Washing my face as best as I can with only one ladle of water, one of the women passing by hands me a piece of fabric to use as a rag. Taking advantage of the moment, I grab another ladle of water to wet the cloth and try to discreetly wash between my legs. Gamba gives me a proud grin when he sees what I am doing. *This guy.* Rinsing the rag one last time, I slap it to his chest to get the look off his face, which only makes him smile wider. *Cocky bastard.*

Gamba is suddenly called away by some of his men and I am left standing by the well, unsure of what to do. I wonder if Duma is already halfway here? This bloodshed still has to stop. Just as I turn around, I hear the screams of the women running towards the middle of the village dragging children in hand while more warriors run towards the outer lying areas. Everything around me erupts into chaos as a horn is sounded nearby. Warriors are grabbing bows and spears or whatever else is around them.

Shit, Duma's already here.

"Mata warriors coming from the west!"

Mata warriors. It's Chiemko.

Everyone is positioning themselves for battle while I'm still standing here like a fool. Where am I expected to go? This is just ridiculous. War at every damn turn? Making up my mind that I need to do something to stop this, I run behind some of the warriors that are headed towards the front of the village. I barely make it a couple of yards when the sounds of battle cries and flesh hitting flesh carries in the wind.

That close? Crap. I need to move!

Running faster and dodging warriors behind some of the huts, I safely make it to the last hut before the village ends and stop to stand behind the grassy wooden building to watch what's going on. Blood is being sprayed like a high definition movie in front of my eyes as some of Gamba's warriors spear and shoot arrows into the fray, while some of the Mata warriors are on top of Namwana and stabbing them with their hand to hand weapons.

It's already a bloodbath, and it has only just begun.

My eyes are scanning the men around me, hoping I'll find a familiar face. He sees me a few moments after I see him, like our souls are tied to each other.

"Chiemko!"

At my call, he roars and viciously kills three men on his way towards me. My guilt is building the closer he gets. Am I the reason for this particular war? For all this death? My heart aches as the thought crosses my mind. My hands might as well be painted red along with everyone else here.

"Chiemko! You have to stop this! Stop this!"

With a knife in each hand, Chiemko slashes the next warrior to come between us, spilling his intestines onto the ground without a second glance. He grabs the warrior's short dreadlocks, pulling his head back and gives him one final deep slice across the neck, almost cutting it right off. The spraying blood hits him all over his chest and splatters his face. But his eyes never leave mine as he races towards me.

I need to stop him from killing too many more. Making up my mind, I start running towards him in case any other Namwana warrior tries to come between us.

A flash of white skin has me zoning my sights in that direction. A child's cry carries on the wind towards me. *No no no no! The children! Someone protect the children!* Gary is in a battle with a Namwana warrior in hand-to-hand combat and the child is too close! I move my feet to try and save him when I see Gary's eyes land on the child, leaving his defenses open for a second. The other warrior, in his blood haze, uses this lapse in judgement to pick up a spear off the ground nearby and throws it towards Gary's direction. I cry out with my hand outstretched just as Gary grabs the child in his embrace and rolls onto the ground. A red streak of blood blooms across his back as he comes back to standing and pushes the child towards the village before turning back into the fight. The spear still sticks out from the ground, tripping the next two warriors caught in battle.

This is utter madness.

The sound of hundreds of bird wings flapping in the sky intermingle with the sounds coming from the battleground and I look up to find creatures of the air that resemble a mix of a vulture and a crow circling. Their black feathers gleam in the suns, reminding me of a dark cloud of death hovering above our heads. Sparcra. They hover around death.

There is a bird call — one I've heard before, coming from a distance. It's the same call Duma's scout let out, and I know the Chintkku tribe has joined in the bloodshed. *This is insane. Everyone will die here today, and for what?* Chiemko is just about a few feet away from me when the ground starts to vibrate and the sounds of war drums can be heard over the sounds of battle and death around us.

Dum drum. Dum dum dum drum. Dum drum. Dum.

Dum drum. Dum dum dum drum. Dum drum. Dum.

Turning my head to the left, I see him before I see anyone else. He towers over his men, black as night like the grim reaper. His teeth are bared like a feral beast that's been starved for centuries about to come upon a feast. My eyes widen when I see what he's doing. His arm pulls back with his spear in hand and my mind goes into slow motion as the momentum of his swing throws it directly towards Chiemko.

"Nooo! Chiemko! Watch out!"

I see his eyes sharpen when I say his name, and he looks quickly to his right. I've never seen a man move as fast as he dives to the blood-soaked ground to roll under the path of the spear. The sound of the impact is sharp in my ears when the spear strikes the ground, sticking up right where Chiemko's path would have been.

"No Duma! You need to stop this!" *Someone, hear me!* "Chiemko! Gamba! No more!"

At the sound of their names being cried out, all the men I call turn their heads to look at me. The distraction costs me dearly as two warriors fighting for dominance to the death stumble into me, throwing me onto my back and knocking the air out of my lungs. *Oomph. That hurt.*

Chiemko pulls his warrior off of me while he slices the throat of the Namwana warrior, spraying his lifeblood all over my body still on the ground. My adrenaline must be what prevents me from feeling the pain of the impact because as I lay there trying to catch my breath, it just registers in my mind a few moments later that there is a sharp pain in my abdomen and my thigh.

Roars, grunts, flesh on flesh sounds, and battle cries slowly die down as the war drums stop their musical beat. Everyone's eyes are on their respective war chiefs, and each war chief's eyes are on *me*. Duma is first to break the trance of shock and drops to his knees by my side when his feet reach me. His hands hover over my body, unsure of where they should go. My eyes haven't left the short blade hilt protruding out of my gut as well as a larger open wound from the tip of a spear on my thigh. There isn't anything I can say, and I'm not sure if taking out the knife would do more damage than good. My eyes prick with tears as I stare into the sky, trying to calm my erratic breathing. The warmth of my blood flowing out of my wounds is what I concentrate on at the moment.

"…My Juri…" Duma's voice cracks.

"This is the fault of the Namwana! She would have been safe if she stayed with me!" Chiemko's voice is raw and the sound of flesh hitting flesh starts up again, but with only two.

"No, Mata warrior. I knew you would bring her danger! The Gods have spoken, and she was meant for me."

"You dare fight like beasts in heat when Juri lies in a pool of her own blood? Cease!"

Duma's booming voice and body are a formidable presence when he is commanding men. It almost feels like his dark aura is seeping from his pores, spilling the feeling of gloom onto every warrior here. The reaper of death on his knees next to me.

"You motherfuckers!"

Gary? I almost forgot about him. He saved that poor child — my God, he saved him. My heart hurts for what could have been something so tragic if it wasn't for Gary. How deep was his wound? Is he okay?

I suddenly feel so damn tired. Tired of these men and their never-ending thirst for war. Duma's warm hands caress my face softly, like I'm a treasure about to break into pieces before him. It just makes my emotions more weary. Letting out a sigh, I close my eyes for a minute to try and overcome the pain I feel, inside and out.

At this moment, I can hear my mother's voice in my mind saying, "Har kali raat ke baad ek ujli subah hoti hai." *After every dark night arrives the brightest morning.*

I hope you're right, mother, because we need it right about now. There is only darkness around me, even the skies fill with black wings that circle around us.

"She needs a fucking doctor, you bastards! Don't you have a healer?"

"You fool! This is war!"

"Yeah, well, what good is your fucking war if what you are fighting for might be dying before your very eyes!"

The silence is thick, and the only sounds to be heard are the continuous flapping of wings from the crow-like birds overhead, circling the scene we've made.

"What would you have us do then? You are not of our lands. What can you do to fix this? How do we find this … doctor?"

"We need to get her back to our world. It's the only way."

"How do we make this happen? She cannot die!"

"I will slaughter your entire tribe before she breathes her last breath!"

Am I crying? I guess I am, but I thought laying down my tears would just drip down the side of my face and not my cheeks?

Opening my eyes slowly, my vision focuses on Duma's broken expression.

"My poor Duma…"

More wetness is splattered on my face and body in light sprinkles, confusing me. When did the sky get so dark? Storm clouds roll in and it's starting to drizzle on us. The sky is crying — crying for all the lives lost this day.

Duma's eyes suddenly sharpen on me like steel, and I can see his jaw clenching. "We must bring her to Kwame, the Chintkku's sight seeker. Now! Warriors, the drums will be beat to make a path home."

"I am not leaving her."

"You must be a fool to think I trust her with you, war chief."

"I'm not leaving her with you fuckers."

Duma isn't listening to the other guys one bit; his focus is solely on me laying here as still as I can. Reaching his hands gently under me, he slowly lifts me bridal style until he is back up to a standing position. The jostling hurts, the pain throbbing almost like a heartbeat, but I think my adrenaline is still kicking in because it doesn't hurt as much as I think it should.

Without another word spoken and with a stoic expression, Duma turns to walk back towards the west. His men, who have started a different type of drum rhythm, part like the red sea to let him through to lead the march in the front.

I don't know if the other war chiefs are following, but I assume they are. These guys are too cocky, too possessive, and much too jealous to let Duma have his way without some sort of "supervision".

The pain is starting to register even more about ten minutes into our march. I grit my teeth to hold down any moans that want to escape my lips because it's not going to make it hurt any less.

Being around warriors who don't even flinch with these kinds of wounds, I don't want to show any weakness in front of them. The raw emotions crossing their expressions at the situation were enough to tear my own heart apart. It was not my intention to cause so much pain, so much hate.

Mother, what do I do? How do I fix this?

The drizzle that started earlier has now turned into a light rain. Wrapping my arms around Duma's shoulders, I squeeze him tighter as I bury my face towards his body, letting out a slow sigh. Though he smells of metallic blood and death, Duma still smells of strength and man. It's a comfort to me in this moment, this moment of weakness.

The steady cadence of the march makes my mind wander to everything that's happened since it all started. Why was I chosen to fall into a world of war? Am I the only one? How can I find an emotional connection to these war chiefs who only crave blood and retaliation? How did their people even survive this long if that is the case? What is causing my movement and travel between the two worlds? How did Gary end up here with me? Was it because he was touching me at the chosen time of phasing out?

The more I think, the more confused I get. Releasing Dumas neck with one of my hands, I finger my choker as I concentrate on the answers I seek. About five minutes of problem solving go by when we hear the sound of distant thunder. Lightning cracks and flashes, illuminating the path ahead. My mind pricks with memory. Another moment that left me confused.

Someone bumps into my shoulder. "Oh dear! I'm so sorry." I tell whoever it is. Once I rearrange my glasses back to their rightful place, I open my eyes to find... No one. Huh? I turn around 360 degrees and it doesn't look like anyone is stopping or rubbing their shoulder from the impact. Oh well, sorry anyways whoever you are.

Where did it come from? Didn't that old man mention some-thing about it?

"You wear a mark on you that I do not recognize myself. What tribe are you from? The talisman around your neck seems familiar, but I cannot place a name to it." He is staring where my hands are near my neck and I realize he means the choker I'm wearing is the talisman he is referring to.

"Talisman? This thing around my neck? It came to me out of nowhere. I don't know why I always feel drawn to touch it. It brings me comfort."

Talisman. I haven't even thought about it much since I started wearing it every day the same way I used to put on my glasses every day. Once I got my eyesight corrected, it must have been a new habit I created to replace my old one — putting on the choker. My hands caress it again. *Is it this? Is this what brought me here? Who gave it to me? I remember not being able to find the person who lost it.*

Duma's wise decision to see Kwame might solve a lot of things after all.

THIRTY-FOUR

When we reach the edge of the Chintkku camp, there is an increase in the noise of weapons moving around us. Turning slightly with me still in his arms, Duma's warriors turn around as well towards the east, raising their shields and pointing their spears towards the other tribal warriors who have followed our march west — specifically, the Namwana and the Matalo'toa Tribe.

"What are you doing?"

"As war chief, I cannot let enemy tribes into my village. There are women and children here under my protection."

I tell you, these war politics.

"She is mine, war chief."

"The God's have chosen her as mine."

"I don't care how big of a fucker you are; I'm going where Juri goes."

The sound of weapons being shifted and men changing into fighting stances carry in the wind around us, amplifying it. The rain is coming down harder now as these boys fight over the metaphorical sandbox.

"Boys! Stop!" I hiss at a sharp pain going through me. "Look, just bring the old man out here, okay? And let's keep this neutral ground! Put your weapons down!"

Duma's nose flares, emphasizing his nose piercing. With a sneer, he nods his head and his warriors do as they're told. *Sheesh.*

"You still hold my men as prisoners, war chief." Gamba snarls this statement as he continues to stand in a fighting stance. No fear in his eyes. He actually looks like he's hoping for a fight.

"Dammit Duma, just let them go! There are more important matters right now!"

Duma's nostrils flare again on a big exhale, his jaw flexing in anger. After a few silent moments, he finally responds.

"It will be done for you, my Juri. Chiku! Bring the prisoners out of their hut. Jomo, go find Kwame!"

Gamba straightens up with a cocky grin as he continues to stare at Duma in challenge. He won this battle. Chiemko and Gary are standing side by side in front of the Matalo'toa army that followed us, also staring at Duma in challenge.

The sound of scuffling feet comes towards us as a few beaten and bloody Namwana tribe members limp towards Gamba's group of warriors.

Duma turns me back to face his village as the old man slowly walks towards the group with his wooden staff being used as a cane. How is this man still alive? He looks frail and old as time with sun worn skin making him look like dark leather.

"Duma, I have told you that your destiny moves and crosses

with hers, the light spear that hails from the skies." He's shaking his cane to the sky as emphasis, his face all seriousness.

"What else do the old words and tales say, Kwame? What must we do? She needs to return to her lands to heal or there will be no destiny!"

Kwame sounds crazy when he just mumbles the same phrase over and over, like a broken record. His face is serious as he stares at me, and it's kind of creeping me out.

"It is said the lands will be united by the strongest of light spears that hail from the skies. The last tribal war; the war to end all wars and unite our people as one. To finally bring peace to the lands!"

Everyone around is looking at everyone else because no one knows what to make of it. *How do I get back?*

"Kwame, what of my talisman?"

Kwame stops his repetition when the word talisman comes out of my mouth. Thunder cracks in the skies and we're all getting drenched standing out here in the rain, but none of the warriors seem to care, so I won't either.

"There is something to that. I feel it. But there is nothing that has been said in the old stories that I remember."

Let's hope the old man remembers everything he's been saying because if his memory is going now, how can I trust anything that has come out of his mouth thus far?

Duma stares at Kwame with a stony expression, and I can tell the wheels are turning. When a decision is mentally made, he walks me towards Gamba's old prisoner hut. Ducking into the doorway with me, Duma calls for a warrior to bring a grass mat. Once the mat is placed on the ground, he lowers me gently onto it. The jostling of my wounds and knife that's still sticking out makes me hiss in pain. Duma's jaw clenches and he bares his teeth like he's feeling my pain right along with me.

Suddenly, the hut shrinks as all the war chiefs force themselves inside as well. *Gosh, as if I don't have enough blood splattered on me already.*

"No fighting!" Hissing in pain again, all the men around me stand in silence, baring teeth at each other without a word. Everyone except for Gary, who is solely staring at me with a fire in his eyes I haven't seen since we first appeared back in this place. His white skin is coated in dust and blood, and I'm not sure if any of what I'm seeing is his. The rain has washed some of the blood off the guys, but not all, leaving streaks of stains behind.

"Call the village women to help clean her wounds."

The sound of someone outside moving lets me know they are following orders from Duma's booming voice. The rain sounds like it's steadily slowing down outside with the beat of the rhythm on the roof of the hut.

The boys are forced into the same proximity as a couple of the village women come in with bowls of water and rags. The rain washed away most of the blood that splattered on me, luckily, so they shouldn't have much to clean. None of them turn away when the women clean my intimate areas and breasts. *Thanks guys.* Once done, the women leave and the tension inside the hut rises again — so thick you can cut it with a butter knife.

Gary moves to my side and the other men growl in their disagreement. Ignoring their threats, Gary looks directly at the choker on my neck, trying to figure out a way to unlock its secrets. His ocean blue eyes stand out even more against his dirty, blood-coated skin. I can see cuts on his body, some deep enough to still be oozing blood freely. I wonder what his back wound looks like?

"I have no clue, Gary." I know he's trying to help figure things out.

"We'll figure it out. I'm too selfish and love you too damn much to let you die on me."

How…sweet, stalker boy.

"I'm so tired."

"Do we remove the knife?"

"It is a Mata knife. I should kill you right here."

"It was a Namwana spear that struck her leg. I should kill *you*."

"Enough!"

"So you say, Chintkku. But it is your very people who are the most bloodthirsty of all."

I didn't realize my eyes drifted close, but knowing another battle is about to break out in this little hut has me on edge. My eyes pop back open and I am staring every man here down with a glare that would cut them all right on the spot. *I am damn tired of this shit!*

Keeping my voice calm, I issue my own command to these men. "All of you, out. Now."

"There must be one to remain by your side if you come in need of something. Your voice may not carry through the walls of the hut."

I see what you are doing, reasonable Chiemko, you sly dog.

"Okay fine, everyone out but Chiemko."

"I'm not fucking leaving you out of my sight, I don't trust this island bastard."

Fuck! I can't take all this bickering!

"Fine! Chiemko and Gary stay. The rest of you, go! YES, THAT MEANS YOU TOO DUMA! NO BLOODSHED!"

Both Duma and Gamba look so offended, it's cute and I might have laughed if the pain from yelling at these fools didn't start up again. They both stare daggers at each other before they leave, one after another like pouting babies. *I'm so damn tired.*

Gary and Chiemko give each other nasty looks too before they decide to compromise and sit down beside me on opposite sides of the mat. I'm honestly done with these guys right now, I'm so damn tired! My eyes start to flutter again, and I succumb to the coming darkness, listening to the pitter pattering of the rain coming down on the roof of the hut.

THIRTY-FIVE

Juri has fallen asleep. This day has been a trying one for us all. Many warriors have been killed and there are losses from all of our tribes. The cuts on my body bring me sharp pain, but I remain by her side. Staring at her, I see her breaths slowing by the rise and fall of her chest. Good, her body needs rest to fully heal from her wounds. Then something strange happens. Right before my eyes I see her body becoming the mist — like the wet air you breathe before the sky cries. Something inside of me is telling me I need to touch her — that string that ties me to her is being pulled again, *tightly*.

Quick movements before me have my body ready for battle, but it is only Gary who puts both of his hands on Juri's shoulder as if he can keep her from disappearing. I am reminded of the moment Juri left me on that boat during the last rainfall. I do the same as Gary and put both of my hands on her knees to stay away from her injuries.

It seems like only a few moments when my body feels light, the same way it feels when I jump off my boat right before I hit the waters.

Now it feels like the suns are being stabbed into my chest — it burns from the inside but I do not let go of my Juri. The pain makes me hiss and my eyes close to try and control it.

As fast as it came, the moment is gone — like it did not happen at all. Opening my eyes, I look around as the blood pumping in my ears becomes louder and louder. I do not know where I am. I do not recognize anything in my surroundings — I have not seen these things before.

"We're back." The one called Gary knows where we are. So this is Juri's land?

"This is where you come from? And my Juri?" What is under me is the softest thing I have ever been on. It is a bright white with a lot of fabric or softened hide. I am unsure. What beast has fur this pure?

Gary is looking over Juri, and so I do the same. She is still in the clothes I fashioned for her when I found her on the mainland. But the wounds are gone. *It is impossible.*

"Where are her wounds?" *Where are ours?* I no longer feel the sharp pain of my battle wounds.

"Looks like teleporting back brought her back the way she left. Whole. The same goes for us."

I do not understand, but I am glad for it. I am glad my Juri is no longer in danger.

"Juri is still sleeping, so I'm going to make use of my time. I'm going to shower; you can have it after me."

Gary walks into a doorway of a connected hut. Is this her hut? The walls are not made of wood. It is whole, with no light to come in but through a straight hole made with four sides in the wall on the opposite side that you can see through. Similar to my hut back home, but not. There is something else that covers this hole but it does not block your sight from what is on the other side. What my eyes see makes me want to be prepared to fight, in case something or someone else can see inside of Juri's home. *If we can see out, then surely others can see in?*

The sound of water falling like hard rain against rocks reaches my ears. This must be what Gary means by shower. How does he control the water from the skies?

The sound of water falling stops and there is a small thunder coming from the room. Gary returns with something white around his lower body. *Why is everything so white?*

"Look, I don't fucking like you, but we both need to take care of Juri right now. Come over here and let me show you how to work this shower. We'll take turns watching over her until she wakes up."

This is a sound plan. I will need him on my side while I am here. There may not be things I understand, and that may put Juri in more danger. I must make my enemy my friend in case there are other enemies I have not prepared for.

Once Gary shows me how to do this shower in the extra room, I clean the dried blood off my body and watch it go down a small hole in the ground. *Where does it go?*

Grabbing the white fabric I saw Gary with, I find it is just as soft as the bed we fell on. Dropping the fabric onto the floor, I return to the room with Juri sleeping. She remains in the same position with her eyes closed, but I can see her chest moving with her breaths which settles my heart. It aches to know if she is okay, but she must need this sleep.

"Alright, look. While we're here, I am going to be giving the orders. I still have some clothes here, I'm going to go to my apartment and grab some clothes for you so you don't end up walking around this place naked and run into someone you shouldn't. Stay by Juri's side until I get back."

This fool thinks he can control me. I do not care for coverings, but I am also not going to leave Juri vulnerable like this. I will stay by her side. I lift my lip his way to show him I heard his command and for him to leave us. Gary lifts his hand in the air and folds his fingers down, but not his middle one. I do not know what this means, but I know he means offense. Making a show of biting the air, I bare my teeth at him in challenge.

"Whatever fucker, I'll be back. Stay here."

He gives my Juri one last longing look before he leaves her hut through another door. There are too many doors here and I do not know where they lead. It is better I stay right by Juri, so she does not lose herself looking for me when she wakes.

Climbing onto the bed she lies on, my knees sink down like the sand beneath my feet back on my island. Unlike the sand, it tries to push me back, but my weight is too much for it to fight. Is it alive then? I should protect Juri closely, in case the bed pushes her. I slowly make my way over until I am on top of her. My weight should hold her down since my Juri is a small female. When my skin touches hers, a slow fire burns inside of me. I almost lost her. My chest feels tight from the image that replays in my mind. Her warmth surrounds me and calms my soul but only by a little. My curiosity at this ... will of the Gods to put someone like her in my path has my hands roaming her skin to make sure she is real.

Why is all of this happening? Why would the Gods need two worlds to meddle in when there are enough troubles in one?

Her skin is as soft as the bed beneath us. This is where she belongs — a place where there are no wars and bloodshed at every turn. She belongs in a place where she can wake up and rest easy knowing that the day will only bring simple tithings.

But the beast instead of me rages at the thought of her being away from us. It is the Gods' fault for putting her in my path because now I will never let her go. My hands continue to roam the plains of her body, causing my own to heat up from the inside. *What is it about you, Juri? How can something so small and fragile calm a warrior's soul?* It is not as hot as when we left the Chintkku hut, but I feel it all the same — a tension between us, despite her eyes remaining closed.

Her skin is smooth, soft and woundless. Thank the blessed suns she no longer needs a healer. When my body is fully on top of hers, I touch her necklace and take a closer look. Is it this, then? I heard her talk to the old Chintkku sight seeker about a talisman — the talisman that makes her travel to different worlds. Turning it in my hands and staring at it closely, it looks very old. I do not recognize the pattern carved into it. The details are rich with life and stories that I do not recall hearing about around the fires as a child.

Something catches my eye and my fingers stop moving. Leaning in, I stare closely and see the shape of what looks like the sun and moon coming together. Similar to our past, the images show two beings on different sides.

Did this come from our lands? It seems so similar to the tales of our father of the skies and our mother of the ground. But how did Juri find it here — in a land so far away and so different?

Juri moans and my fear of hurting her has me slowly crawling away. The bed does not push her off as I suspect it would. Instead, it continues to cradle her like a babe. Once I am sure she is okay, I begin to explore around her hut.

There are so many strange things here. Why must there be so many obstacles inside of a home? *Perhaps there are more than one that lives here.* Growling under my breath, I refuse to believe this.

Trying to ground myself, I take deep breaths in and out. My Juri smells of a rare flower that hides among the plants in the suns — the scent only to be carried by the breeze. If you are close enough to it, you will find the luck of smelling such a sweet smell.

This entire hut smells only of her.

This is my Juri, a soul carried by the breeze where only the lucky are able to smell and feel her. I am a lucky man to have the Gods choose her for me. My heart always settles when we are together. I miss her lips on mine. It burns me to know it could have been one of my men to have almost ended her life because of a false step that tumbled him on top of her. The thought of another man on top of her makes me anger and rage. My beast inside is wanting to kill again.

Is Juri right about us? — Those of us from the land of nothing but bloodshed. The Matalo'toa have lived peacefully on our isolated island away from barbarians like the Chintkku and Namwana. *But yet you found yourself on a warpath in the mainlands.*

Walking around the hut, my eyes land on objects that sit inside of a wooden tomb. Crouching down to take a better look, my confusion slowly disappears into old childhood memories around the fire. The images and glyphics on them remind me of something I've seen before. My mind flashes back to memories of the elders who used to draw in the sand while they told stories to the children.

It is an art that has slowly been lost in the generations. The elders mentioned that it was a form of communication without actually speaking. Is this a sign from the Gods? Looking over my shoulder, I watch as Juri continues to rest on her bed of white.

She looks like she is floating in the skies and clouds — the image of a goddess herself.

GARY

It feels like we've been gone ages and yet not that long at the same time. My apartment is only a couple doors away from Juri, though she never realized it.

"Gary! I haven't seen you for a while. You go on vacation or something?"

"Yeah, something like that."

"Someone came by to see you and I had to tell them you weren't home."

I had hidden a set of keys in a secret location, if ever I found myself needing to change out of my clothes for whatever reason. Unlocking the door, the neighbor continues with his ramblings.

"Yeah, they looked like detectives. But I told them that you were a good guy and that you were always coming and going to work, that's about it."

My ears sharpen but I keep my expression calm.

"Oh yeah? Thanks man. I appreciate it."

"Of course."

Stepping inside my apartment, I don't wait for our goodbyes when I slam the door shut and lock it. That's the problem with living in an apartment. Everyone is all up in your business. The only damn reason why I even chose to come here was for Juri, and Juri alone.

Tossing my keys onto my side table by the door, I continue into my bedroom to find come clothes that will fit that fucker that's still in Juri's home. I need him alive at this point, if only to watch over my girl while I have things to do.

Speaking of things to do.

Digging around, I find one of my spare phones in the bottom of my dresser. Scrolling through the screen, I see that I have about ten percent of battery left on the charge. How long were we gone? Tapping the screen, I put the phone up to my ear and continue to grab clothes out of the other drawers.

"Pantom Cybernetics."

"Transfer me to floor five for Anderson's office please."

"Please hold."

The hold music grates my nerves. It's too fucking cheery for how the building sucks the life out of you.

"Hi, you've reached the office of Mark Anderson. How may I assist you?"

"Is this Amy or Jessica?"

"This is Amy. How may I assist you?"

"I'm calling in for Juri Chakrabarti."

"Is there something wrong? Juri hasn't been at work for the last couple of days. Is she okay?"

"She's fine. Look. Let Anderson know that she recently got married and will be taking a little hiatus for the unforeseen future."

"What? She got married? When — this doesn't make any sense. I was just with her the other day."

"Yeah, she told me about that. Anyway, let Anderson know she probably won't be coming back and he's going to have to find a replacement." No matter what happens, I'm not letting her go — Not when we've come this far together. I can't wait to get back to her, to taste her again, to stick my fucking dick in her so deep she wont be able to walk for days.

"—hello? Are you still there? Who did she get married to?"

"Thanks for your time." I end the call and hit redial.

"Pantom Cybernetics."

"Transfer me to the IT department, please."

"Please hold."

"IT."

"Yeah, this is Gary from floor five."

"Gary? Where the hell have you been man? You were a no call no show and the boss is pissed."

"I had an emergency come up with family. I'm going to need to call in for the next few days as well."

"Fuck, and you want me to give the big guy the news, right? You're an asshole, Gary. Why don't you just come and tell him yourself? I don't want him to kill the messenger."

"It's your damn job, dick. Just tell the boss my message, alright?"

"Yeah, whatever. Hey, while you were gone, there were some detectives that came by to question everybody."

What are the chances of hearing about detectives twice in one day?

"Yeah? What about?" Playing it cool, my mind is already going through the planned out scenarios I had in my head with kidnapping Juri and marrying her on a deserted island off the coast of Jamaica anyway.

"You remember Jack and Chris?"

Of course, it would catch up with me. I just didn't think it would catch up this fast. Maybe it was a good thing I ended up teleporting wherever with Juri that day.

"Yeah, kinda. I didn't talk to them much."

"Yeah, they were a bunch of douches anyway. But anyhow, they both haven't shown up for work in a while which is why the boss was so pissed when you were a no call no show."

"What do I have to do with them?" I've learned that you need to feed people what they need to hear in order for them to respond the way you need them to respond. Manipulation tactics. They've come in handy way too much in my life living with my father and having to convince everyone everything was okay at home.

"I feel you, man. I'm starting to think those two ran off together. That's probably why they were so close, right? But what do I know?"

The perfect alibi — at least for a little while longer.

"You know what? I always wondered why they were so close. Anyway, tell the boss my message. I don't know when I'm coming back yet."

"The hell? Why don't you —"

I end the call and toss the phone on the bed. I'm tired of that Cybernetics building anyway. Thinking about the asshole boss who piles all the cases on our desks while he sits in his and eats all day — I should have cut that fuckers head off when I had the chance. *Maybe I still can.* Shoving everything into a backpack, I exit the front door and lock everything up.

I need to stop leaving a trail behind me. Those detectives are already sniffing a little too close. Maybe it's a good thing there's another way to escape this stupid life.

...

THIRTY-SIX

CHIEMKO

A whimper comes out of her. She must be lost in her dreams. Does she dream of the bloodshed our tribes have brought to our lands? Of the knife that pierced her delicate soft skin? Quickly walking back to her side, I watch as her body twitches and her face frowns. I cannot bear it, she deserves to feel good and not to be in pain. I will do this for her — my Juri, with much pleasure.

Climbing back onto the bed, I lay my weight down on her and rub my head against her shoulder. It isn't fair of us to pull you into a battle as old as the tales of the beginning. The Gods must have laughed as they threw you into the pit to be devoured by beasts like us. The thought of the others taking her away from me spurs my jealousy. Why have I been sentenced to such a life of solitude, then given the biggest temptation only to have to almost be taken from me once more?

Pushing my lips to hers, I demonstrate my love and hunger for her through our kiss as my hands roam the soft round curves of her side, making sure that the wound is really gone as my eyes have told me.

She takes a moment, still struggling in her dreams before her soul relaxes into my body and molding herself to me as if she feels my call. Her lips begin to slowly dance with mine and I know I have woken her. But it is no matter, now that I have started, the fire is burning hotter and I cannot stop. When her tongue enters my mouth, I move mine towards her. We are connected and my heart aches for her — it aches to become one again. I have never felt this way about any female before, it is addicting and brings on my battle instincts at the same time.

When she moans into my mouth, my hips thrust against her, making her legs open wider for me. Things are becoming out of my control — my body moving on instincts as old as time. My hands move from the curves of her side to push her lower covering away as I crawl down. *I need her; I need her now.* It is a stubborn thing, this covering, as my Juri has very appealing round hips. I don't wish to do it, but I must take my lips off of her to grab the covering with both of my hands and remove it completely. Juri's lids open halfway, showing me her eyes the color of light spears. The look she is wearing on her face makes my cock harden more than it already has.

Is this what it's like for all males? To hunger this much and feel like it's never enough?

When I finally throw the offending material aside, Juri takes off her top covering and now lays bare before me like an offering. I groan at the sight before me — if the Gods trick me, I will have to hunt them and kill them myself. Closing my eyes, I take a deep breath to hold my beast in, who wants to eat her like his last meal. My face is close enough to her center between her legs that I give in and do just that. Her smell is driving me mad, the smell of a woman in heat. My beast craves it. When my tongue licks up her wetness from her bottom lips, Juri's legs open wider for my shoulders and I hear another moan in her voice.

JURI

What a way to wake up. I don't feel as tired as I did after the battle. The softness under me tells me we've returned to my bedroom, and waking up to Chiemko on top of me is the best thing a girl can ask for. When did I become afraid to wake up alone when I've been doing so much of it in my life?

This particular time, I'm glad Chiemko saved me from myself. Nightmares were plaguing my mind, everything was red and the only thing I could see was a sea of dead faces staring back at me accusingly. My heart was breaking for the guilt I felt for what I've caused. I'm sorry, I'm so sorry. My face heats up from the moment of weakness I'm having, my eyes beginning to burn with that tell tale sign of tears pricking at them. Taking a shuddering breath, I try to control my emotions and just get lost in the moment.

Chiemko brought me out of the darkness of my nightmares with his kiss and is now eating my pussy like he's done it all his life. Though from the conversations I've had with him in the past, it sounds like he's never been attached to a woman before. My thoughts scatter when his tongue flicks and circles my clit, making me lose my train of thought with a gasp. My hips begin to writhe towards him, silently asking for more and he does not disappoint. He is really good at reading my body language because he starts concentrating on my clit with gusto the more I squirm.

I hear the front door of my apartment open and close with a bang, but it doesn't stop Chiemko one bit. He's lost in what he's doing to me. Almost like he knows his time is running out, he climbs me quickly and shoves his hard dick inside of me. *Holy shit.* His thrust almost made my hip pop. He's clearly very excited for this moment and you know what? So am I. Caressing Chiemko's face, he brings his head down to place another kiss on my lips. His mouth moves along my jaw and he's starting to suckle on my neck as his hips continue to thrust in a dangerous intensity. I can't help but widen my legs even more so he doesn't pop them out of their sockets with his efforts.

"You fucker!"

Gary?

Chiemko only chuckles into my neck as he continues thrusting harder inside of me, creating a very delicious friction. *So naughty.*

"Fuck if you're the only one who's going to have this moment. Turn her over on top of you."

Chiemko does just that. *What, are they friends now or something?* In this new position, Chiemko pulls me into his embrace and he kisses me senseless with his new found skills, making me forget about Gary being in the same room for a moment.

A hand pushes my body into Chiemko even harder as another hand spreads one of my asscheeks. *What the hell is going on?* I groan into Chiemko's kiss as a tongue probes my back entrance making me whimper against Chiemko's mouth. *It shouldn't feel this good, should it?* The slight flexing of Chiemko's abs grinds his dick inside of me and his happy trail of hair rubs against my clit in the most perfect way. I'm getting lost in all the sensations around me — from below and from behind.

"Mmm." Gary's hum while he's tonguing my ass makes me tighten my muscles. It doesn't stop him though. With a hard bite to my asscheek, Gary smears the wetness from my pussy into my ass with a finger. Using his tongue to make a wet trail towards my lower spine, Gary sticks another finger into my ass in a slow thrusting motion. It's starting to feel good and I don't want him to stop, becoming hungry for whatever he has planned. Chiemko distracts me again as he trails his kisses along my jaw towards my shoulder — the same shoulder where Gamba marked me. I hear a growl escape him before he bites over the old mark, making my body tense and my ass clench around Gary's fingers.

Gary sticks a third finger into my ass and starts scissoring them, opening me up wider as he places his whole body over my back, covering me in his warmth. Peppering kisses on my other shoulder, I can feel him pull his fingers out and replace it with the head of his cock. *Am I really doing this?* Two virile men wanting my attention so badly they're fighting to get inside of me. *Hell yes, I'm doing this.* I'm going to seize the day. I flex my ass towards him, dragging Chiemko's shaft out of me a few inches.

Gary's voice is gruff as he whispers against my ear with his warm breath. "Fuck yes, I knew you were fucking dirty Juri. I'm going to bury my cock deep in your ass since this greedy fucker over here already filled your pussy."

Why is that so hot? Gary and his stupid stalking — his stupid sexual explorations with me. Maybe I secretly enjoyed it on the inside after that second time together and never allowed myself to voice it to the front of my mind. It doesn't matter now; we're doing this because I say we are.

Chiemko is sucking on my nipples and biting them while his hand plays with my other breast. I feel renewed. I feel brazen. After what I felt like was a near death experience, all my filters and walls are down.

"Shut the fuck up and stick your dick in me Gary."

He groans into my shoulder before he bites down and pushes the head of his cock, that's been teasing me with his precum this whole time, beyond my ring of muscle. *I feel so fucking full.* Chiemko groans into my breast as he starts to increase his pace.

Gary, not to be outdone, does the same. In this game of tug of war, these boys are wrecking my body in the most delicious way.

Maybe it's good they're jealous of each other then, if I get to reap the benefits.

I feel pleasure climbing the metaphorical cliff and my orgasm is getting so close it almost hurts as much as it feels good. My pussy is starting to pulsate while they're both fucking me like it's *me* they hate and not the other guy. My mind clouds over, lost in the haze of lust and desire, as I imagine what this scenario would be like with Duma and Gamba. *Oh my god.* The image is too much and my climax hits me like a freight train.

"Ahhh! Don't stop!" The waves are just as strong as the initial climax itself. The guys do as I say and start fucking me harder. If this is what it's always going to be like, then I'll be happy to cause a little mischief between them all.

Chiemko is the first to finish as he groans into my other breast, biting down on my nipple and making me moan.

"Fuck!"

Gary's cock starts to expand and throb in time with his thrusts, his balls hitting me with every push. I can feel the hot jets of his cum splashing the inside of me and my body flushes from everything we've done. I push Chiemko's face off my breast so that I can lay myself down on top of him more comfortably. Gary's a deadweight on top of my back, sandwiching me between two hot bodies as his dick continues to throb from his climax.

Holy crap. That was wicked and wrong on so many levels — but feels so damn good and so right.

We lay there for a long while, and my eyes feel like they want to drift off to sleep again even though I just woke up. The boys are drifting to sleep as well because Chiemko's breaths have evened out from what I can tell with my cheek snuggling into his chest. Gary is snuggling closer to me from behind, rubbing my shoulders languidly without bothering to pull himself out of my ass. Everything he's doing to me right now feels really damn good and I mentally give him brownie points for the impromptu massage.

My last thought before succumbing to the darkness is: I hope Duma doesn't kill Gamba while we're gone.

THIRTY-SEVEN

JURI

One of the boys is stirring, and it's starting to wake me up. I think it's coming from below me. He's so warm and I don't want to open my eyes just yet, so I snuggle a little closer.

"We have returned."

"Fuck, stop moving, I'm still sleeping."

I can feel hands are caressing and playing with the side of my breasts — breasts that are currently being squished into Chiemko's chest. I can feel a hard dick pressing against the crack of my ass and I think it's Gary. I better get him off me before he decides to go another round.

"Get off me Gary, let me get up."

He chuckles into my right shoulder like he knows what I'm thinking, kissing it, but continues to let his hands roam, anyway.

Chiemko moves from under me gently, and suddenly Gary's weight is removed off my back like a bandaid being ripped off. The sound of flesh hitting flesh makes me finally blink my eyes wide open and look behind me. *Shit.*

Gary's got blood trickling from his mouth and Chiemko is in a fighting stance, looking like he's about to throw another punch. Is that Chiemko's knife in Gary's hand? Looking back at Chiemko, I see a bloody red streak on his thigh.

"Boys, stop! It is way too early for this. I forbid you from any more bloodshed!"

The ground rumbles and two extra bodies enter the hut we appeared in, making it feel really crammed. Was this the same hut we were in last time?

Pushing myself up into a sitting position, I'm quickly lifted by two strong arms banding around my midsection. The searing kiss Gamba gives me tells me he didn't think he would see me again. *Poor thing.* I kiss him back just as ferociously because I did miss him and his cockiness very much. I still don't know how this stupid necklace works and I am almost afraid to go to sleep now since I always seem to wake up in a different place. *Is that the secret?*

"My female, I thought I lost you again. I would have killed that Mata warrior, but he was gone as well." *You say the sweetest things.*

When Gamba's tongue starts dueling with mine, I hear a growl come from behind him. I know that growl very well. Duma is about to shed some blood. Pulling my face away from Gamba before someone gets hurt, I look over his shoulder at my brooding war chief and give him a smile.

"Duma, I've missed you! Put me down, Gamba." I have to slap him a few times on the shoulder hard, but Gamba grumbles and does as I ask so that I can run into Duma's waiting arms, giving him a passionate kiss as well. A girl can get used to this kind of welcome.

All the other men are grumbling and growling behind me but there are no more sounds of flesh hitting flesh or fights, so I keep on telling Duma how much I missed him through my kiss.

When he finally pulls away, he puts his forehead against mine and his nostrils flare slightly from breathing me in. I missed his smell too, the smell of comfort and protection. I lean in and sniff his neck. Duma groans and I laugh at the effect I have on him.

"Put me down Duma, you can't hog me all to yourself."

"Yes I can."

"No, you can't. Down, now."

With a growl under his breath, he does as I ask so that I can turn around to face the rest of the men in the hut.

They all stare at my stomach and thighs, where the wounds should have been. Nods of approval go around and I find it funny that this is the only thing they can all agree upon.

Clapping my hands together to get their attention since they seem to have become distracted by my nudity, I give them all glares when their eyes meet mine. At least Chiemko looks sheepish.

"Boys. Stop staring at my boobs. Now, what are we going to do? I can't disappear again. And if there is more bloodshed, who's to say I won't be hit again, hmmm? You guys catching my drift here? If you guys keep warring with each other, and I am hit — again, who's to say I don't get stuck on the other side when you guys decide that's the only way to fix my injuries?"

Everyone is quiet and still staring at my breasts, but I can see the mental wheels turning in their heads. One can only expect so much.

"Our tribes have been fighting since the beginning."

"What does that matter? You don't need to fight now." What kind of excuse is that, anyway?

"You are mine, my Juri, I fight for your honor."

"Oh, and I do not? The Gods chose her for me."

"By the blessed suns, what is wrong with you two? She is my female."

"I'm standing right here, fuckers."

The men start bickering again, staring each other down and sticking their chests out. I'm not going to wait around for the dick measuring contest, so I grab the fabric that's hanging in front of the hut door, design a makeshift cover for myself and walk out. I can hear them still arguing and I don't even think they realize I'm gone yet. *How sad.*

Seems I've come back to the Chintkku village, and the rain has stopped. The air still smells like rain and the wet earth makes it feel kind of nasty to walk on barefoot. But my time with Chiemko and Gamba have changed how sensitive I am to these things now.

Wandering around, my eyes search for the oldest guy with a long white beard. Some of the women villagers greet me with smiles as they go about their duties. Baskets full of what looks like dried meat and berries are carried over the head of one of the girls. The sight and smell of it reminds me that I do feel kind of hungry. Catching up to her, I ask her for some and she kindly gives me a handful.

"Of course, anything for the war chief's bride."

Bride, huh? I didn't even get a ceremony or anything. I'm going to have to get on Duma about that one.

Grubbing down on a meat stick, I continue the search for the sight seeker.

Maybe it's this one. Scratching at the hut, I push the cloth aside to peek in only to catch someone's ass pounding and legs in the air. *Eep!*

Running as far away from the hut as I can, I try a few more. After scratching a good handful of wrong huts, I was finally given the direction to Kwame's hut by a kind young Chintkku male. I don't even bother to scratch outside of his home when I get there because I just bet he was expecting me.

Moving the fabric aside, I call out. "Hello? Kwame? Are you home?" I let the fabric fall back down behind me and it immediately becomes extra dark inside.

"Ah! The one who hails from the skies has returned. By my eyes, you look healed." I can hear him moving around but my eyes are still adjusting to the change in lighting. "So the healer did his job well. I do not even see any markings."

When my eyes finally adjust, I can see the old man getting up from wherever he was sitting to walk towards me. When he's close enough, he pokes me in the thigh with his boney finger. *This is kind of awkward.*

Trying to politely swat his hand away from my thigh, I ask, "Kwame, how do I stop all this from happening? I don't want to go to sleep and wake up somewhere else I don't recognize. This has to end. How do I work this talisman?"

My fingers automatically start rubbing against the carved designs as I mention it. Now that I think of it, it never crossed my mind that the habit of fingering it for comfort has started to die down over the course of coming back and forth to these lands. Is this a sign?

"There is a tale I have heard, of a time after the old wars. The war chiefs had a spot they all gathered, to talk of peace." *No way.* "They were never able to talk far because bloodshed always soon followed their gatherings. You might find something there." *Of course.*

Old man Kwame is rubbing his beard while he's lost in thought. How the heck am I supposed to know where this spot is?

"Where is this spot that you mentioned?"

He stops rubbing his beard and looks like he's staring into nothingness for a few seconds. *Is he okay?*

"Kwame?"

"It is a cave between the Chintkku and the Namwana tribe, by a river. No one has ventured there in a long time." He turns to me and there's a weird look in his eyes. "Be wary, female, we know not what has remained there."

Creepiness aside, why does this place sound so familiar?

"You are not going anywhere alone, female. We are coming with you."

Shadows cover both myself and Kwame as all the guys start piling in this poor old man's hut that's even smaller than the last hut we were in. Turning around, I look over them and see that a few are sporting some trickles of blood in places and bruises on others. The cuts don't look too deep or life threatening, no guts are hanging out, so I'm not worried.

"Well, I'm glad we're all alive to join this meeting at least. Have you boys settled your dick measuring contest?"

"Is this what your people do?"

"I already know I win that battle."

"Not when my knife is done with you, Namwana."

"What the hell is wrong with you two?"

I can't take these guys anywhere, not like this.

"If you guys don't make an effort to stop killing each other, no one is coming with me but Kwame."

That shut everyone up quickly. Who knew I just needed to threaten them, hey?

Turning to Kwame, I see him smoothing down his beard again but with eyes full of sparkle. He's standing up a bit straighter and…is he blushing? *Dear lord, not you too.*

Turning back around to face the guys, I see them still staring each other down, but no one is voicing any concerns or disagreements. This is progress.

"So what will it be? Speak now, because I am about to go to this cave, with or without you."

"You will need us to guide you, little Juri. It is where I found you last, tied up in ropes and beaten."

A cough sounds from Gary, and we all look at him. He's pretending to look anywhere but at me. The bloodthirsty aura coming off the other guys is making the air thick again, almost choking me. Frowning at Gary, I'm just going to ignore that little…blip in our relationship and come back to that later. I have more important matters to think about right now.

Duma is starting to growl like a feral animal at Gary, and he's baring his teeth back in challenge. All of these guys are like animals — their instincts driving their responses.

"I'll get back to you on that, Gary. Don't think I've forgotten." The moment the words leave my mouth, all of the guys turn to look at him with fury in their eyes. *Oops.*

Duma pounces on him from behind, while Gamba sweeps his feet, making him fall flat on his face in Kwame's hut. With one knee pushing him towards the ground, Duma pulls one of Gary's arms back, about to break the damn thing in half while adding a twist. Is Duma trying to bite Gary's fingers off? Chiemko quickly maneuvers himself on one knee, grabbing Gary's neck and pulling him back while placing his knife under his chin. Some blood is already dripping down from the contact point.

Gamba has a sinister smile on his face, looking as if he's just letting the other boys have their murder foreplay before he takes his own time with Gary.

Is the old man laughing right now?

Clapping my hands as hard as I can to catch their attention, I clear my throat before things escalate. "Alright then!" Once their eyes are on me, I clear my throat again. "Lead us, War chief Duma!"

Even though I told him to lead, I end up being the first to leave the hut in hopes that the fresh air will cool the boys down. As I expected, they all follow me out — even Kwame. *Oh dear.*

"Kwame, are you joining us on this trip?" He smiles wide and I see he's missing some teeth but his eyes still sparkle with mirth. I bet he's just hoping the guys mess up so he can swoop in for the chance. I give the guys a look that says this is exactly what's going to happen if they don't follow the rules.

"We'll take care of it from here, old man. Why don't you go back into your hut to rest. Juri will be much protected with warriors surrounding her."

Brownie points to Chiemko for his quick response. These other boys better try harder if they want to catch up.

THIRTY-EIGHT

JURI

With Duma's insistence, we gather weapons, food and whatever other supplies we need even though it didn't sound like the cave was that far of a trek. But it was another thing all the guys agreed upon, so I just went with it. What do I know? I'm just a girl from the city.

We've been walking eastward for the past hour and I think I can hear water running in a stream. We must be close; I swear I've been here before — with Gamba to be exact. The guys don't let me walk in the front, but rather they've created a barricade around me. Even Gary is strapped down with weapons and a Chinttku loincloth. His bicep straps hold knives given to him by Chiemko. Gamba seems to favor his bow and arrows, while Duma only has a spear with no shield. Duma is a beast of a man though, I'm sure his body is his weapon and a shield in itself.

They seemed to have cleaned up whatever scuffle they had when I left them in the first hut. Some strips of cloth are tied in random areas to stop the bleeding wounds, while other areas are left to the elements. Nothing is actively bleeding out profusely. It could have been worse; everyone at least still has their heads. I heard the Namwana warriors who were milling outside the village talking about Duma's perchance of putting heads on spikes as warnings around the perimeter of the village. I should be more upset about that, I know I should, but Duma has a hard time holding in his volatile emotions. Heads on spikes is just a coping mechanism, at least that's what I tell myself. It's probably what made him war chief for the tribe, his willingness to go the distance in order to secure victory.

Gamba's tale weaves into my mind. Could it be that Duma's volatile emotions stem from the fact that he's connected to the original children on this land? It would explain a lot. And what of Chiemko — a warrior from an isolated island. Is this why he's more easy going in some ways?

When we reach the opening of the cave, the group stops and stares. I try to peek behind Duma's back, but the bodies on each side of me make it hard to get a good look. A tap on my ass makes me squeal and I turn to find Gary trying to stifle a grin while not looking at me. *The bastard.*

When he does turn to look at me, he mouths, "be good," and boy does it do something to me. Who knew I'd like this kind of stuff? Well, maybe if I dated more, I would have found out. Seems, the universe had other plans for me and didn't want me to die alone as a spinster. Four men is more than enough to keep me occupied. Keeping them from killing each other is a full-time job in itself.

What would mother think about me now? I wonder how my family is doing.

Duma mumbles something towards Gamba and it seems the boys decided on dividing the team in two. Cheimko and Gary both come to stand at my left and right once the other two go into the dark entrance first.

Things are beginning to feel a little ominous. There is still sunlight out, but I can't see beyond four to five feet inside the cave. I wonder how far it goes?

Gamba jogs back out and waves us in. I let Chiemko and Gary walk a foot ahead of me, not wanting any weird creatures to jump out unexpectedly. The entrance of the cave is hard and jagged but smooth enough to not pierce the bottom of my feet when I walk over it. It smells strange and I can put my finger on it, but it is something I've smelled before because it tickles a memory. Whatever light that is able to come inside is enough to show some drawings on the walls. We're still within three feet beyond the entrance and all the images are catching my curiosity. They're so faded that it's hard to make out.

Lifting my hands to touch one of the pictures that looks like a sun or moon, Chiemko grabs my hand abruptly, startling me. I'm about to ask him what his problem is when the necklace I'm wearing begins heating up and burning my skin. The whimper that comes out of me doesn't help speed my hands behind my neck, trying to take the makeshift choker off. Squealing, the sound of my voice bounces off the walls and the other two guys come running towards me. Everyone is trying to figure out what I'm doing. I probably look like I'm performing some crazy ritual. It would be kind of funny if this thing didn't burn so much.

It's Gary who figures it out first and takes a knife from his armband towards me. The growls from the other guys start up and Chiemko is about to throw a fist at his face, when I yell "take it off of me!"

Chiemko grabs the wrist on my closest hand and brings it up to his face. My hand is freaking dematerializing in front of our eyes and I'm beginning to freak out. Oh no! It's never happened while I was awake before! What do we do?

My disappearing hand distracts the men enough for Gary to cut through the choker with his knife, making the talisman fall to the floor with a clank. The sound echoes and I jump again when it sounds like something echoes back in response.

"Did you guys hear that?"

None of the boys answer me — all of us staring at the necklace on the floor. I'm still breathing hard from the pain I was feeling earlier while Chiemko nuzzles my now solid hand into his face. *My god, that was close.* That was extremely frightening. Did it always burn during my teleportation and I just didn't know it? But that would leave behind scars, wouldn't it. My hand automatically goes to my neck and rubs my skin there. I breathe a sigh of relief when I still feel smooth skin.

Duma takes his spear and uses it to push the talisman away from me.

"Wait!"

"It is evil, my Juri."

"But —" I look to Gary for help with what I'm feeling. I'm not sure if he even understands what's going through me right now.

His piercing ocean blue eyes watch every move I make and I let out a sigh. What will happen to my family? How will I be able to see them again? If I do see them again, what if I can't return? My body has been moving on its own accord as I crouch down towards the choker. Lifting my eyes to all the boys here, my heart aches at the thought of never seeing them again. They've all buried themselves in me in one way or another — their own heartaches at my loss the last time still hurts me.

My eyes land on Gary again and there's a frown on his face.

"Juri. I go where you go."

"She is not going anywhere."

"What is he speaking of?"

"You would not make it out of this cave alive."

Ignoring their bickering, my hands touch the talisman lightly. It's cool. Grabbing it in my hand I bring it back up with me to standing, staring at it. What just happened before? And why is it so different now?

Suddenly, I'm screeching again from the pain but this time, my hands feel heavy and I can't let go of the damn necklace.

The boys all watch in horror as, not only my hands, but the necklace begins to dissipate into thin air.

"No! No no no!"

Duma's voice drowns out my panic and fear as his low baritone begins to chant something I can't understand. Tears are spilling from my eyes as I watch him watching me. Will I ever see him again? My rock, my protector. My lips are trembling as my eyes shoot to Gamba who joins in on the chant but in a different cadence and language. Duma's spear is pounding on the rock solid ground to create an ancient beat and Chiemko joins in with a more lyrical chant.

I'm so lost, the pain ebbing and flowing with my arms dematerializing. I can't even wipe my own damn tears because I have no hands.

My shoulders shake as a sob escapes me. Gary's warm arm comes around me from the side with his other hand on Chiemko's shoulder. All the men are touching each other's shoulders as the chants echo into the cave mouth.

"Whatever happens, Juri. I go where you go."

"Gary, I'm —I'm so scared."

"I got you."

The mens' voices raise higher and higher, the combination of sound almost deafening my ears. I can feel my eardrum pop when suddenly, the talisman cools in my hands. *My hands!*

They're back! Dropping the offending piece onto the floor, I bury my face into Gary's chest.

My heart is still beating out of my chest but I take a peek at the thing on the ground. Gamba takes his bow and pushes against it, scraping it across the floor. It looks like it's almost pulsating with a subtle glow — pulsating like it has its own heartbeat.

"It needs to go back where it came from. Do not touch it any more, my Juri." With a sneer, Gamba uses his bow to toss it farther into the heart of the cave. The echoing sounds of the piece hitting walls bounce back to us until it stops.

What does this mean? This is it, isn't it? That was my only ticket out.

Looking at each of the guys' faces while Chiemko is planting kisses on my palm, I know my heart isn't that sad about it.

"Duma. What was that chant?"

"I am unsure. It used to be done around the fire when I was not of season. The elders would perform the ritual away from the village at strange times. My young disobedience led me to follow them, and that was when I saw it."

"But you all were chanting together."

Duma looks at the other men but doesn't answer. Gamba looks at me with something in the depths of his eyes but it looks like his pride is holding him back. Chiemko ignores everyone and holds onto my hand as if he needs to physically feel that I'm still here.

What I do know — whatever happened here was proof of all their blood ties to the original families. And I think they realize this as well.

Letting the subject drop, I leave Gary's embrace and start walking towards the exit. I will miss my family, but I've been on my own for the past decade already. My mother wanted me to consider starting a family, but city life and not finding anyone interesting, held me back. I was drowning in the monotony of life in the city and working for Anderson.

We continue our walk back towards the west in silence and my mind plays through different thoughts of everything that's happened in my life.

Looking at Gary, I tell myself that I really wasn't as alone as I thought I was — someone found me interesting enough to hold on tight. We started shakily, I have to admit. The creep followed me around like a stalker and had his way with me in the beginning — essentially forcing himself into my life. But it was his quick thinking with his knife and then with his contact inside the cave that probably saved me from disappearing. His words during my rising panic have seared itself into my heart.

"Whatever happens, Juri. I go where you go."

How often can a woman say she's found a man who would give up everything for her? Even if the unknown could have meant death. Looking at all the guys around me — what woman can say she's found men who would face death just to be with her?

As we all walk away from the cave, a thought crosses my mind. Where *do* we go from here? All the boys have their own tribal lands, and Gary is as stuck here as I am. How is this going to work? There's no point in even asking because it will just lead to another knuckle drag out with these guys. Someone might lose a limb.

Our walk back is slower than our trip there. The breeze picks up and pushes my hair off my back with a whisper of crisp coolness. It makes me think of Chiemko, a son of the waters and an islander. He lives in the farthest lands. Bringing to mind all I know so far about these guys, I tick off the facts: Duma is from the west, while Gamba is from the east. There's really only one solution and I don't know if the guys would go for it, but what other option do we have? *Seize the day, Juri.*

I stop walking and stand here until the boys notice I'm not trailing back with them. When they turn around to look at me, I take a deep breath and just go for it.

"We need to make another village, right in the middle of the land. Not east, not west, not on the island. Right in the middle. It's the only way. You can't ask me to choose one of you because it's not going to happen. It's all or none." Crossing my arms over my chest, I wait for their answer.

All the guys look like they'd rather chop their own arm off than live with the other warriors around them. All the guys except for Gary, who is in the same predicament as I am, finding himself stuck in foreign lands. Gary walks up to me first, taking my face between his palms and giving me a slow and sensual kiss. When he pulls away, he looks at me and smiles.

"I'd follow you anywhere, Juri. Whether you want me to or not."

Well, okay then. I didn't doubt that one bit from our history together.

He must have done this on purpose because now the other guys, who will not be outdone, start shoving their way towards me like toddlers fighting over a toy. *Oh, for goodness sake.* Gary is still holding my face and I can't help but laugh out loud at this ridiculous moment. The guys stop their squabble and I just start walking eastward toward the destination of our new home.

Gamba jogs until he's in front of me to stop me from continuing my march. He places both hands on my shoulders, bends down towards my face and tells me something I didn't even think about.

"We must rest a while at the Chintkku village before heading to the middle of the lands. The war chiefs will send warriors to remove the bodies and mix the blood into the soil before our arrival."

Oh dear.

EPILOGUE

JURI

Much to the men's dismay, not only do the guys have their own personal huts, I have my own as well. Why? Because if these guys can't play fucking nice, then I won't either. *Too bad.* I'll just stay in my she-shed until they come to an agreement. I'm probably hoping for too much, but it doesn't hurt to try.

The warriors that were sent out to 'clean the mess' did an amazing job, and very quickly I might add. Perhaps they didn't have much to clean up since the sparcra were following the bloodshed. I've been informed that they feed on the dead, nature's garbage disposal. By the time we gathered supplies back and forth, the land was tilled and mixed in with the blood. I can't even tell this was a battleground.

A few warriors from each tribe decided to join us in our new village, bringing along their attached females and families if they had any. Those that are still bachelors enticed unattached females to join them. We now have a pretty decent size village, not as big as the other more established ones, but it is perfectly located to promote trade between the tribes. It's another step towards bringing peace to the lands, I hope. I'm surprised the guys didn't think of this before. They just needed the right incentive.

Despite Gary's pouting, he had his own hut built as well. I will not be picking favorites. I'm currently out with a couple of the other village women today, looking for berries to dry. My basket isn't full yet, so I've wandered a little farther out in case I find more.

As I'm bending over to get a closer look at the bush in front of me hiding behind a boulder, I feel big sun warmed hands grab my hips. Looking over my shoulder, I see Duma with a feral expression and it makes me clench my pussy in anticipation.

The boys have taken to playing this game with me, to see who catches me off guard and then have their way with me since I refuse to visit them in their huts in case it incites another world war. It was alarming at first, but the guys are very good at persuading me to play their game of Command And Conquer.

Seems Duma's caught me today, making my basket the lightest with the least amount of berries picked when I return to the village. I've taken to wearing a makeshift wrap skirt with some of the fabrics found hanging over hut doors in the other villages. The women were kind enough to give me their tattered pieces — pieces that were very much salvageable to make clothing. It covers me enough but bares one of my thighs when I walk, enticing the eyes of my men.

The only thing I couldn't make was underwear that would stay up, much to the guys' delight. Duma pushes my skirt over my back as he rubs his hard cock at my pussy entrance from behind. I'm already wet knowing what's to come. One of his hands covers the back of my neck, bending me further at the waist over the boulder in front of me. In one quick thrust, he's in me to the hilt and I swear I can feel him hitting my lungs. This man is a beast all over. He must be mad that he wasn't the one to catch me yesterday because he's pounding into me like he hates me. His other hand grips my hips and pulls me towards him as he thrusts deeply into me, making slapping noises as our combined wetness coats his shaft allowing for quicker thrusts. Duma's accumulated a few more warrior marks since I've met him — below the belt towards his shaft. I have to say it feels fucking amazing during sex, and I think he knows it too.

Gamba found me by the pass the other day, lost as usual, and decided to fuck me against the rocky wall as punishment. The rough texture at my back and his temper at endangering myself made for some amazing rough sex. Gamba has a way with his hips that always hits me in the right spot, making my screams echo into the pass. Again, he leaves a bite mark on me to rile up the other guys. The bastard only gives me a cocky grin when he sees me try to hide it once we are back at the village.

Duma and Gamba ended up in a bloody fist fight when Duma caught sight of the mark.

Duma is grunting now every time he enters me, and I can feel his cock thickening as he grips my hair from the tension of his orgasm. Gone is the soft lover I knew before. Duma's competitive and jealous spirit makes him fuck me instead of make love to me. I pretend I don't like it and it makes him wild, wanting to mark me the way Gamba does. Duma doesn't bite me though, instead he's taken to giving me small "warrior marks" on my hips, his favorite part to pet me when we're like this. The first time he did it, a fight broke out between the guys — body parts getting cut and sliced, blood splattering every which way right in the middle of our village causing everyone to run and hide until I told them no one was getting lucky tonight and left for my hut alone.

I've also taken to wearing a band around my thigh to hold the knife Chiemko gifted me. It hides under my clothes well. It turns him on to feel it there while he's ravishing me. The first time I took his cock into my mouth, I brought him to his knees for a few minutes before his beast took over and started fucking my face with unrestrained passion. I loved every minute of it and now Chiemko looks at my mouth with a different type of raw hunger every time I walk by.

Gary, though? That bastard just uses his ninja stalker skills to sneak into my hut in the middle of the night while I'm fast asleep to tie a gag around my mouth, preventing the other guys from hearing all the sinful things he does to me. I was afraid the first few times, but I have to admit his kinky ways have grown on me the way he has. *Like a damn fungus.* How he manages to sneak around with skin as white as his against everything else is a damn mystery, but he does it. His ocean blue eyes always sparkle like the waters glistening under the suns when he catches me unawares, whispering all his dirty thoughts into my ears as he drives me into the ground. *The psycho bastard.*

How we haven't scared the other villagers away, I have no idea. Most of the women just look at me with wide eyes when they see the marks I carry from all the war chiefs, as well as all the marks on them from all the fights that break out. At least none of the women have attempted to flirt with my guys anymore since the last incident.

She was a younger female who must not have known all the details of what's happened between my men and I. I caught her trying to touch Gamba on the arm and the knife on my thigh found itself at her neck, piercing her skin. The trickle of blood dripping from her wound and the cocky smile from Gamba scared her away for good. Oh Gamba was punished for that, believe me, even though he smiled throughout it all as I rode his dick and cut him on the same location he likes to leave his mark on me. *Cocky bastard.*

The moment the other guys saw my mark on Gamba, another bloody fight broke out with spears in hand and arrows getting stuck on the side of huts. I had to level the playing field again by marking them all with my knife after having my way with them.

Big babies, the lot of them. Like beasts fighting over a bitch in heat. *Sheesh.*

…And I wouldn't have it any other way.

The memory of my mother's wise words comes to mind in these bittersweet moments. "Ye ishq nahi asaan Bas Tina samjh lijiye Aag ka dariya hai Aur dob ke jana hai.

This love ain't easy…just understand this. It's a river of fire and you have to swim through it.

Little did I know, just how right she was.

THE END.

Ma
Chintkku
Nam

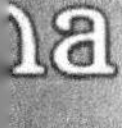

Other Earth

PLAYLIST

Lorde - Royals (African Tribal Masqerade Cover) Alex Boye
Lindsey Stirling (VenTribe) - We Found Love
Shakira - Empire
Veridia - Still Breathing
The Five Strings ft. Alex Boye - Amazing Grace
The HU feat. Lzzy Hale - Song of Women
Garbage - #1 Crush (Nellee Hooper Mix)
Sarah Mclachlan - Possession
Lindsey Stirling feat Amy Lee - Love Goes On And On

ABOUT THE AUTHOR

Y.D. La Mar is a poet, writer and author of The Scent of Jasmine, the first book in the Street Arrhythmia Trilogy. She's been known to write eccentric book reviews online and can be found recommending even stranger books in her reading groups. She lives in sin city as a wife, a homeschooling mother, seamstress, knitter and dog owner. She enjoys reading a wide range of books from fluffy stories to pitch black reads.

www.ydlamar.com

ALSO BY YD LA MAR

www.amazon.com/author/ydlamar

THE ESSENCE OF ESME SNIPPET

RAW AND UNDEDITED

I can't breathe.

I'm drowning.

My mind gets lost in the sorrow, lost in the void of agony.

The pain in my heart threatens to consume me.

I can't do this. I just can't. I'm not strong enough. The tears streaming down my face do nothing to cool the burn inside my chest. Is this where I lose myself? Is this the last of me? What was the purpose of it all? Was I always destined down this road of agony and torment?

I scream out at the top of my lungs until my throat feels raw. Raw with emotion, raw like I've been shredded to pieces from the inside out. My sobs taper as I lay here, feeling like a shell of myself.

I can't let them down. But Lord, I'm not strong enough. *Mother, what do I do?*

Her voice floats through my mind as I close my eyes.

Esmeray, honey. Rejoice in hope and be patient in tribulation. Lean not on your own understanding.

The sound of air releasing niggles the back of my mind. I'm too lost in the darkness of my mind to even care what it means. After a few moments, a shadow comes over my body, shrouding me even more in physical darkness as my mind continues to get lost in the void. No matter how lost I get it's not enough to numb me like I want it to. It doesn't stop my tears from continuing to stream down, wetting the sheets beneath me.